THERE WAS A LIGHT IN HER WINDOW . . .

Holding his gun in one hand, Longarm stood on the edge of the adobe house with his back to the street, leaned out against the taut line, took a deep breath, and kicked himself out and away.

He swung down, feet first, and crashed through the window as his boot heels sent discs of glass flying like scattered poker chips. His feet-first swing dropped him smack in Pepita's bed as the man seated on it sprang off with a yell of surprise.

The bedsprings gave way and Longarm wound up on the floor, atop the mattress and under a shower of glass. Then it started to get noisy . . .

→•← TABOR EVANS →•←

ON THE OLD
MISSION TRAIL

A JOVE BOOK

First Jove edition published October 1980

10 9 8 7 6 5 4 3 2 1

Printed in the United States of America

Jove books are published by Jove Publications, Inc., 200 Madison Avenue, New York, NY 10016

LONGARM

ON THE OLD
MISSION TRAIL

in its infinite wisdom, did not see fit to try him in an election year."

"Yeah, he mentioned something about controlling a mess of votes while I was pounding some sense into him," Longarm said with a disgusted grimace. "Are you saying you want me out of town because the senator's out gunning for me, Billy? I ain't afraid of the son of a bitch."

"I know you ain't. That's why I feel that Denver will be a lot more peaceable if the two of you don't meet up until the senator's had time to cool down some. He specifically asked for you as he was leaving the federal courthouse yesterday afternoon. But I figure he'll have other fish to fry in a few weeks, what with the election coming up and his other enemies accusing him of everything but smallpox."

"Hell," Longarm snorted, "if you just want me to hide out a few weeks, I have some vacation time coming and a lady up on Sherman Avenue who says she wants to improve me. I could just stay out of sight and—"

"At the opera?" Vail cut in, raising his bushy black eyebrows. "This case out on the Coast will not only keep you off the streets of Denver for a spell. It's the sort of case you're good at."

"Catching cow thieves, Billy? Hell, anybody can catch a cow thief."

Vail shook his head and said, "Not these rascals. They're sort of slick and spooky, and the local lawmen out there are stumped. Do you remember those high-graders stealing gold out there a while back?"

Longarm nodded. "Sure. Federal gold was sort of vanishing off guarded ore cars on its way to the San Francisco Mint."

"These cow thieves are pulling a similar game," Vail said. "Do I have your undivided attention?"

"No. I promised I'd take the lady to the opera to-

9

night and there's a train leaving in the morning, but go ahead."

Vail said, "The Indian bureau has been buying beef to feed the Modoc, in Northern California. The Modoc just signed up for rations and such after playing tag with the army until a couple of years ago."

"I know about the Modoc War, Billy."

"Right. Anyway, the BIA gets the beef cheap down near Pueblo de Los Angeles, herds it up the Old Mission Trail to Frisco Bay, and ships it from there by steamboat, as needed."

"Where are the cow thieves hitting the herds, on the long drive up the coast?" Longarm asked, his interest piqued in spite of his annoyance.

"That's the spooky part," Vail said. "Nobody's been attacking the contract drovers. They form the herd down by the Los Angeles River, move 'em out, and nothing much happens along the way. But when they tally the herd at the north end of the drive, they end up with a third or more of the cows missing."

Longarm pursed his lips and whistled. "That's a lot of beef if we're talking about the usual trail herd, · Billy."

"It is and we are. The last herd that sort of evaporated on the hoof left Los Angeles with three thousand head counted and trail-branded. A month later, when they ran 'em in the tally chutes at San Francisco, they had less than two thousand."

Longarm frowned and asked, "Didn't they tally on the trail, for Pete's sake?"

"Sure they did," Vail said. "It's hard to get more'n a rough count on the hoof when you bed 'em down for the night. But the drovers knew they were leaking cows along the way, they just haven't been able to figure out how. The spooky part is that not a cow has been stolen at night, when you'd expect it. The BIA has its own investigators riding with the contract drovers. So they tally before each day's drive."

10

Longarm took a thoughtful drag of cigar smoke before he said, "Let's back up and study these contract riders. The easiest way for cows to wind up missing in broad daylight is with a little help from their friends."

The marshal shook his head and said, "Interior is ahead of you on that. They fired the first trail boss who limped in with all that government beef missing. They fired the second one too. They've checked the credentials of everyone they've contracted with, ever since. They even tried to drive one herd north with army personnel, but the cavalry spilled the herd just trying to cross the San Fernando Valley, so they had to go back to hiring cowboys. Which is getting to be a bitch, by the way. The good old boys around Pueblo de Los Angeles don't cotton much to being called cow thieves, so a lot of 'em have refused to work for the BIA. They say the job is jinxed. Some fool Mex tells everyone who'll listen that the ghost of some Mexican bandit is still haunting the Coast Range."

Longarm shrugged and asked, "What about *real* bandits? That's rough country and a hell of a long drive. Has anybody bothered to *look* for those stolen cows? You did say they were trail-marked, didn't you?"

"Sure. The government agent buys scrub Indian beef at a good price from the hardscrabble rancheros in the Los Angeles Basin. Then each one gets a big old ID branded on it as they run 'em into the holding yards. As to looking for them, the county and state lawmen all the way up the trail know the brand. They've looked over the herds of every outfit the trail passes anywhere near. None of the local rancheros seem to be expanding their herds at the expense of the U.S. taxpayer. Before you ask if I think the local lawmen are crooks, I already considered it. I'll buy a crooked sheriff here and a corrupt state brand inspector there. But the Old Mission Trail is over four hundred miles long, and if every lawman along it is a crook, we are in trouble."

11

"Two out of three men with a badge seem to be reasonably honest," Longarm agreed. "You can't pin down just which counties along the trail we're talking about, can you, Billy?"

"All of 'em. The cows just dribble away, all along the line. Hell, I wouldn't need to send my best hand if we could localize the problem. But nobody can. A cow vanishes here, a cow vanishes there, until after a while a hell of a lot are gone. I figure some of it's normal wastage. You always lose a stray or two a day on a long drive. But when you get there with a *thousand* missing, some son of a bitch has *got* 'em! So I want you to go out there and make them stop. Do you figure your best move would be a straight investigation, or would you feel more comforted if you worked under-cover?"

Longarm considered this for a moment, then said, "Well, everybody knows the BIA has its own officials riding with the herd, so the thieves will likely be watching them. I'll just see if I can sign on as a trail hand and play her by ear."

"I figured you would. I'll notify Interior that you're coming."

"I wish you wouldn't, Billy. I work best on my own and there's something fishy about the whole deal."

Vail looked surprised. "Jesus, do you suspicion somebody from the Indian bureau might be in on it?"

Longarm said, "Don't know. If they are, I'll stand a better chance of catching them if they don't know I'm watching them. Like I said, I'll just mosey out and wrangle myself a job. When is the next drive forming up?"

"About a week. The sooner you get there, the better."

"Maybe. Forget the case for a minute. Since you are an unsuspected opera fan, Billy, maybe you can fill me in on something the widow Brown was jawing about this morning as we parted fondly. She said this opera

12

I was to escort her to was White Tie. What in thunder do you reckon she meant?"

Vail laughed loudly. "Hell, that's easy, old son. If she's got herself a season box, it means she listens to her music fancy. The folks sitting up in the boxes wear clawhammer coats and boiled shirts with little white ties, like the waiters at the Pullman House Hotel."

Longarm looked thunderstruck. "Sweet Jesus, where in hell would I get me a dude outfit like that, Billy?"

"I reckon she expects you to rent one," Vail said, shrugging his round shoulders. "She said she aimed to improve you, remember?"

Longarm stubbed out his cheroot grimly. "She sure did, but I didn't suspicion she meant she wanted me to dress like her butler. You did say there's a noonday train leaving, didn't you?"

"I did. I take it you aim to get an early start on them cow thieves?"

Longarm stood up and adjusted his gunbelt grimly, as he nodded and replied, "Yep. Duty calls, and what the hell, you told me what the opera was about, anyway. I could likely sit through a couple of hours of Italian screeching to please a lady, but not in any infernal boiled shirt."

Longarm was a deputy U.S. marshal, not a member of the Secret Service, and he didn't like to lie. Even if he had, some defense attorneys could cloud up a case with a mess of dumb charges about entrapment. So Longarm had to walk a narrow line as he got off the train a few days later in Pueblo de Los Angeles.

He wasn't wearing false whiskers and he used his right name when he checked into the Angel's Rest Hotel on Olvera Street, near the main plaza and around the corner from the old Church of Our Lady, the Queen of the Angels. But he had shucked his frock coat and the fool tie the Justice Department made him wear, and the luggage he had toted over from the depot included a fifty-dollar double-rigged stock saddle he had borrowed from a public-spirited citizen riding for the Diamond K near Denver. The government-issue McClellan he usually worked with was inclined to hint at army or federal connections. A well-broken-in manila rope and a used pair of gunbarrel chaps tied to the stock saddle spelled out High Plains Cowhand to the curious who knew how to read such things. Longarm didn't intend to ask right out for a job with the contract drovers who were due to leave in a few days with the government herd. Folks would be less suspicious of a hand who had to be recruited almost against his will. Longarm knew already that the outfit hired to make the next drive was short-handed, and he figured that if he played his cards right, he wouldn't have to go to them; they'd come to him.

He paid a week's rent in advance for the room he hired, but he wouldn't be there. If any nosy cuss discussed him with the rummy-looking room clerk, they'd pick up on the fact that the tall stranger's original plans didn't seem to include riding off with just anybody at a moment's notice. Longarm locked his gear in the room, stuck an inconspicuous matchstick in the doorjamb to see if anyone visited his borrowed cow outfit while he was gone, and went back downstairs. The lobby was a small adobe cavern, but as usual, a couple of seedy old gents were camped in chairs, reading yesterday's papers by the light of a potted palm. Longarm handed his room key to the clerk and said, just loudly enough to be overheard, "I'll be back sort of late. What time do you lock the front door?"

"We don't," the clerk replied, "Everything is up to date in Los Angeles, now that us white folks are running it. We're open twenty-four hours a day. But if you get back all that late with a lady under your arm, we'll expect you to pay for a double occupancy. We don't make moral judgments, but you cowboys have to understand that we are not in business for our health.

14

That room rents for fifty cents a head. So don't go trying to sneak no heads by us, hear?"

Longarm chuckled and said, "I did hear tell there's a little action over on Hill Street."

The clerk warned him, "Don't you *dare* come back with one of them greaser gals from Bunker Hill! We don't rent rooms to Mexicans, Chinamen or colored folks, male or otherwise."

"Don't get your bowels in an uproar. I ain't looking for a woman right now. I'm looking for a job. I hear tell there's some oil sign here in the basin, and I worked one summer drilling oil, so—"

"Oil?" The clerk laughed incredulously. "There ain't no oil wells in California, cowboy."

One of the old loafers lowered his paper to opine, "He must mean them tar seeps out on the Hancock spread, Pete."

"Hell, them ain't oil wells," the clerk scoffed. "They're tar pits. They sell a few barrels of the goop down at San Pedro, now and again. The tar's all right for ship's bottoms, but it stinks too bad for burning and such. They ain't hiring out on the Hancock spread, young feller. Why don't you try over to the railroad yards? I hear tell Cracker McBride is hiring trail hands for a drive north. Just ask around the yards and they'll direct you to him."

Longarm shook his head and replied fervently, "I thank you for the thought, but I have done all the trail herding the Good Lord ever meant to pile on one poor boy's plate."

"I noticed the grass-rope saddle. I understand old Cracker McBride pays pretty good, if you're a top hand."

Longarm raised his blue-gray eyes heavenward and milked a forlorn sigh for all it was worth. "I've rid high and I've rid low. I've chased cows up the Chisholm and the Goodnight, and froze my ass on the Montana. I've

15

rid for the Hash Knife and the Jingle Bob. I was ramrod on the Middle Fork when the Shoshone tried to eat all our beef one winter. I have been rolled, stomped and dragged by a vast collection of ten-dollar ponies the bosses expected me to work on. I tell you, boys, I have et my last trail dust and milled my last midnight stampede. There *has* to be an easier way to make a living."

The room clerk frowned suspiciously, but since Longarm had paid in advance, he decided it wouldn't be polite to ask the dumb cowboy if he had any visible means of support. The old man who'd filled him in on the oil industry of Southern California said, "I understand your pain and anguish, son. I used to be a cowhand, before I wised up. They do say there's a little color being dug over in Calico, a desert town not far from here."

The other old man put down his paper and broke in, "Now just hold on. The boy says he's looking for a *sensible* job! Gold mining is more work for less pay than herding cows!"

Longarm tried to look eager as well as dumb when he said, "Not if you strike it rich. How do I get to this Calico town?"

The room clerk rolled his eyes and said, "Jesus H. Christ, you must have worms or something. You ain't slept a night on your hired pillow, and already you're talking about tear-assing out across the desert in the dry season! You'll fry your brains out, boy. If I were you, I'd give this growing city a chance. There's all sorts of jobs hereabouts. Los Angeles is growing like a weed."

"I reckon I'm just itchy-footed from the train ride," Longarm replied sheepishly. "I did promise I'd have me a good look at that ocean you folks have around here. How do I get to this here Pacific they keep talking about?"

"It's a mite late to start this afternoon, son," one of the older men said. "It's a day's ride out to Santa Monica along the Sunset Trail. If I was you, I'd hold off until morning."

The other oldtimer agreed. "It's a nice ride, this time of the year. But you wouldn't see much if you reached the ocean after sundown, and there ain't a durned thing to do in Santa Monica. It's just a stage station on the coast trail, and they charge captive-customer rates for beer."

Longarm took his Ingersoll watch out of his vest pocket and consulted it before he said, "I suspicion you're right. I'll just mosey over to the plaza or maybe find me a card house or whatever."

As he was leaving, one of them called after him, "Stay out of the La Paloma. The wheel over there is rigged beyond common courtesy."

The clerk and the loafers exchanged a chuckle as Longarm left. One of them said, "He might land a job in construction. He looks strong."

His companion opined, "Hell, can't you see he's a born cowboy? What'll you bet he winds up working for McBride's outfit?"

"Well, McBride pays pretty good," the other said, "and none of the local spreads would sign on a grass-rope hand if they could help it. But the boy says he don't want to work cows this season."

"Hell, they all say that, and it's true. Nobody *wants* to work cows. Not if they have any other trade, they don't. But that boy is over thirty if he's a day, and I've got him read to a T. He's been working cows since they was invented. Did you notice how busted-up his stock saddle was when they brung it in?"

The old man looked a little wistful as he raised his paper to close the discussion. "I was like him once. A cowboy starts to think of the future as he leaves his twenties behind him. But that boy ain't ready to settle

17

down just yet. He's dumb and restless. They make the best kind. All McBride has to do is mention San Francisco at the other end of the trail, and you'll see. He'll sign up."

The room clerk glanced at the register Longarm had signed. "I'll mention there's a top hand staying here, next time I see Cracker McBride. McBride has sent me business in the past, and one hand washes the other."

Chapter 2

It was just as suspicious for a grown man to be too dumb as it was for him to be too smart, so Longarm let the City of the Angels work at taking a new arrival to the cleaners. Marshal Vail had given him a hundred dollars to lose while setting up shop as an out-of-work drifter, so Longarm shot a couple of lines of pool with some hustlers who should have been ashamed of themselves. He shot a straight game to keep from looking like a total idiot. So, while he couldn't beat the usual pool shark, he'd only lost a few dollars by the time the sun went down and it just got too tedious to go on. He left and drifted over to the La Paloma Saloon that the oldtimer had warned him about. It was a ticky-tacky joint that reminded him of the Long Branch in Dodge, save for a big Wheel of Fortune against the back wall. A bored-looking gal in a red fandango dress was in charge of the wheel, but nobody was playing it. Word had likely gotten around. The gambling gal was seated on a bentwood chair, trying not to fall asleep.

Longarm ignored her and the Wheel of Fortune at first, and bellied up to the bar and asked for Maryland rye. As he'd expected, a man with enough in his jeans to order by brand drew a thoughtful look from the lady sitting by the wheel. It cost an extra cent a shot, too. But what the hell, he was on an expense account.

It was early yet. The only other customers were a couple of gents at the far end of the bar, near the doorway. They'd sized him up as he came in. He'd run their faces through his mental file of wanted posters and figured he wasn't after them, either.

They were dressed like cattlemen. The one who liked black duds had an interesting sidearm hanging low on his Border gun rig. It looked like an old Le Mat revolver. Longarm hadn't seen one for years. It was a French-made weapon that had never really caught on. The Le Mat was expensive and carried firepower to the point of ridiculousness. The big pistol couldn't make up its mind whether it was a revolver or a sawed-off shotgun. It weighed a ton and had two barrels, over and under. The top barrel fired .40-caliber slugs from a nine-chamber cylinder. The lower barrel fired a back-up .66-caliber buckshot round. The shotgun part was single-shot, but how much lead did any one man need to throw in peacetime? The jasper in black either had a mess of enemies to worry about or, more likely, he just liked noise.

Longarm noticed that the gal by the Wheel of Fortune was giving him the eye, so he downed his drink, ordered another, and moseyed back to her, glass in hand. "Howdy, ma'am," he said. "What's that thing and how does it work?"

The girl stayed seated, but she smiled up at him as she said, "You can't tell me you haven't played Wheel of Fortune, cowboy."

He said, "I tried it at a carnival once. I got whipped disgraceful. I've heard it said that you folks can stop that wheel on any number, as long as it ain't the one I bet on."

The girl said, "This wheel is as honest as the day is long, cowboy. I will tell you true that the odds are against you. You look like a smart gent and anyone can see that there's more numbers you can lose on than there is one number you can win on. But I don't use a brake on my wheel; I don't have to. Do you want to pick a number, just for fun?"

Longarm vacillated as visibly as possible. "I don't know. I don't have much of my grubstake left, and I'm out of work, too."

The girl stood up, letting him see how tight her dress was, and gave the wheel a spin. "Come on, I said we'd just try it for fun. Pick a number, cowboy. It won't cost you anything."

Longarm shrugged as he stared at the spinning wheel and said, "I'll pick seven, if it ain't costing me anything."

The wheel slowed down. The clacker atop the rig started hesitating as the nails set in the wheel between the painted numbers passed it. Lucky seven inched into place, looked like it was going to stop, and then moved on one space as the wheel stopped. The girl said, "You almost won. You want to try again?"

"For free?"

"Sure, why not? Business is slow and I like you."

Sure she does, Longarm thought, as the girl gave the wheel another whirl and he picked eleven. She was a pretty little thing, with too much henna in her hair and too many men's faces in her world-weary hazel eyes. He admired a good con artist's skill, but she wasn't as good as she thought she was. That was likely why the owner of the wheel had a gal working it. The wheel stopped on eleven and the brake was so obvious that it would have gotten a male gambler killed in Dodge or Cheyenne by now. She laughed and said, "Oh, you *won!* It's too bad you didn't have real money riding on eleven."

Longarm felt as foolish as hell, with the bartender and two grown men watching. But he reached in his pocket and took out a quarter. He put it on the beige counter in front of the wheel and said, "Well, maybe my luck is changing. Let's try six this time."

The girl shook her head and said, "Table stakes are a dollar a spin, cowboy. If you don't have real money, don't play. I'll spin it again for you, just to see if you'd have won, but put the two bits back in your pants. My boss would scold me if he caught me, but like I said, I like you and we're just doing this for fun."

She spun the wheel as Longarm thought: *Sure we are, you sly little bitch. That crack aimed at my manhood was slick as hell. I bet you charge extra for taking off your socks in bed, too.*

The wheel stopped on six. Longarm was surprised. Did he look *that* country? The girl said, "I don't know how you do it! Not many gents pick two out of three. It's a good thing we weren't playing for real money." Then she bent forward as if to whisper to him, but really to give him a look down her low-cut bodice as she added, "Or other things."

Longarm raised a hayseed's knowing eyebrow and grinned toothily as he asked, "Oh? Do you mean I might win, well, a pretty dolly, if I beat your wheel?"

She'd baited the hook and he'd nibbled, so she eased off with a light laugh and said, "Don't get your hopes up. You'd have to beat the bank before I'd be forced to bet anything like that. I've got a hundred silver dollars you'd have to win off me before we'd get to higher stakes."

He knew that she knew he had lower stakes in mind as he grinned and put a silver dollar down. "Powder River and let her buck," he said. "I feel lucky as hell about seven. I used to ride for the Lazy Sevens, up Colorado way."

The girl spun the wheel and managed to look worried when the number seven won. "Oh, dear," she said, adjusting her bodice to cover her cleavage as she covered his bet. He said, "Let it ride. But this time I'll try eleven again."

"I can see you know how to figure the odds," she said, as she spun the wheel again.

Naturally he lost, and naturally he'd only lost a dollar of his own, so naturally he put another down as she raked in the spoils and sighed, "I sure don't want to lose the boss's money and have to bet my all. Big men like you are sort of scary."

"I'll be gentle, honey," he reassured her. "Spin the wheel and hope it don't stop on six."

It was an interesting little charade, and Longarm was enjoying her act. But as the wheel was still spinning a voice behind him yelled, "Cowboy! Duck!" and all hell busted loose!

Longarm dropped to the floor and rolled, drawing his Colt .44 as the big smooth-bore Le Mat roared deafeningly in the confined space a split second after a smaller gun put a .45 slug in the spinning wheel above Longarm's head. He crabbed sideways along the floor to join the girl crouched behind the corner of the bar, as he stared into the smoke that filled the saloon from halfway down the bar to the entrance. The girl whispered, "Jesus Christ, you win! You didn't have to shoot my wheel!"

"I didn't," he answered, as the smoke started to thin and he could make figures out in the blue haze. The bartender had sensibly dropped out of sight behind the mahogany. The two men who'd been drinking together when he came in were still on their feet. Another man lay mangled on the floor, with his face in a spittoon and a Walker Conversion a foot from his clutching dead hand. The man in black was still holding his big Le Mat, and the awesome mass of steel was still smoking. Longarm saw that the thing wasn't pointed his way, so he got up, holding his own muzzle politely down, and asked, "What happened?"

"Beats hell out of me," the man in black replied. "This gent came in the door, took one look at you, and slapped leather. I didn't want him to shoot Trixie and she was lined up with you too close for comfort, so I shot him. I hope he ain't a friend of yours, stranger."

"Not hardly. I'm new in town. My handle is Custis Long. Let's see who this gent was."

The man in black said to call him Boomer. As Longarm rolled the bloody corpse over with his boot, the aptly named Boomer asked, "Anybody you know?"

Longarm lied. He had to. The man who'd tried to shoot him in the back was a well-known train robber that Longarm was surprised to see out of jail. "Do Jesus, I think I have seen him before. We tangled a year ago in Ellsworth. It was a friendly fistfight and I'm surprised he took it so serious. The dance-hall gal the discussion was about was sort of bowlegged, as I remember."

"You've an eye for the ladies, Long," Boomer observed as he started to reload the bottom chamber of his Le Mat. "It's lucky for you the galoot was too mad at you to consider us innocent bystanders."

Longarm put his own gun away as he said, "You are right as rain, and I would say I owe you more than a drink, Boomer. But a drink will have to do you. I'm bashful about kissing grown men."

A couple of men in blue uniforms came through the swinging doors. One of them sighed and said, "We heard there'd been a shooting in here and I can see we heard right. Is anybody here going to explain all the noise, or do we have to guess what happened?"

Longarm stared, frozen-faced. He knew he could flash his federal badge and make them listen to reason, but that meant giving his whole show away.

"I shot him," Boomer volunteered rather proudly.

"We were just about to have a drink to celebrate. The cuss on the floor was trying to murder this cowhand when I stopped him."

"That was neighborly, I'm sure, but we try to discourage gunplay on Olvera Street, and I'm afraid you boys are all under arrest," one of the coppers said.

Boomer reached in his pocket and calmly took out a billfold. "I see no reason to pester the judge. I'm a government man. Long, here, didn't know it, but he managed to get on the wrong side of a wanted man. The cuss on the floor is a Texican gunslinger named Jennings. I've seen his face on the federal flyers they send to every office."

Longarm found it easy to look astounded as he asked Boomer, "Are you a lawman? No wonder you're so good with that cannon!"

Boomer looked a trifle smug as he patted his holstered Le Mat and answered, "I reckon I can handle most two-bit owlhoots after Uncle Sam's gold. I'm the boss guard here in L.A. for the BIA."

"You're an Indian agent, Boomer?"

"Not exactly. I work for a purchasing agent who buys for Uncle Sam. They pay cash on the barrelhead for Indian beef, so that means a mess of cash on hand at our office over by the railroad yards, and since cash on hand attracts thieves on the hoof—"

One of the coppers said, "Say no more about it. What we have us here is an open-and-shut case of whatever. Do you reckon this boy was out to rob the Interior Department?"

"Hell, no," Boomer snorted. "The cowboy here got in a fight with the rascal once, not knowing he had a rep as a badman. Jennings came in here for a drink or whatever, spotted a man who'd whipped him, and became ancient history. Why don't you get somebody to drag him over to the morgue? There may be a reward on him; I'll see when I get to the office."

The two coppers looked wistful. Longarm knew that most federal men shared reward money with the locals for good will. But when one of the coppers mentioned sharing to Boomer, the man in black laughed easily. "Hell, go shoot your own outlaws. I nailed the son of a bitch fair and square, and any money due on him is mine!" Then he nudged Longarm and said, "You come with us, old son. Let's go someplace quiet and talk about your future."

Longarm still owed him that drink, so he followed politely, but when they got outside, he said, "I can thank you for such future as I may have, but I don't want a job as a guard, if that's what you have in mind."

Boomer laughed and said, "Hell, I can see you're a cowhand, not a gunslick. This here is Mr. Carver, by the way."

Longarm nodded at the silent man who'd stood by through it all without appearing to take much interest. As Boomer led them to another joint across the street, Carver said, "I'm with the BIA too. I'm the gent you see if you have any cows to sell us."

Longarm didn't comment. The three of them went in and took a corner table. Longarm put a coin on the table when the waitress came over, and he ordered drinks all around before saying with a frown, "Damn. I left a whole dollar back there and I never found out if I won or not."

Boomer laughed. "Nobody wins with Trixie. I found it sort of amusing to watch you try."

Carver said, "Forget your lost stake, Long. We might be able to put you on the trail of real money, if you're a top hand."

Longarm looked carefully dubious. "I don't know. I'm getting kind of old for chasing cows. I didn't know the Interior Department hired cowhands, anyway."

"We don't," Carver told him. "Not direct. But I just

bought a mess of cows for the Modoc and some other Indians, and I'll be buying more in the next few days. We've hired a professional drover named McBride to herd 'em north for us. He's having a time getting a crew together. Interested?"

"Not hardly. Trail herding is the only chore I know more disgusting than stringing fences. What's wrong with this McBride jasper? There's generally something wrong with a trail boss who can't sign on enough kids to ride drag."

The two Californians exchanged glances and Carver waited until the girl had placed a bottle and some shot glasses on the table between them before replying, "We don't want green kids herding our Indian beef this time, Long. We want the cows to arrive at the far end of the trail."

Longarm poured as Boomer explained, "Our beef is getting strayed or stolen. This time we're sending some law along to watch for cow thieves. We'd feel better if we knew the herders knew their business, too. You may as well know we were looking for you when you wandered into the La Paloma. I was fixing to approach you when that rascal tried to shoot you." He paused meaningfully. "We know all about you, Long."

"Oh?"

"That's right. Spider Gardner, over at your hotel, told us all about you," Boomer said. "You're a tie-down roper who's worked cows in Indian country. I read hats good, and that's a High Plains Stetson if I ever saw one. Anybody who could hold a herd on the High Plains should have no trouble on the Mission Trail. It's practically a paved street through tamer country."

Carver took a sip of Maryland rye and confided, "McBride would sign you on if I told him to."

Longarm shook his head. "I thank you for the kind offer, but I ain't sure I aim to take you up on it. Maybe

I will if I can't get something better, like nailing up shingles."

Before anyone could answer, a man in blue with bars on his shoulders came over to the table and said, "Damn it, boys, you can't just shoot a man and walk away in this town. I know you federal gunslicks think your shit don't stink, but we run things more civilized than that."

"I gave a statement to your beat men, Lieutenant," Boomer replied evenly. "The cuss I gunned has wanted papers on him, and I'm a paid-up lawman."

Longarm pointed to the bottle. The police officer said, "Not on duty," and turned back to Boomer. "I need a *written* statement for the coroner. The boys at the morgue are sort of confused about that cuss on the slab tonight. They say he looks like somebody took a crosscut saw to his spine, but he hardly bled enough to mention."

Boomer patted the impressive weapon on his hip and said, "Old Frenchy cauterizes as she cuts. I almost had the muzzle up his ass when I fired."

The copper looked uncomfortable. "Yeah, the morgue crew said something about him being shot in the back."

"He was," Boomer admitted without batting an eye. "Fair is fair. He had his gun trained on another gent's back at the time, and I did not see fit to wait for his seconds to call on me. As it was, he got off a round as I tried to put him out of business. He parted the air where this old boy here was standing with his back to the door."

The officer looked at Longarm, who nodded and said, "Yep. Remind me never to do that again. Old Boomer saved my life. That's why we drink together a lot."

Carver looked like he had other fish to fry as he consulted his watch. "Boomer, you run over to the police station and make some sort of statement for the boys.

28

I'll meet you in the yards at sunup. We've got those cows coming in off the Verdugo spread, and Don Manasco's bringing in a dozen from the Cahuenga Hills."

Boomer shrugged and rose to his feet. "Sure, boss. Watch out for them Cahuenga cows if they beat me to the yards. They're mustard-fed and skinny as hell from running up and down them canyons over there."

Boomer followed the copper out, looking like the Angel of Death, and Carver turned back to Longarm. "I'll have one more drink on you and then I have to move it out, cowboy. I was about to say that McBride pays as high as two dollars a day and found, for a top hand."

Longarm pursed his lips and said, "That's pretty good, if a man knows he'll get the money at the far end of the drive. I made the mistake of driving for the Thompson Brothers once, and—"

"The wages are guaranteed by the U.S. Government," Carver cut in, explaining, "McBride is a private contractor, but he's funded by the Interior Department. He doesn't get his final payment until the San Francisco office is satisfied that he's lived up to his contract and satisfied all accounts and judgments due against the drive."

Longarm hesitated, then decided that even a dumb cowboy was allowed some sensible questions. "You tell me you've had trouble getting the herds north. Does that mean the losses come out of our pockets, saying I was desperate enough to sign on?"

Carver shook his head emphatically. "No. Wages and expenses are funded by us. McBride gets a flat fee for his own trouble, plus a bonus if he does it right. *He* loses money on lost cows. *We* lose money on lost cows. You hired hands can't lose no matter how it goes, but of course, any drover fucking up the drive can be fired on the spot."

"I rode herd for Captain Goodnight, once," Longarm said. "I know the way a fair outfit works. But like I said, I'll pass on this next drive. How many a year do you have?"

"Two, when things go right. One of the reasons I'm out recruiting for McBride is that this next one is an emergency ration for the Indians. The last beef we sent 'em arrived in a shrunken condition and the Indians are muttering about our tongues being forked."

"Didn't you tell 'em your trail herds were robbed?"

"Cowboy, we don't ever tell an Indian shit! The Great White Father is supposed to be infallible! How would it look if the Modoc found out we couldn't stop a handful of brush-busting free-enterprisers?"

"I can see how it might make some braves reconsider their options. But surely they can't be starving? Even losing a third of your cows, you've still run a mess of beef to them since they made peace. I don't know much about the Modoc War, but as I remember reading in the papers, it ain't that big a tribe."

"You're right," Carver said. "But the BIA has other Indians up north who draw beef rations, and some of what we buy is consigned to the armed forces around Frisco Bay."

"Meaning the Indians get what's left after quartermasters from the army and that big navy base up there cull the herd for prime?"

Carver shrugged. "War pays Interior for what they put aside. We buy and send enough for everybody, if only the goddamned cows could get there!"

He lowered his voice as he leaned forward and confided, "I wouldn't want this to get around, but Washington's about to shut down this operation. They can buy all the beef they need in Northern California, albeit at a much higher price. I've been told that if we can't get our cheap border beef to market, there's no savings worth mention. If they shut down the BIA yards here in L.A., a lot of little local spreads figure to get hurt. We're the only big buyer around here."

"Well, I'll study on it," Longarm promised. "But I aim to have a look-see around the basin before I sign on for any month-long drive. I'll let you know if nobody here in town will hire a strong back and a weak mind. But to tell you true, I'd rather dig post holes all day, and have my nights free, than spend my next four or five Saturday nights alone in a bedroll under a fool bush."

They finished their drinks and jawed politely about less important things until Carver left to head on home. Married men were like that.

Chapter 3

Longarm went back to the La Paloma, but Trixie wasn't there and a canvas tarp had been thrown over her shot-up Wheel of Fortune. So he found another clipjoint and let a tinhorn rob him of another fifty dollars with a friendly smile and a marked deck. Then, not wanting to look *too* stupid, he headed back to his hotel to turn in.

The hall upstairs was dark, so Longarm noticed right away that a sliver of light glowed under his hired door. The matchstick he'd stuck in the jamb was lying on the floor, edge-lit by the mysterious light.

He drew his gun as he moved in on the balls of his booted feet. He saw more light coming out through his keyhole, so he dropped to one knee for a peek inside.

There wasn't much to see, at first. The keyhole was lined up on his saddle, piled on a chair by the window. The shade was down, as he'd left it. But he sure hadn't left a light for himself to come home to. A flash of red winked across his line of vision. Longarm stood up

33

with a puzzled frown. He remembered that Trixie from the La Paloma had worn a fandango skirt that shade of red, but he didn't remember inviting her up to his room.

Men who open doors in a pussyfooting way are just asking for a bullet from the far side, so Longarm grabbed the knob in his free hand, found that it turned, and kicked the door flat open. Trixie whirled to face him. He saw that she was alone and didn't have a weapon in either fist. She'd spread his bedroll open on the bed and had been going through his possibles. But her voice was calm as she said, "Oh, it's you. You startled me."

Longarm stepped inside and closed the door, still holding his .44 pointed politely at Trixie's toes. "I'm a mite startled, too. It's a good thing I carry my cash in my pants, ain't it?" he said.

Trixie shrugged defiantly. "I couldn't find you out on the street, so I came here. Fortunately the door was open."

He smiled crookedly. "I hope you won't take this as bad manners, ma'am, but while I'm only *sure* I locked the door as I left, I'm dead *certain* the bedroll was lashed to that saddle. I notice the buckles on my saddlebags have been opened, too. You likely didn't aim to break your nails buckling to the same holes, huh?"

"Damn it, cowboy, are you calling me a liar?"

"Yes, ma'am. You seem to be a burglar, too. I reckon you didn't expect me home so sudden. But I'm sort of disappointed in Los Angeles. It gets colder here at night than Dodge in the summer, and the people ain't as friendly."

Trixie licked her lips and started to unbutton her tight satin bodice as she said, "Look, I only wanted to ask you to pay for the damage to my Wheel of Fortune. You can see for yourself that I haven't stolen anything."

34

Longarm knew that was probably true. His Winchester was still tied to the borrowed saddle. His remaining front money was in his hip pocket with a wallet he could spare. His badge, ID, and emergency gold certificates were sewn into the lining of the vest he had on. So he said, "I never shot up your wheel. But even if I had, why are you taking off your duds, ma'am?"

Trixie's eyes were defiant as she answered coolly, "I have to look disheveled. For if you call the law on me, I mean to say you tried to rape me."

Longarm stared morosely down at her as he digested this and tried to think how an innocent saddle tramp would react to her stale old dodge. As a lawman, he knew how often female suspects fell back on it. But he wasn't supposed to be a lawman, or even very smart. Trixie stopped when she had one breast exposed. He grinned and said, "Keep going. You got nice tits and this is just getting interesting."

Trixie sat on the bed, raised a knee, and rolled one of her black stockings down around one ankle as she said, "There. Anyone with eyes can see how you pawed me as we wrestled. How was I to know you'd threaten me with calling the law when I refused your ungentle advances?"

Longarm nodded, threw his hat toward the coat tree across the room, and said, "How indeed? But don't you reckon the police court would wonder what such an innocent damsel was doing up in my room at this hour?"

He could see that Trixie was pondering that, so he went on, "I doubt like hell that the clerk downstairs will witness you slipping up here innocent. So it'd be my word against yours, and I don't have a record."

That hit her where she lived, but she still looked brassy as she demanded, "What makes you think I have a record, cowboy?"

"Oh, hell, I'll admit I never went to college, but your opinion of my education is downright insulting. I meet you spinning a crooked Wheel of Fortune in a red satin dress, I catch you red-handed burglarizing my digs, and you ask me how I know you've been in jail before!"

He took off his gun belt, hung it on a high hook she'd have trouble reaching, and started to unbutton his own duds. Trixie looked aghast and asked, "What are you doing?"

"Just following your suggestion, honey. I might have paid for fixing your wheel if you'd asked me polite. But first you tried to rob me and then you accused me of rape. So we ain't friends no more and I don't have to be nice to you. But like I said, you sure do have a nice pair of tits. The ankle you flashed to befuddle me is nicely turned, too."

Trixie rose from the bed as if it had suddenly turned into a hot stove. Longarm stiff-armed her back, sprawling her across his open bedroll and scattered possibles. She started to scream, but thought better of it, and tried some tears as he climbed aboard her, hauling up her skirts as he pinned her hair to the mattress with his other hand and kissed her.

Trixie tried to bite his face off, but he was too quick for her and her teeth just trimmed his mustache. He grabbed her exposed breast by the nipple and tweaked it, growling, "You try that again and I'll see if this twists off."

"Please," she whimpered, "I'm not that kind of girl." So he kissed her again, and as she responded politely this time, he let go of her nipple to run his hand down her trembling torso and up under her crumpled skirts. Trixie wasn't wearing anything under her fandango outfit. It was just as well. Longarm wasn't used to raping ladies, and by the time he was getting the hang of it, they were both hotter than two-dollar pistols. Every time he took his fingers out of her to unfasten another button, Trixie tried to cross her legs and cooled off a mite. So between buttons he'd stroke her some more and go for another button as he felt her starting to relax. She must have found it exciting too. Between kisses she said a dreadful thing about Longarm's mother and moaned, "You're teasing me cruel as hell, you brute."

But when he took her up on it to start getting seriously undressed, she crossed her knees and tried to sit up. She sure was a contrary little thing. Longarm shucked his pants down around his booted ankles, forced his free hand between her clamped-together thighs, and worked on the passion-wet little spitfire until she moaned and opened wide.

He got aboard again and thrust home. After that, who was raping whom was sort of up for grabs. Trixie was still making funny noises about not being that sort of gal when she got on top, planted a heel in each of his armpits, and began to bounce as if she were aboard a corkscrewing bronc and riding for prize money. Then she fell forward, legs jackknifed with a knee beside each of her ears as she groaned, "Oh, bastard, bastard, bastard, this is heaven and I *hate* you!"

"I noticed," he said, as she climaxed in a long, shuddering orgasm. Before she could cool off, he rolled her underneath him and started grinding with her ankles locked around his neck.

"Jesus, not so deep!" she cried. And as he eased off to settle in for a longer siege, she sighed and said, "Oh, that's just right. Don't stop. Don't ever stop. By the way, what's your name, cowboy?"

He said, "I'm Custis Long, as you should have figured out by now. I have it written in block letters on my saddlebags."

"Don't be nasty, Custis. I thought we'd agreed to forget about the past."

"Well, I've still got some hard feelings," he chuckled. "But I'm fixing to come and they'll soon be gone. More's the pity."

She laughed, contracted some inner muscles skillfully, and said, "You just keep *those* hard feelings as long as you're able. You're quite a man. But I suppose you've been told that before, eh?"

So she was getting used to him in the saddle and had started to con him with flattery. But, next to a gal in the first warm flush of enthusiasm, nothing screwed as good as a trail-town twist trying to make friends. It had been a long, dull train ride getting here, and it promised to be a long, dull cattle drive, leaving. It was too bad he didn't *like* Trixie; she was great in bed. But Longarm couldn't help his romantic streak. He closed his eyes and tried to pretend she was somebody nice. Somebody like that librarian who'd said no, that time.

But it was hard to imagine that prissy little virgin blonde with such an experienced love-pit. So he thought of Roping Sally and other gals he'd have liked to stay with longer, and when he got to the pretty Mexican gal who'd cried when he rode off, he knew he was almost there again and opened his eyes. Trixie looked exciting as hell in the faint light from the window-shade slit, with one black stocking still on and hellfire gleaming in her eyes, so he just decided to forgive her and they both enjoyed it.

When she suggested going sixty-nine, he said he was tired. Cunnilingus might be common courtesy with a gal a man respected, but Trixie was a thieving little tramp who didn't smell pure enough to eat for dessert. Besides, he knew she was just trying to wear him out too much to call the law on her, so he said they'd talk about French lessons in the morning, but he aimed to sleep on the idea.

They flopped atop the bed and cuddled while they shared a smoke. She told him the usual long, sad tale

38

about coming west with a man who betrayed her. He didn't make up much of an autobiography for himself. He snuffed out the smoke and lay still as she droned on and on about the way life had mistreated her. After a while Trixie asked, "Are you asleep, darling?"

Longarm didn't answer.

Trixie snuggled and talked quietly some more, until she saw she wasn't getting any answers. He lay doggo as she cautiously slid out of his arms, sat up, and started dressing with the lightning speed of a gal who'd done this sort of thing before.

Longarm watched under slitted eyelids as she got to her feet in the semidarkness. Trixie looked down at him thoughtfully, then bent to pick up his pants from the floor. He wasn't too surprised when she lifted his wallet. He watched her place the pants neatly on the foot of the bed before she tiptoed out, closing the door gently behind her. He waited until she'd had time to get well clear before he sat up with a wry chuckle and relit the lamp. He prided himself on never paying for a piece. But he hadn't paid; she'd rolled him. He had a plausible reason for needing that job with McBride's outfit, now. The brassy little bawd would doubtless brag to the street about her trick. That was likely why they called her Trixie.

He got to his feet and started to neaten up, rerolling his possibles and tying them behind the cantle of the stock saddle. He picked up his scattered duds, hung them on the wall hooks, and noticed that she'd slipped the empty wallet neatly back in his pants. It was comforting to know she wasn't all bad. He took out the wallet to see if she'd busted the stitching in her eagerness. He opened it and gaped in blank surprise.

His money was all there! The only things missing were some meaningless business cards he'd tucked in the wallet for the hell of it. He wondered what in thunder Trixie wanted with the business card of a

Denver whorehouse and the price list for the Black Cat Saloon.

He sat on the bed to reconsider his recent guest. Trixie hadn't come up here to steal, and it hardly seemed likely that she'd gone to all that bother to get laid. So what *was* her game?

She wasn't working for the law. A lady detective would have screamed when he took her up on that rape suggestion. At least, a *nice* lady detective would have. But somebody had sent her to check him out, sure as hell.

Longarm lit another smoke and ran the whole evening by for another look. Trixie couldn't report anything but the size of his pecker to anybody, since she hadn't found his badge or ID. But what had made anybody suspect him in the first place?

That train robber had recognized him; it was possible someone else in L.A. had. But if they'd known for sure who he was, why send Trixie to take such a chance?

He restudied the gunplay in the La Paloma. If the two government agents had spotted him as the law, it hadn't bothered them much. Old Boomer had saved his life. So that meant Boomer was either ignorant of his true reasons for being here or, if he suspected, hadn't wanted to see a fellow lawman murdered. If either government man had been worried about his being an undercover man checking up on them, they'd have let that outlaw kill him, so he decided to put Carver and Boomer on a back burner for now. That just left almost everyone else in Pueblo de Los Angeles. He shrugged, blew out the lamp, and decided to worry about it in the morning.

Chapter 4

Knowing he was being observed for some reason, Longarm had decided by the next sunrise to play his cards even closer to the vest. He'd aimed to drift over to the yards and see if anyone made him an offer. But instead he lugged his saddle to the nearby livery, hired a chestnut mare, and allowed that he aimed to have a look around.

The little town was tucked into a bend of the Los Angeles River where it wound around a range of chaparral-covered hills to meander off across the flats, a quarter-mile wide and a couple of inches deep.

Longarm headed west past frame and adobe houses strewn helter-skelter on the river's flood plain and steep hillsides, following the Sunset Trail they'd told him about. He ran out of town in no time. He rode with the hills on his right and the flat semidesert basin on his left. The flats were covered with stirrup-high wild mustard, a range plant considered a pest in other parts. He knew the Californians grazed their Spanish cows on it; that was likely why California beef wasn't popular back East. A cow could live on wild mustard and cheat grass, but it made for stringy beef that tasted gamy as hell. The Mexicans were used to it, and the Indians had no say about what they ate, so he could see how it could be a bargain for the BIA, but it was a pure puzzle why someone was going to so much trouble to steal it.

The brown hills to his right were called the Cahuenga Mountains for some reason. Longarm had no idea what a cahuenga was, but they sure weren't mountains to a Colorado rider. They rose about as high as the Cumberlands he'd tramped over as a boy in West-by-God Virginia. He studied them some, knowing he'd be looking for stolen cows in country related to them. The local Mexicans had burned off some of the chaparral for sheep range here and there, but it was mostly rough, leg-ripping brush. Greasewood and scrub oak covered most of the high country, with California laurel and stuff they called coast holly choking the draws. The folks around here called those brush-filled gullies canyons, though they didn't look like canyons to Longarm. He noticed that a little water ran out of some of the bigger "canyons," to dry up and die on the furnace-hot flats between the Cahuengas and the Baldwin Hills to the south. He saw that local small-holders had built little spreads here and there, where there was water, and some of them had a few acres of what looked like beans fighting the wild mustard for survival. He stopped to ask for water at an adobe house in the shade of giant live oak trees, and the Mexicans who lived there insisted on his having some home-grown wine. But when he asked the friendly Mexicans if they knew about any jobs, they just looked sad. So he rode on.

He was about five miles out of town when he spotted the glint of sunlight on a spyglass. He pretended not to notice, but there was a *mirador* up there on the ridge above him, anyway. Longarm had run into *miradores,* or rather, spotted them before. They sort of went with

Spanish country. *Mirador* meant "gazer" or "watcher." The Mexicans who'd explained this to Longarm said they had no idea what the watchers were watching, either. Nobody ever admitted to being one, and of course there was no way to ask a gent scouting you from a distant ridge, since he'd just drop down the far side and vanish if you tried. *Miradores* were sort of spooky, but they never seemed to hurt anybody. They just seemed to go with the country and the people, like red peppers hanging on the walls.

Longarm rode on, waving to some Mex kids herding goats. They waved back and, like him, seemed to accept the mysterious watcher up on the ridge as a part of nature they were used to.

A while later, just as he was getting thirsty again, he spied the remains of what the map said had been a stage station near the Cahuenga Pass. Another rider was watering his own mount, pumping a hand pump into a weathered wooden trough. Longarm rode up and said howdy, since the other looked Anglo. The stranger smiled and said, "Howdy your own self. My handle is Pronto Boyde, and the water here is free, if that's your notion."

Longarm said to call him Long as he dismounted in front of the roofless adobe station. He led his hired mare to the trough and said, "I'm new in these parts." And Pronto said, "I noticed. I see by your double rig and grass rope that you're a tie-down roper."

Longarm nodded at the center-fire saddle and braided leather reata on Pronto's gray and said, "I see you ain't. Do all you California hands ride Mexican?"

"We have to," Pronto told him. "These Spanish cows ain't as delicate as they look, but the rancheros don't let us bust 'em Texas or High Plains style."

Longarm said, "Hell, I rode out here looking for a job. Would you know where I could find the Hancock spread? I hear tell they're American folks, like me."

43

"They are, but you're headed the wrong way." Pronto pointed at a distant smoke smudge, out across the flats to the south. "Yonder's the Hancock ranch. But you're wasting your time, pilgrim. They already have more Mex vaqueros than they need. I ride for the Hollywood ranch, up there in the pass. I'll save you a ride by telling you *we* ain't hiring, neither."

Longarm sighed and asked, "Who owns what's over there to the west?" Pronto said, "It's open range till you get to Don Manasco's place. He'll coffee and grub you, but he won't hire an Anglo, grass-rope or reata. If I was you, I'd look up Cracker McBride, back in town. I hear he's forming up a big cattle drive and he might need help."

"I heard mention of that in town. Don't you reckon he'll have already hired all the hands he needs?"

"Not hardly. Boys who already have good jobs ain't about to sign up for a long drive this time of the year. If you're any good he can likely use you."

"I'm tolerable good," Longarm allowed, "but I don't admire eating dust all the way to San Francisco, either."

Then, having established that he was still reluctant about the job he really wanted, Longarm bent down, took a handful of water for himself, and said, "There's some gent with a spyglass staring at us, Pronto."

Pronto said wearily, "I know. He's up there on Mount Lee playing Vasquez."

"Vasquez? Wasn't he a bandit you folks had trouble with out here one time?"

Pronto laughed easily. " 'One time' was long ago, back in the Gold Rush days. Old Vasquez used to hold up stages running through Cahuenga Pass to the Mission San Fernando on the far side. As you can see, there ain't no stage line anymore. Vasquez was shot back in the fifties. They cornered him in the Santa Monicas, just west of the pass, in a place called Spider Canyon. Hell of a fight, the way the oldtimers tell it."

"What's that fool up there doing if he ain't riding with the late Señor Vasquez, then?" Longarm asked.

"Beats the shit out of me. We call them fellers *miradores*. They just ride around up there looking spooky for some fool Mex reason. They might be kids, you never get close enough to see. But since they seem content to just sulk up there, we don't pay them much mind."

It was a natural opening, so Longarm said, "Well, I don't know much about Mexicans, bandits or otherwise, but they do make me sort of thoughtful, staring down at us like that. Have you been missing any cows lately?"

Pronto shook his head. "Hell, it's hard to steal cows in *this* country, Long."

"Do tell? Seems to me a man throwing a community loop could hide a mess of critters up in all those brushy draws you grow out here."

"*Stealing* cows ain't the problem," Pronto said. "*Hiding* them ain't the problem. *Getting away with it* is the problem. Aside from the fact that every water hole is claimed and knowed, there's no place to sell a stolen cow around here."

"Couldn't an old boy who'd gone into business for himself claim a modest spread and sort of wait until the brands he'd run healed a mite before he allowed he had some beef to market?"

Pronto smirked and leaned back on the pump, arms folded. "I can see you sure don't know California, cowboy. I just told you all the water rights are sewed up tight, and these old families out here are so inbred that you can't fart without a neighbor in the next county commenting on the smell. The Anglo and Mex rancheros are thick as thieves, and they all belong to the same vigilance committee. You throw a rope on the wrong critter in these parts and you'll wind up hanging from it on a live oak tree!"

Longarm held up a hand, palm outward. "Hell, I

never said *I* had a running iron in my saddlebags, old son. I was just asking because of that jasper spying on us and because I'd heard something about cows getting stolen from those trail herds you mentioned."

"Oh, them," Pronto said. "I heard that, too. But that's different. You have to expect to lose some beef, driving all the way north along the Old Mission Trail. The country gets downright uncivilized, north of San Fernando. Wait till you see the busted up badlands between here and Santa Bob. You can lose cows up there without any help at all."

Longarm thanked Pronto for the advice and allowed that he didn't aim to join the trail herd anyway. He mounted up and rode on to the west. He meant to ask for a job all the way out to the ocean before he turned back, "defeated" and ready to be talked into it.

Longarm wasted most of the day getting turned down by a mess of otherwise friendly folk who'd remember that he wasn't interested in joining the cattle drive. He wasted so much time that darkness caught him on the trail and the damp sea mists chased him into the little town as all the nice folks were getting ready for bed. He wondered what the *bad* folks were doing. So he returned the hired mount to the livery and his saddle and rifle to his room. This time the match in the doorjamb said he hadn't had any visitors while he'd been out. That meant they'd decided there wasn't anything worth looking for, he hoped.

He went back out. He glanced into the La Paloma and saw that Trixie wasn't there; another gal was spinning the repaired Wheel of Fortune. She wasn't bad, but even a dumb cowhand would hardly push his luck by returning to the scene of a shootout. He crossed over to the saloon where Carver and Boomer hung out. They weren't there, but he bellied up to the bar and ordered anyway.

A big, beefy man in faded blue denim and a Texas

46

hat big enough for a family of Indians to live in got up from a corner table and walked over to Longarm. Longarm noticed he was packing an S&W .45 in a cross-draw rig, but the stranger put his hands on the bar politely and said, "If your name is Long, I've been looking for you."

"I hope you mean that friendly," Longarm said, and the other replied, "I do. The bar gal said you was in here last night with Boomer and his boss. I don't like Carver much, but Boomer is a pal of mine."

"He's sort of a pal of mine, too. While he was describing me, did he mention saving my ass?"

"He did. My name is McBride, but you can call me Cracker. I rode for the Georgia Militia in the War Between the States."

Longarm said, "I disremember who I rode for. You can call me Custis, and I hail from West Virginia by way of Colorado and other parts too tedious to mention."

"Border guerrilla rider, huh? Well, it was a long time ago, whichever side you rode for. Boomer told me you were looking for a job, and it's his opinion that you look like you know which end of a cow the shit falls out of."

Longarm signaled the bartender for an extra glass and told him to leave the bottle before he told McBride, "Boomer told you true. But he said you were headed out on a long drive in high summer, too. I'm looking for less tedious work."

McBride helped himself to a drink and said, "You won't find better around here. I pay top dollar and I need at least three more drag riders."

Longarm snorted in carefully feigned disbelief. "I'll still drink with you, but let's not swap no more insults. I ride as a top hand when I ride at all."

McBride took a sip of redeye and said, "I'd have to know you better before I hired you that high on the

47

totem pole, Long. You sound like you think you're good."

"I'm tolerable. I ain't rode drag since I started shaving regular. Any ragged-ass kid can hold the tail end of the herd. If Captain Goodnight was here he'd tell you about the time I turned a stampede with Shoshone yelling from the far side of the herd. I'd tell you myself, but that'd be bragging."

McBride shrugged and said, "I never said you looked like a sissy. Why don't you drift down to the yards, come morning, and let us see some cutting and roping?"

Longarm shrugged right back. "Maybe I will and maybe I won't. Like I said, a man would have to be a mite desperate before he chased cows so far in all this heat."

"We're leaving day after tomorrow, early. If you expect to be signed on as a top hand, don't come crawling to us at the last minute."

"I don't crawl much, McBride."

"Whatever. *I* don't take much shit, either, Long. I'm telling you friendly that you won't get a better job in this basin than the one I'm offering. If you don't want to ride for me, ride for somebody else. If you think you're good enough to sign on as a top hand, get your ass over to the yards and let me see you work cows. Anybody can *talk* like a cowboy, but it's tedious as hell to watch folks rope their own mount's head, or just fall off."

McBride put a silver dollar on the bar and said, "You drink and study on what I said until this is all gone. If you can cut the mustard, you'll find me a good man to work for. If you're all wind, we'll just say no more about it, hear?"

McBride stalked out, spurs ringing. The back of his neck was a mite red. Longarm decided he either needed hands or else he was a damned good actor. It hardly seemed likely he'd be going to so much trouble to hire a lawman, if he knew Longarm was a lawman, and if he had anything to hide.

Longarm wasn't about to put away a dollar's worth of redeye alone. So he pocketed the cartwheel and left some small change in its place before he left.

He lit a smoke as he got his bearings on the dimly lit street, and decided that home was as good a place as any to go. He had to be bright-eyed and bushy-tailed when he showed up at the stockyards in the morning. He knew he was in for some hazing, and it was important that he passed all tests with flying colors. Unless McBride signed him on as a top hand, following the herd north undercover would be a waste of the taxpayer's money. A top hand got to ride all positions, looking for trouble. A common trail hand rode the one position assigned to him. A hand riding left flank would have a hell of a time spotting anybody cutting beef from the right, and a drag rider saw little more than dust.

He started for his hotel. But as he passed a narrow, dark slit between the buildings, a whispering female voice called, "*Hsst!* Señor Long!"

Longarm didn't think much of being seen standing out in the lamplight jawing with somebody invisible, so he glanced around, saw that nobody on the street was looking his way, and ducked in to join the dimly visible form of the *mujer* who'd invited him. It was a tight fit between the adobe walls, but he slid his back against one to face her. The far end was as black as a coalbin at midnight, but anybody using it for a bowling alley had a good chance of nailing the gal, if she was a decoy.

The girl said, "I had to warn you, Señor. They are waiting for you at your hotel near the church."

"Thanks. Who are they? And while we're on the subject, who are you?"

"Don't you recognize me, Señor? I am Pepita, the waitress from next door?"

"Oh, right," he said. "I can hardly see you in this

49

light." In truth, he wouldn't have known who she was at high noon. Longarm had learned a long time ago that most waitresses were a lost cause, so he never flirted with them unless they started it. He had a vague mental picture of a mousy little Mex gal in a flounce skirt and an off-the-shoulder, pleated cotton blouse. Now that he was belly-to-belly with her, he could smell the rose in her hair. She said, "I heard them talking as I was serving their table in the back room. One of them said you had killed his friend. The other one said not to start a fight in there. He said he knew where you were staying."

Longarm frowned down at her and asked, "What did they look like? More important, were they with Cracker McBride when I came in?"

"Señor McBride was at another table," Pepita told him. "He had asked me to point you out to him, so I did. Those others did not hear this. They are strangers to me, so I would have hesitated in any case. One was short, with curly blond hair. The other was almost as tall as you, with dark hair and a scar on his left cheek. I did not hear any names except yours. What are we to do?"

"That's a good question, Pepita. They ain't in there now, huh?"

"No. They left as you were speaking to Señor McBride. I was afraid to approach you until I was sure they had left for good. I did not wish for to warn you inside, in case they have other friends who might tell on me. I sneaked out the back and came through this passage, knowing you would pass this way."

"Hmm, does your boss know about all this, Pepita?"

"No. I thought it best to trust no *gringo* with a secret that could get me killed if the wrong people heard about it."

Longarm nodded, but said, "You sure take chances for a dime tip, Honey. How come you stuck your pretty

Spanish nose into a tussle between us Anglos, if you're scared?"

"*Por favor,* I did not wish for them to hurt you because . . . because I think you are pretty!"

Longarm digested this before he said, "I think you're pretty, too."

She gave a shuddering sigh. "Oh, this makes me so happy. How may I call you, *querido?*"

"My folks named me Custis, but *querido* suits me fine," said Longarm. Then he kissed her, to show his neighborly feelings.

Pepita responded warmly as he glued her to his body with one hand between her shoulder blades and another cupping her tailbone. Then she pushed him back, which wasn't far because of the slot they were standing in, and said, "We cannot stay here, and if you go to your hotel they will kill you, *querido mío.*"

"Where do you reckon I should be heading, then?"

"My room is not far, *querido.* You will be safe there. Nobody I work with knows where I live."

Longarm sighed and said, "I sure hope you won't take this personal, honey lamb, but the last time I followed a Mexican gal I'd just met down a dark alley, a couple of hombres swarmed all over me with knives. They wanted my boots, I reckon."

Pepita stiffened in his arms and gasped, "*Nombre de Dios!* Do you think Pepita is a wicked woman?"

"I sure hope so. But I've got this fool habit called thinking twice. Your words have put me in a thinking pickle, and that's a fact. If I head back to my hotel and you're telling me the truth, I could wind up dead. On the other hand, if I follow a strange lady into a pitch-black maze and she's *not* telling the truth, I could wind up just as dead and, even worse, looking foolish."

Pepita started to cry. He reached out and stroked her shoulder. "Aw, don't do that, honey. I ain't saying you're a liar. I just said I had to study on it."

51

"You think Pepita is a wicked woman. You think I told you I liked you for to lure you into a trap."

Longarm reeled her in and started kissing the tears from her eyelids. The kissing part was fun, and it also proved that her tears were real. He pinned her back to the wall with his weight and started patting her down for concealed weapons or anything else interesting under her clothes. As he cupped a firm cantaloupe-sized breast in his wandering hand, she gasped, "Oh, what are you *doing*, Señor?"

He said, "I like it better when you call me *querido*. I thought you said you liked me."

"I do, but we are out in public and—"

"Hush, now, we ain't in public. We're snug as two bugs in love in here. Nobody could see us, even if they hadn't started to roll up the sidewalks. Most of the town's in bed, and the streetlights are starting to burn out."

He kissed her some more as he slid his hand down her trembling flank and opened her thighs with his knee. Pepita moaned with her lips against his, and he started working her skirt up a fold at a time while massaging her groin. She kept trying to say something, but he kept shutting her up with hot kisses until suddenly there wasn't any skirt to lift and he had two fingers in her. He waited until she started moving her hips in time to his petting before he got his other hand down to unbutton his fly. Pepita spoke into his mouth as she protested, "No, this is impossible!"

"It ain't impossible," he replied. "It's just improbable and a mite ingenious."

He had to spread his own legs wide to lower his center of gravity as he got his love tools out and into position. Pepita thrust her pelvis up and out to meet his entry even as she protested, "We can't do it standing up!" And then her eyes opened wide and she gasped, "Oh, *Madre de Dios*, I see we *can!*"

In truth, it was more teasing and clumsy than Longarm liked. Between her bunched-up skirt and his gun-belt, it was impossible to get in all the way, standing up or not. The gal's legs were too short, and his own were too awkwardly placed to do things right. He braced her against the wall behind her, reached down for her right thigh, and lifted. She asked what he was doing as he hooked her knee over the sixgun riding on his left hip. He answered with a deeper thrust. Then he swung his right hand down to grab her left leg, and as he lifted her remaining foot completely off the ground she said, "Help, I'm going to fall!"

But she didn't. Longarm hoisted Pepita's left leg high, hooked an elbow under it, and slid her higher up the wall to do it right, with his legs straight and Pepita moaning like a cougar in heat. She was wide open, with her rump braced on the brick wall. He came hard, ahead of her, and kept going to be polite. He was getting the hang of it by now. He had his hands flat against the adobe wall on either side of her and she'd cooperated in getting the other leg off his gun and over his left elbow. She goaned, "Oh, I am dying!" and he admitted, "I can feel it. This would be a lot more fun if only we could find someplace to lie down and talk about it."

Pepita didn't answer until her orgasm subsided. Then, cradled limply in her grotesque spread-eagle position, she giggled and said, "You are loco, but *muy toro*. Let us go now to my room and do it right, eh?"

So Longarm went. He was still suspicious, but at least he'd sort of established that she liked him. His crude alley seduction had been more than lust, as nice as it had been. He'd learned that Spanish-speaking gals almost never betrayed a man they were fond enough to screw. Treacherous Anglo gals seemed to start right out by making love to a man they aimed to take advantage of, but while a Mex gal might be out to mess an old boy up, it seemed a point of honor with them that all the sucker was entitled to was batted eyelashes and dirty talk. He knew that border-town gangs used female decoys to get a victim alone in an alley, but the hard-cased little *señoritas* who worked that game never gave themselves. Pepita might still hit him for money, of course; Mexican whores liked to say it was love. But Mexican whores were otherwise honest working girls who seldom robbed a customer.

Of course, many a man had been buried in the past for trusting too much to local custom, so Longarm had his derringer palmed in his hand and was walking on eggs as he followed Pepita through a maze of back alleyways up into the old Spanish quarter on the hill-side northwest of the main drag. He let her go first. When they got to her door, he stood to one side as she opened it. Then he moved in fast and flattened his back to a blank wall as he waited for her to close the door and light a candle.

The room was small and empty. The only furniture was a bed against the wall, some crates with bottles and such on them, and a plaster *santo* set in a dug-out niche above the bed. There were no other doors. The window was made out of beer-bottle bottoms set in cement, and was impossible to see through. It sure looked like she was telling the truth. He tested the door anyway. It was solid oak and had an iron bar to secure it on the inside, so Longarm did.

Pepita sat on the bed, staring up at him confusedly. Now that they were friends, Longarm studied her back. It was sort of funny, but he'd had a totally different picture of her face, getting to know her as he had in the dark. Pepita was a short, shapely girl, which came as no surprise, but she was prettier than he remembered from the casual glances he'd given her in the saloon. She had Spanish features, with Apache eyes. Her hair was blue-black and shimmered down to her bare shoulders. Her skin was that sort of peach-orange shade that *mestizas* with a lot of white blood tended to have. She said, "I feel so strange now."

54

"Do you want me to leave?" he asked.

"No, of course not. You know I wanted for you to come here with me, but everything happened so suddenly, and now I feel so low in your eyes. Why do you look at Pepita like that? You have such knowing eyes. I feel like they look right through me."

He smiled gently. "Just through your clothes, honey. Let's get out of these fool duds and get to know each other better."

He suited actions to his words by taking off his hat and gunbelt. Pepita held up a restraining hand. "Wait, I must put out the light. I feel most bashful."

She snuffed out the candle and they undressed in the dark. The moonlight through the beer-bottle window dappled the bed in brown and green, and Pepita was outlined against it as she took her clothes off and folded them on a crate. Then she got on the bed, looking sort of like a naughty stained-glass window in the funny light as she warned, "Don't look at me. I know I am too fat."

Longarm scattered his duds to the four winds but made sure his gun was where he could get at it before he joined her. He still had his derringer palmed, and as he slid it between the head of the bed and the wall, Pepita asked, "What is that, *querido?*"

"My watch," he answered. It wasn't a lie. Longarm had his derringer and Ingersoll attached to either end of the gold chain he usually wore across his vest front. "A man never knows when he may want to see what time it is," he said, then he rolled her into his arms and kissed her.

She responded warmly but asked, "Do you think I am too fat, now that I am naked?"

"Honey, you are built like a brick nevermind," he reassured her. "It's natural for a short gal to be sort of curvaceous, and you curve just right."

"I suppose you are used to those tall skinny Anglo women, no?"

He started petting her into a more sensible frame of mind as he replied, "Honey, if I didn't like enchaladas I wouldn't be here." Then he got a finger where they both wanted it and added, "You got a hot little enchalada here, and that's a fact."

She sighed and surrendered by opening her thighs as he mounted her with no further ado. It was a lot nicer this way. She acted like she thought so too, so they just went crazy for a while.

Later, as she nestled her head on his bare shoulder while he enjoyed a smoke, Pepita asked, "Do you really like Pepita, Costees?"

Here it comes, he thought. *I wonder how much she's going to ask for, and how I'll write it off on my expense voucher.*

Pepita started playing with the hairs on his chest as she asked, "I have been wondering why those hombres were after you tonight."

"Me too," he said. "It likely has something to do with that shootout in the La Paloma. I was sort of an innocent bystander, but Boomer said the man he shot was a wanted owlhoot. Maybe those other gents are pals of his and think I had something to do with it."

"I think so, too. But I heard the men speaking of the fight. They say the man who was shot was trying for to shoot you, no?"

"I reckon so. I didn't notice until Boomer nailed him. I thought he was a cowhand I had harsh words with, once. I didn't know he robbed trains on the side. Since he was after me, he must have been that gent I tangled with back East. But that's all I can tell you."

"All you can, or all you *will, querido?*"

"What's that supposed to mean, Pepita?"

"Oh, I was just wondering. One of the men said you were a lawman. That would explain many things, no?"

Longarm took a deep drag on his cheroot, let it out,

56

and kept his voice light as he chuckled and said, "It'd sure save me having to look so hard for a job. If these owlhoot pards of the man who got shot suspicion me for law, it explains why they're so unforgiving. I wish I did pack a badge. I'd march over to the police station, gather me a posse, and surround that hotel before I had a talk with them."

"I didn't think you were a range detective, *querido,*" she said.

Who did she think she was bullshitting? Longarm wondered. He felt both better and worse now, as things fell into place. There wasn't anybody gunning for him; he'd thought that story about a scarfaced killer sounded a mite dramatic. A Mex gal working as an honest waitress seldom dragged a total stranger home to bed just because she thought he was pretty. Somebody had sicced her on him. She wasn't asking for money because she'd already been paid!

Well, two could play at the same game. If push came to shove, he could probably scare her into talking if he couldn't match their price.

He took another pull on his cheroot as Pepita started to fondle him. He didn't know if she wanted more or if she aimed to lull him between shrewd questions. He decided to stay a dumb cowhand. If the folks she worked for had him pegged as a lawman, they wouldn't have asked her to work on him. If he took the gloves off and started playing rough, they'd know for sure. Even if he unmasked them, the game would be over; he didn't have a charge he could make an arrest on. Hell, he could frog-march the whole bunch in front of a judge and the case would be thrown out of court. Nobody had stolen a cow since he'd arrived. Nobody was *about* to steal a cow with a lawman anywhere near it. Instead of trying to find out who Pepita was working for, he had to convince them he was just a saddle tramp they didn't have to worry about.

He put his hand on Pepita's wrist and said, "Hold it. I have to finish this smoke and get my strength back. What makes you so nervous about lawmen, honey? Even if I was a sheriff or such, I couldn't hardly arrest *you*, could I?"

She was good and she knew it. She was a natural chess master who moved into any opening. Not knowing he was even better at her game than she was, she bit.

She sounded genuinely worried as she said, "I had to warn you. But, for to tell the truth, Pepita is glad you are not with the *gringo* law."

"Oh, have you been up to something, honey?"

"Nothing really wicked. Just a silly *gringo* law about . . . I don't know if I should tell you. Can I trust you?"

He hugged her closer and murmured, "With your life, you pretty little thing, but don't tell me if you think I might blab on you."

She started to fondle him some more as she said, "Oh, I know you would not tell. You see, I am not supposed to be in your country."

He threw his head back and laughed. "Hell, is that all? I thought you'd done something wrong."

"They say it *is* wrong. I have been so frightened. If they find out, they will send me back to Sonora, and we were so poor there."

"Hell, who's going to find out?" he asked with a shrug. "Who'd be looking? Half the folks in California are Mexican. I reckon it's left over from us taking the place from Mexico a while back. I can't even get a job because of all the Mex vaqueros working here for next to nothing."

"What would I do if some *gringo* lawman asked to see my citizenship papers, *querido*?"

He started to explain that nobody would, because sorting native-born Mexican-Americans from immigrants was impossible. But then he remembered that he wasn't supposed to know all that much about the law, so he said, "Ask to see *his*, I reckon. If push came to shove, I'd have a time showing proof of my citizenship. I was birthed at home and nobody took official notice of it. I don't see why anybody would want to turn you in, honey. You're too pretty, and friendly as hell besides."

He snuffed out the smoke and prepared to remount, but now she wanted to talk some more. "Are you going to ride with McBride's herd, *querido?*" she asked.

"Nope. All the riding I want is right here in bed with me."

He rolled atop her as she protested, "But you said you could not get a job here in the basin. I am afraid you will be forced to take that job with McBride, and then what will happen to Pepita?"

He entered her and said, "If I'm forced to, you know I'll come back to you by and by. And speaking of coming, let's quit talking about *mañana* and enjoy the here and now!"

Chapter 5

Cracker McBride had twenty-five hundred head penned in the yards when Longarm moseyed over the next morning. Twenty-five hundred doesn't sound like such an awesome number, just saying it right out, but milling and bawling on the hoof, it was one hell of a mess of beef.

Longarm found McBride and the government buyer, Carver, seated on a top rail near the branding chutes. The yard behind them was filled with cows and cowshit-scented dust clouds. A fainter smell of scorched hide and burnt hair drifted on the light breeze from time to time. A couple of kids who worked for Carver were stamping a big ID on the flanks of each critter they poked through the branding chute. Longarm noticed that the varicolored scrub cows had older, healed brands, which came as no surprise. The herd was being put together from dozens of surrounding spreads, but now that they belonged to the Interior Department, the fact was being properly advertised. The boys shoved a calico into a holding yard, its big new brand still smoking, and poked a crooked-horned ladino in to take its medicine. The critter bawled like hell when the hot stamping iron hit it. McBride asked, "Have you come to help them kids trail-mark? I notice you're on foot."

Longarm planted a boot up on a lower rail and said, "I've been sort of studying on that. You know I'm a tie-down roper. Aside from being leather-jawed crow bait, all the ponies over at the livery seem to be Spanish-trained. A man could get hurt roping tie-down with a mount expecting him to dally."

McBride nodded. "I know. Our remuda holds seven or eight mounts for each hand. Every one is trained California style. They might hold still for a double-rig saddle, but you'd play hell trying to bust a cow aboard one, your way."

Carver looked confused. The tie he wore likely explained it. He asked what they were talking about and McBride explained, "Old Long here is a High Plains roper who ties his grass rope to the saddle horn and pops 'em down direct. My dally ropers use reatas, wrapped, not tied, around their bigger horns. A braided leather reata throws better but it ain't as strong, so you have to sort of play the critter like a fish as it hits the end of the line."

Carver looked as confused as ever, so McBride gave up his attempt to explain the intricacies of cowpunching to him, and said, "I'll tell you what, Long. I'll sign you on as a drag rider anyway. You won't have to do any roping back there, and I'd feel better with an older hand watching the kids. I'm sort of worried about a couple of 'em. A cow*boy* is one thing. A cow*baby* is another. There's one who swears he's sixteen, but I was bigger than that at ten."

Longarm shook his head and said, "Not hardly. I came over to see how you boys were getting along because you invited me. I'll allow I can't seem to land a job as top hand anywhere else, but if I ride for you at all, it'll be top hand or nice talking to you."

"Damn it, Long, you know a top hand might be called on to do some roping."

"I do. I said I *liked* to rope tie-down. I never said I couldn't dally."

McBride eased his bulk off the fence and stood, arms akimbo, in front of Longarm. "You consider yourself the bee's knees, do you? Well, let's find out."

Longarm followed as McBride led him down the fenceline to where some other riders were perched like crows, spitting and whittling. Longarm noticed that they were a mixed bag of Mex and Anglo riders, with one lone Chinese who looked a trifle odd in batwing chaps and a flat Spanish hat. McBride yelled, "Boys, I want you all to meet up with Custis Long, who says he knows how to ride and rope like Buffalo Bill and Captain Goodnight rolled in one. Could you find it in your heart to find him a mount, Fong?"

The Chinese cowhand grinned slyly but nodded politely to Longarm before he called out, "Sanchez, why don't you saddle up old Gila for our guest? We'll drift over to yard seven. There's a couple of cows over there that just came in. They're still trail-spooked, and maybe a little exercise would steady them before we run them in with the others."

Fong got down and the others fell in behind as the Chinese led the way. Behind them, Longarm heard one snicker something under his breath. It was going to be like that, was it? He hadn't expected it to be any other way. Signing on as a new hand was tedious as hell. That was one of the reasons he'd quit to work for Uncle Sam.

Fong turned out to be the boss wrangler. Longarm knew he had to be good, and didn't fret about what he knew was coming. He knew it wasn't just cruel humor or cussedness. Half the fool kids in the country seemed to run out west to be cowboys, and anyone who'd read Ned Buntline's Wild West Magazine could get the lingo reasonably right. But it was important to know how good the man riding next to you was, when things got scaly out between the townships. More than one old boy had been killed when a comrade he depended on had let him down. So men who worked with cows were leery as hell about riding with a man who just *said* he'd seen the elephant.

Fong stopped at a nearly empty yard and pointed out three longhorns bunched in a far corner. He said, "These are the spooks I mentioned, Long. Tell me what you see."

Longarm looked the critters over and said, "The two that ladino has against the corner rails are just scrub heifers. The ladino was castrated clumsy. He don't know he's supposed to be a steer. He thinks he's a bull and he's protecting his lady loves."

McBride said, "Anybody can see that. What do you aim to do about it, Long?"

Longarm said, "Cut him out, bust him, and drive the she-critters into the next yard. If you weren't fixing to start the drive, I'd say to finish by cutting him right. As it is, I'd cull him and ask for my money back. You can't drive a fresh-cut steer, and a half-bull on the trail figures to make more trouble than he's worth."

There was a general growl of agreement, but Longarm knew he wasn't out of the woods yet.

A Mex vaquero came up to them, leading a walleyed bronc with nervous hooves. Longarm saw that the saddle was center-fire and the rope was braided leather. He took the reins and said, "I'll mount up if one of you gents would be kind enough to open the gate."

Then he forked himself aboard and all hell broke loose.

Gila headed for the sky, sunfishing, as the others laughed like hell. Gila was a gila monster, all right. He came down stiff-legged and started crow-hopping along the rails, trying to scrape Longarm's leg off as the jovial crew got out of the way. Somebody yelled, "Ride him, cowboy. He's frisky in the morning, but he wants to be your friend!"

"Son of a bitch," Longarm muttered at both the wise-ass and the horse as he raised a knee while the bronc smashed into the rail. Gila saw that *that* wasn't working, so he settled down to some serious bucking.

Longarm was serious about staying aboard, so he cranked the brute's head against his right boot to make him dance in a tight, predictable circle. Gila tried to bite his toes, and Longarm kicked hard and drew blood from Gila's nostrils. Nobody likes to be kicked in the nose, so Gila quit fooling around and just stood there, his flanks heaving, waiting to see what his new master wanted. Longarm gave him some rein, braced for a sly buck, and when Gila raised his head and stayed polite, he wheeled him and ran him up and down the fenceline a few times as they got to know each other better. As he passed McBride once more, the trail boss shouted, "You're hard as hell on horseflesh. Do you aim to ride all day in the park or could you see about that damned ladino in there?"

Longarm slid Gila to a stop near the gate, shook out some reata, and said, "Open the gate."

One of the hands slid the gate on its rollers and Longarm rode in. The ladino charged, as he'd expected. Gila had been expecting it, too. He was a good cutting horse when he wasn't in a homicidal mood. The ladino missed as he tried to hook the sidestepping pony, then whirled and charged again like an express train. No Spanish matador would have lasted against the brute. The ladino didn't play by any rules. He charged with his head up, looking where he was going and hooking back and forth, trying to corner the horse. Longarm left the dodging to his mount as he whirled his reata, holding the loop open and high for an opportune moment.

The moment came as the ladino banged into the rails, bounced off, and shook his head to clear it. Longarm dropped the loop over his horns, took a dally, and heeled Gila into a running circle as he shook out more slack. He had the noose tight on the ladino's head. He whipped the slack like a kid playing with a jumprope, and when he got it under the ladino's legs, he yanked hard and spilled the critter. As the sloppily castrated steer landed on its side, bawling, Longarm vaulted from the saddle, ran over, grabbed the top horn, and twisted the critter's neck to give it an unobstructed view of the sky as he quickly whipped the slack of his reata around its flailing hooves. Two other hands ran in to help hogtie it. Longarm stood up, dusting his pants with his hat, and said, "I'd have done that sooner and neater with a proper horse and some pigging string, but what the hell."

He saw that the others had the ladino under control, so he walked over to his mount. Gila rolled a thoughtful eye at him. "You just stand *still*, you son of a bitch!" Longarm warned the horse, who took the warning seriously.

He mounted up, and since nobody had seen fit to open the other gate, he rode over and did it himself. Then he circled, waved his hat at the heifers and called out, "After you, ladies."

He drove the two she-critters into the empty neighboring yard and was sliding the gate shut when behind him he heard someone shouting, "Sweet Jesus, *hold* him!"

Longarm turned in the saddle to see that the rogue ladino had busted the reata and was on its feet again, moving.

Hands scattered as the ladino charged. Some damned fool had left the other gate open. Cracker McBride was exiting through it at surprising speed for such a big gent in high California heels, but the ladino was right behind and gaining as McBride tore out through the gate, hooked a fencepost with a hand, and swung himself around on the outside of the fence. Longarm spurred his mount in pursuit, realizing at the same time that he had no rope, but playing it by ear. Most critters would just have headed out for parts unknown, but the ladino was a killer who likely felt abused. He slid to a halt, wagged his horns, and charged after McBride down the fenceline, with Longarm following at a dead run.

McBride kept glancing back, wide-eyed, as he tried to put enough distance between himself and those horns to haul himself up on the fence. But everybody, including the bull, could see that if he stopped running to start climbing, it would all be over. Longarm rode alongside, giving up on trying to cut the critter away from the fence. It ignored him and Gila in its hot pursuit of McBride, so Longarm swore and threw *himself* at the critter, head first!

He wrapped his arms around the ladino's horns and hung on until his bootheels came down and dug in. The shock twisted the ladino's muzzle skyward again, and they went down in a hell of a pileup, but Longarm wound up mostly on top, with the ladino's horn tips stuck in the ground.

McBride stopped, turned around and drew his gun. "Roll aside, old son," he said, and when Longarm did, McBride shot the rogue between the eyes. Then he said, "That's that." His face was the color of buttermilk.

Longarm got to his feet and said, "I should have worn my chaps. I tore my damn pants out at the knee."

McBride took off his hat and mopped his brow with his sleeve. "I noticed. I owe you, pard. But what in the hell was that you just done?"

Longarm shrugged. "Don't know. Saw a colored cowhand do that once, and not having a rope, I figured it was worth a try. If you boys are through funning with me, do I get to ride as a top hand?"

McBride holstered his gun, held out his hand, and said, "Son, I am putting you on the payroll as my segundo. You are one pure cowboy, and I aim to have you backing my play if them cow thieves are dumb enough to hit us on the trail again!"

Chapter 6

The great depression of the seventies seemed to be over, and the price of beef was rising, so the salad days of the working cowhand were in the offing. Casual help, working on foot around the spread, still worked for little more than their keep, but anyone good enough to work on horseback expected from fifty cents to three dollars a day plus found. The outfit supplied unlimited coffee and three meals a day. No working hand could have afforded to keep the six or eight horses he needed to do his job, so while the outfit boarded his personal mount free, if he had one, it also owned and furnished his mount or two of the day. The selection of mounts, like the choice of desserts, was up to the boss wrangler or cook, depending.

But the cowhand was expected to provide some things for himself. He bought his own smokes, such medicinal liquor as the boss tolerated on the job—subject to the hand's good behavior—and of course his own clothing and equipment, including his working gear. He used the outfit's branding irons, and in fact a man caught between jobs with a running iron of his own was subject to suspicion and possible rough justice. His boots and saddle and everything up to and including his hat were highly personal and his own business, as long as he could cut the mustard.

So Longarm went shopping that afternoon, after consulting the amiable boss wrangler, Fong, about conditions on the trail ahead and the horseflesh he'd be working with.

Fong said Longarm's High Plains saddle was heavier than those the Spanish barbs of the remuda were used to. Longarm had figured it might be. He'd only borrowed it because a hand who showed up with no saddle at all was viewed with suspicion. He had to return it to the Diamond K when and if he returned to Denver, so Longarm left it in a safe place by pawning it for a ninety-day loan. He kept his bridle and possibles, of course. Fong had offered to help him choose a California saddle, but Longarm preferred to work alone, and he liked Fong too much to drag him into a gunfight that might not concern him. He'd decided that Pepita had made up that tale about two men gunning for him, but women were sort of treacherous, and a man just never knew when they'd mix him up by telling the truth. Besides, he knew what he wanted.

He found the saddle shop Fong had told him about, and dickered himself a center-fire saddle with slick forks and a fairly low cantle. It was nigh impossible to be thrown from the rocking-chair rig most Mexican and California riders cottoned to, but they made Longarm nervous. There were times when a man might want to vacate a horse quickly, and he knew he could stay aboard with less help if he had to.

The Mexican saddler suggested that if he'd be riding through the Coast Range chaparral, he'd better buy *tapaderos* and *armas,* so he did. He'd noticed that most of the riders around the stockyards favored the short chaps they called chinks out here, but he decided to stick with his gunbarrel chaps, with the taps protecting his toes in the stirrups, and the *armas* hanging from the saddle swells protecting his mount's front end. The saddler was so pleased with a *gringo* taking his advice that he threw in a nice *bayeta* saddle blanket.

Longarm hired another horse from the livery to try out his new gear and get some more feel of the country. He rode across the ankle-deep Los Angeles River to the northeast and tried popping through some brush. The coast chaparral was lower but thicker than the sticker bush he'd ridden through on the Texas side of the Rockies. The stuff they called holly was mean as hell, but his mount seemed used to it and didn't spook at the little lizards that skittered every which way as they passed. The California breed moved like spit on a hot stove and seemed as thick as grasshoppers were on the High Plains. The locals said you seldom saw lizards and snakes occupying the same territory, so the horse likely found them reassuring.

Longarm circled the outskirts of town, reading the brands on the cows he spotted grazing here and there in the wild mustard. He recognized some brands the Indian bureau had already bought and were holding in the yards. Some of them were a mite fancy. Mexicans went in for lots of frills and curlicues and sort of drew pictures instead of the more standardized letters and numerals that Anglos favored. Longarm had no idea how a brand inspector would describe the fancy monograms, but he saw that they'd be a bitch to run. It was easy to change a *C* to an *O* or a 3 to an 8, but what could you do with a brand that looked like a house on fire or a critter chewing its own tail?

He kept an eye peeled for any flank brand that might once have read ID. The government brand would be easy to alter to a T-Bar-Slashed-O or an E-Slash-B. But he didn't see anything like that. Most of the cows he passed were branded on the hip, anyway.

71

McBride wasn't earmarking for the trail. It would have been too confusing, since the scrub that Carver was buying already came with a mixed bag of original earmarks. Longarm considered advising them to brand both flanks, but he decided he wouldn't. He was a new hand for one thing, and it stood to reason that the stolen cows had been branded well enough to spot at a modest distance as government beef, if they got spotted at all.

He rode over a rise and noticed a large party of riders gathered around a lone valley oak in the distance. He rode in slow and casual to see what the powwow was about.

He got some thoughtful looks as he approached. This was understandable. The dozen or so riders included a young Mex sitting on a bareback mule, with a rope around his neck. The other end of the rope was tied to a branch above his head.

One of the riders was a hard-looking but pretty gal wearing a skirted charro outfit. She had a pair of eyes that would spook a Comanche. Longarm reined in and said, "Howdy, folks."

The girl said, "I am Doña Maria Verdugo y Alverado, and you are on my land, Señor."

Longarm tipped his hat deferentially. "I'm sorry, ma'am. I didn't see any signs posted. My name is Long and I ride for McBride. If you folks ain't feuding with *him,* I'll just say adios and be on my way."

Doña Maria shook her head and said, "You'd better stay until this is over. We don't want anyone running to teacher before we string this *pelado* up."

Longarm shot a glance at the victim seated aboard the mule. He was about sixteen and a wet rivulet of piss ran down the mule's dusty flank from his crotch, but his face was expressionless. Longarm said, "Far be it from me to interfere, but if I have to watch, I sure wish someone would tell me why we're lynching this gent."

"It is simple," Doña Maria replied coolly. "I am missing some calves. He had a running iron in his saddlebags when my vaqueros caught him camped on my land."

The boy on the mule licked his lips and croaked in a quavering voice, "As God is my witness, Señora, I know nothing about your cattle. I did not know I was on your land."

Longarm knew better. He knew a running iron in one's possession was as good as a signed confession in the informal hearings cow folk conducted under oak trees. But he heard himself asking, "Did he have your calves, ma'am?"

Doña Maria laughed harshly and without humor. "Of course not. His *compañeros* obviously got away with them."

"If he had any *compañeros*. I'd like to hear what he has to say for himself."

Doña Maria shook her head and said decisively, "He would only lie. We have heard his protestations. He has said his prayers. It is over."

She nodded to one of her hands and the vaquero nodded back and slapped the mule with his quirt. The critter bolted forward, out from under the man on its back, and the accused cow thief was swinging, kicking his feet as his face turned red and his tongue swelled and protruded from his mouth.

Longarm reached for the bowie in his boot as he heeled his mount forward. He rode under the limb and cut the rope. The hanging man fell in a heap near his mount's dancing hooves, sobbing and gagging.

Longarm spun his mount to place its rump to the tree trunk as he shifted the knife to his rein hand, leaving his right free to draw. The motion was not lost on the others. Doña Maria raised a hand to freeze everyone in place as she turned those cold eyes on Longarm. "You must like to live dangerously, Señor."

Longarm spoke amicably, but his gunmetal-colored

eyes were as unfathomable as hers when he replied, "Not really. I'm a neighborly cuss at heart. But when folks invite me to a necktie party, I like to clarify the facts. If this kid's a cow thief, he deserves dying of hemp fever. It's the risk that goes with the game. But you're asking me to be a party to murder if he's innocent. So, like I said, I aim to hear his tale."

One of the vaqueros growled, "Let us kill him, Doña Maria. I think he is a friend of this *ladrón!*"

The girl didn't answer, but her eyes went tick-tick-tick at Longarm. He said, "Sure, you all can see I'm a Mexican like this boy here. As to killing me, I figure the odds on my going down here are two to one in your favor. But once we start slapping leather, some of you are sure to join me on the ground."

"We are not afraid," snorted the vaquero, who seemed anxious. But Doña Maria said, "We do not wish a feud with McBride, *gringo*. Ride on, if this is too rich for your blood."

"I *offered* to ride, lady! It was you who insisted on me showing interest in this case. Now that I'm here, we'll do it right or we won't do it at all. Somebody get that jasper to his feet and loosen up that rope. I mean to conduct my own hearing into his recent activities."

Doña Maria hesitated, then nodded, and a vaquero dismounted to haul the victim erect and loosen the slip-knot, leaving him still bound, with the rope around his neck and trailing on the ground. The boy gasped, stared up at Longarm, and rasped hoarsely, "I am in your debt, Señor. My name is Jesus Garcia, and from this day forward your enemies are my enemies."

"You ain't out of the woods yet, son. These folks say you were packing a running iron. How do you plead?"

"*Por favor*, I had but a fireplace poker for to take home with me. I found it in an abandoned *jacal*, over to the east. I did not steal it. The people who once lived there left it when they moved on."

Longarm looked around and asked, "Does anybody here have the evidence?"

Doña Maria said, "Of course not. *We* have no use for a running iron. We are honest people." She turned to one of her men and asked, "What did you do with that thing, Pedro?"

Pedro shrugged and said, "*Por favor*, I threw it down an arroyo, Doña Maria."

Longarm said, "Well, that leaves us with this boy's word that it was a fireplace poker. We'll set that aside for now and get to your missing critters. Do you know for a fact that they were stolen, ma'am, or could they have strayed?"

"We know our range," she replied heatedly. "We can't find the calves. They must have been stolen."

Longarm cast a thoughtful look around at the rough, brush-covered country and observed, "You sure hang folks casual out here. Here's what we're going to do. I'm going to take this boy back to town and ask the law to lock him up for now. It's still early, so after we have him out of the way, I'll be proud to ride back and help you look for those calves."

"I don't like that at all!" Doña Maria protested. "You know that no *gringo* judge will sentence him to death for theft. They might even let him off on the evidence we have against him!"

"That's true, ma'am. But he's sort of young to die for one mistake, and if he's innocent, it shouldn't fret you if they let him go."

The proddy vaquero who had spoken before spat and said, "I have had enough of this nonsense, *gringo*. I shall count to ten, and if you are still here when I have finished—"

And then the vaquero was staring into the unwinking muzzle of a .44 double-action as Longarm said laconically, "If you aim to be a gunslick, the first rule to remember is that you never *tell* a man you aim to gun him. It's a good thing for you I ain't John Wesley

Hardin or some other moody cuss who takes this sort of nonsense serious."

The vaquero and his friends were looking sort of green around the gills, and even the haughty Doña Maria was staring soberly at the gun they'd just seen appear, as if by magic, in his big right fist.

Longarm told Garcia, "You'd best start walking for L.A. son. I'll say adios for you, won't I, folks?"

Nobody answered, but Doña Maria was looking at him hard enough to scorch his mustache. He grinned at her politely until the accused cow thief was clear and moving at a good clip before he said, "I'll come back around noon and we'll hunt cows together, hear?"

"If I ever see you on my land again, I will have you killed," she snapped.

"Is that any way to talk?" he replied wistfully. Then he lowered his revolver and rode after Garcia. Nobody tried to stop him. He hadn't expected them to.

He rode back to Doña Maria's spread about one o'clock. He didn't think she lived under the hanging tree, so he asked directions to her house. It turned out to be a rambling adobe place, facing the river, with a grassy rise behind it and ancient walnuts shading the front veranda. He'd been spotted riding in, so Doña Maria met him by her front door. He saw that she'd changed to a more feminine outfit, with a rose in her hair and a lace fan to flutter. He dismounted and was tethering his mount to the rail when she joined him, her eyes downcast.

"Well, Jesus Garcia is locked up tighter than a tick," Longarm informed her. "The police tell me he's known to them as a scavenger and *pobrecito* who sort of wanders around poking at trash heaps. He don't seem to be too bright, but they say he's never been arrested as a thief before."

Doña Maria murmured softly, "I am so ashamed. After you left, I sent my riders out to make a more careful search. The calves were sheltering in some laurel, up a canyon. You were right. They had only strayed."

Longarm's voice was gentle as he said, "I didn't feel like hunting for them in this heat, anyway. It was a natural enough mistake."

"But if you had not come along, we would have hung that *pobrecito!*"

"Yes, ma'am. That's why we have courts of law, I reckon. But no harm's been done. When I ride back, I'll tell the police to turn the rascal loose, and next time he'll know better than to act suspicious."

She said, "You can't ride all that way during *la siesta*. Come inside where it is cool, and we'll discuss how I can make it up to the poor boy. I would like for you to carry a gift for him when you leave."

Longarm allowed that that sounded fair, and followed her inside. The house seemed empty. The servants were likely taking their own siesta in the outbuildings. Doña Maria led him to a settee by a baronial fireplace and he saw that she'd already put out some vittles and a pitcher of sangria. He sat down beside her and helped himself to some pine nuts while she poured him a glass of cool-off. She smelled like camellias, and he was aware suddenly that he'd sweated some since his last bath, but she didn't seem to notice.

She waited until he'd settled back and asked permission to smoke before she said, "I was angry as well as foolish when we met this morning. But I admit I was impressed. You seem to be a man who is used to giving orders."

"Takes one to know one, ma'am."

"My vaqueros obey me, as long as I am watching. As you see, they were too lazy to really hunt my livestock before reporting the calves as stolen. It was different when my husband was alive."

"Oh, are you a widow woman, ma'am? I'm right sorry to hear that." It was a small lie. Longarm admired pretty women who were free, but he knew condolences were expected.

Doña Maria acknowledged his condolences with a slight nod and continued, "My husband died two years ago and left me to run this ranch. I have been looking for a good segundo. Hernando, the man who threatened you, is the bag of wind you took him for, and lazy, too."

"Why don't you fire him and get somebody better?"

"I have been sitting here thinking about that, as I wondered if you would really come back. I don't know what McBride is paying you, but I'm sure I could match it."

Longarm struck a sulfur match with his thumbnail and touched it to his cheroot as he commented, "You make sudden decisions, ma'am."

"One gets few chances to meet a real man," she replied evenly. "Where did you learn to be so authoritative, in your *Yanqui* army?"

"Oh, I mostly just took orders when I was a soldier boy, ma'am, and it was a long time ago. I reckon I'm just naturally bossy."

"One of my men said you handle a gun like a professional."

"Well, I've herded cows in Indian country and spent a few nights in Dodge," he demurred. "But let's talk about more interesting things, like yourself. Have you sold much beef to that herd McBride is heading north with, ma'am?"

"Of course. The government has bought some dreadful beef for its Indians, but I think the fifty head I gave them a price on should last until San Francisco." She smiled roguishly and added, "I'd hate to try and *chew* a mouthful of that beef, though. Until you Anglos arrived, we only raised cattle for hides and tallow. The breeds we range in this dry country are tough, stringy scrubs that can survive on fodder a goat might refuse."

"I noticed," he said. "A he-brute wearing your brand gave me some trouble over in the yards. This may not be polite to say in front of a lady, but he was supposed to be a steer."

Doña Maria looked away, fluttering her fan, and sighed, "*Maldito sea!* If a girl wants a bull castrated around here right, she has to do it herself!"

Longarm figured Doña Maria knew a thing or two about the subject, but he didn't say so. He said, "Well, McBride shot it, and since you already got paid for it, let's say no more about it."

She turned back to face him and lowered her fan. "Can't you see that's why I need you? I'll top McBride by a quarter a day, whatever he's paying."

Longarm blew a thoughtful smoke ring. This was getting sort of interesting. Nobody seemed to know where Trixie had run off to, and Pepita wasn't at the saloon anymore, either. It seemed impossible that they'd sicced *this* gal on him, since she hadn't sought him out, but it sure was interesting how every woman he met of late seemed to want to keep him from riding north with that herd.

He said, "I've given my word to McBride, ma'am. But it's only a temporary job and I'll be back directly. Maybe we can talk about it then."

"Don't go," she pleaded warningly. "It's dangerous. McBride is hiring strange hands because none of the boys around here will take a job with him."

"I noticed," he said. "They tell me the herds that went north before have been chewed up by cow thieves, but I disremember hearing about any riders getting hurt. The folks stealing Uncle Sam's beef have been doing it so polite that nobody can see how it's done."

"I heard that, too," she confirmed. "But it's only a question of time before the bandits get ugly."

"Bandits, ma'am? I thought we were talking about sneak thieves. They could be Anglos, they could be

79

Mexican-Americans. They could even be Indians. You do have Indians in these parts, right?"

"Only mission Indians, this far south. They've been Spanish-speaking Christians for so long that your people couldn't tell them from Mexicans. Vasquez was supposed to be part Indian."

"I heard about him. He's been dead a spell."

"Perhaps. But some people say your lawmen never really got him, and he robbed not far from here. In any case, many of his gang members must still be alive, perhaps lurking in the hills."

Longarm puffed pensively at his smoke before answering, "I noticed a *mirador* the other day. I don't worry much about haunts. The thieves who've been hitting the government herds haven't been siting up on the skyline like jaybirds. Nobody's seen hide or hair of any riders near the cows before they just sort of fade into thin air. But you folks would know if any of those stolen cows showed up back here, wouldn't you?"

Doña Maria seemed genuinely puzzled as she asked, "Why would anyone drive stolen Los Angeles cattle back to Los Angeles?"

"To sell 'em again," he began. Then he said sheepishly, "Yeah, that wouldn't work, would it? The biggest buyer of scrub beef in these parts is the BIA, and even they would be too smart to pay for critters already wearing an Interior Department brand. Why don't you folks breed up your beef with some registered bulls? I know this ain't delicate, but you're a cattle breeder, so you must know how calves come into this world. If you bred your stock up, you could start shipping east to the market. The price of beef is rising, but housewives in the East are sort of picky and don't like to set a steak before their man that's half whalebone and half India rubber. Get a little Hereford blood in your California cows, though, and they'd be good for something more than tallow, hides, and food for the desperately hungry."

80

Doña Maria laughed again and said, "I have considered buying a bull or two with papers. But you must understand my position. I am a woman alone, and my men are natural flirts as it is. How would I ever supervise such a program properly? A lady is never supposed to watch when a calf is being castrated or a cow is being serviced."

"Yeah," he admitted, "I can see how you'd like a man about the house that you could talk delicate to."

She tapped him teasingly on the knee with her fan and asked, "Are *you* flirting with me, Señor?"

"No, Ma'am," he replied with a grin. "But if you want me to, you'd better call me Custis. This sure is good lemonade or whatever. How do you make it?"

"You know very well it's made of red wine and crushed fruits, and I think the wine is making you bold . . . Custis."

"Well, since you put it that way, it might be the wine and it might be that perfume you have on, but what the hell." He put out his cheroot, took her in his arms, and kissed her.

When they came up for air, she said, "I'll have you know I'm a respectable woman!"

"I know," he whispered. "I respect the hell out of you." And he kissed her once more.

"The servants might see us!" she protested.

"Let's get out of here, then. Which way is the bedroom?"

"Have you gone mad? It's broad daylight and I hardly know you!"

He let go of her and said, "Sorry. Sometimes a man just reads the signals wrong. But no harm's been done and I thank you for the sangria. I'd best be on my way before I up and lose my head again. That perfume is getting to me, and I sure could use a cold shower about now."

He started to rise, but she stopped him and murmured, "Wait, don't leave angry, Custis."

"I ain't angry, Maria. I just reckon we ought to quit while we're ahead, don't you?"

"Yes. I mean, no. I mean—oh, dear, I'm so confused."

He knew she was about as confused as a weasel in a henhouse, but wanted him to beg for it and take all day or longer. Ordinarily, he'd have obliged. But he didn't have the time for a long, drawn-out fandango, and it wasn't going to kill him if he missed out, pretty as she was. He had a long ride ahead of him and common sense indicated a night alone at the hotel.

It must have shown. Longarm had tried bluffing a muley gal or two in the past, and he played a fair hand of poker. But gals always knew when a man was ready to jump through hoops or not, no matter how he acted. It seemed to annoy the hell out of them when they met a man who was indifferent to their teasing, and Doña Maria was a proud little gal. So when he started to bust loose again, she sighed and said, "Oh, if only I was sure I could trust you. I have my reputation to consider."

Longarm took her in his arms again, kissed her till she started breathing hard, and murmured, "I won't tell on you if you don't tell on me." Then he picked her up and asked, "Which way do we go?"

She said, "The bedroom is through that archway, you idiot. Put me down!"

She wouldn't have told him how to get to the bedroom if she hadn't wanted to go there with him, and he knew the other demand was just small talk she felt she ought to throw at him. So he carried her through the archway, and sure enough, there was her big four-poster, with the counterpane folded down, as if she'd expected to turn in early.

He lowered her to the mattress and kissed her some more before he said, "From here on, it gets sort of clumsy unless we work together. I could probably shuck you out of that tight bodice without busting a hook, but it'd go faster if you did it while I shuck my boots."

"You certainly have a direct approach! I'll admit you're attractive, but I'm not sure I like your attitude! Don't you ever fail to get your own way, Custis?"

He kissed her, cupped a breast gently, and murmured, "Sure I do. You only have to say no and I'll be long gone."

She sighed and told him to draw the shades and make sure the door was locked.

So he did, and after they got to know each other the old-fashioned way he piled some pillows under her and got down to serious business. Maria was sort of skinny except for an astounding pair of firm, rose-nippled breasts. The pillows under her slim hips made it easier to do right by her, and she seemed to like it, even though she clawed the hell out of his bare rump with her feline nails. He'd never met a skinny gal with big tits who wasn't sort of crazy in bed. The build indicated an impulsive woman with a hair-trigger temper. Once he'd arrested a murderess who was built like Maria. He hadn't gotten to sleep with that one, of course. He suspected that Maria could be dangerous, but since he didn't aim to hang around, it was sort of an interesting way to spend an afternoon.

Eventually it became tedious, the way she kept clawing him and chewing on his collar bone, so Longarm rolled her over and they did it dog-style as she tore and clawed at the bed linen. She said she felt undignified taking it like that in broad daylight, but he knew she liked it hot and earthy, and he could tell she hadn't had it much since her husband had died. He didn't ask whether she'd screwed the late Don Verduga to death or poisoned his sangria. With a gal like Maria, it was an even-money bet. Plainly, she liked to be dominated, but dominating her took some doing, and the last man who'd annoyed her had wound up with a rope around his neck.

83

That reminded him that he still had to ride back to town and turn that poor *peon* loose. But the boy was safe enough in a nice cool jail cell, and there was no telling when Longarm would ever see another woman between here and San Francisco, so, facing the Lord only knew how many nights on the lonesome trail, he muttered, "Powder river and let her buck!"

Chapter 7

The government herd started north at sunrise—the first mistake Longarm noticed as he rode on the right swing. Most drovers let the cows graze and settle some in the morning before heading them out.

The stock had been foddered in the yards, of course, but once they were unconfined and being driven through farmland, they kept trying to bust loose after fresh greens. Longarm saw that the other riders were holding them, but it was a needless pain in the ass anyway.

McBride's chuck and hoodlum wagons led out up front as usual, with Fong's corrida leading the spare mounts of the remuda right behind. The point riders, including McBride, left a three-hundred-yard interval between themselves and the camp party, holding the lead cows on the Mission Trail between the barbed wire or brush fencing on either side of the right-of-way. The main herd was strung forty feet abreast and a hell of a distance fore and aft. Here in the flat San Fernando Valley, Longarm could see both ends by riding a mite wide. In broken country, he knew he wouldn't be able to. No one rider could keep track of a herd this size.

McBride had hired almost two dozen hands to be on the safe side, and as far as Longarm could see, they were tolerable. A flank rider to his rear headed off a yearling as it broke loose to pick some beans. Longarm didn't drop back to help. As segundo, he was only there for real emergencies. The boy hoorahed the yearling back into line with the usual cussing and a couple of slaps with his coiled reata. It was hot as the sun burned off the morning mists, and Longarm felt sorry for the drag riders following through the hanging dust back there. From the look he'd had at them, he knew they were the kids one expected to see riding drag. A herd almost never stampeded back the way it had just come. Their job was to whup the slowpokes forward or report any that just lay down and died. He meant to drop back and cheer them up, once things settled down, but he moved forward. McBride was riding point, picking out the route. A couple of galoots whom McBride had pointed out as range detectives hired by the BIA were riding alongside the chuckwagon. Longarm knew they wouldn't miss many meals, but he wondered what the hell they thought they were going to spot from up there. Nobody had stolen any food or cooking gear from the previous herds, and the cows were back *this* way.

But he knew he couldn't make suggestions to fellow federal officers unless he told them who he was, and even then, they might not like it. They rode with the confident air of fools who knew what they were doing. This cheered Longarm, in a way. If the other herds had been guarded by boobs and idiots, there might not be such a mystery after all.

Fencelines along the right-of-way both helped and hindered them. The fences tended to keep the herd bunched on the trail, but the beans and irrigated corn on all sides tempted the critters to stray. He spotted an outlaw cow with a crooked horn making a determined run for some fenced-in beans, and whipped his mount into action with the ends of his reins when he saw that the rider who should have been watching was asleep at the switch.

The outlaw got to some Mexican's fence and just kept going as the other rider chased it. Longarm cut in from the north. He jumped his mount over the fence to keep from doing further damage, and as the outlaw saw him it stopped, knee-deep in beans, and snorted at him, wild-eyed. A Mexican was running across the fields, waving a pitchfork and cussing fit to bust.

This was a tactical error. Most range-bred cows considered a man on foot a natural thing to charge on general principles. So the outlaw did. The Mexican saw that he was in trouble and started running the other way, another damn fool thing to do. Longarm yelled out, "Stop and face it, damn it!" as he chased the damn fool cow that was chasing the damn fool farmer. He saw that neither of them was listening, so he shook out some rope, swung a Mother Hubbard loop, and threw.

It was a sloppy way to rope, but he knew the farmer was dead if he missed, so he didn't. The big loop dropped over the whole cow, and when he dallied and yanked his pony to a halt, he had the outlaw by all four legs, lying in the beans and looking surprised.

The other contract drover joined him as he sat on the cow, and said, "I'm sorry as hell, straw boss. I thought for a minute I'd lost that son of a bitch."

"You did," Longarm said. "I caught it. Have you got any loose change on you?"

"I got six bits or so in my jeans. Why?"

The angry Mexican was coming their way, cussing and complaining, as Longarm pointed at him with his chin and said, "*He's* why. We busted his fence and tore the shit out of his crops. I reckon he'll settle for six bits, though."

"Hell, straw boss, nobody never pays Mexicans if they don't have to."

"You have to, cowboy. What happened was your fault, not his."

The Mexican came over as Longarm was still sitting on the stray. Longarm said, "Howdy. Before you stick that pitchfork in anybody, I want you to listen. You're right. We're in the wrong."

The farmer said, "Your cow broke my fence, Señor, and look at all my poor little beans!"

"That's what I just said, amigo. We're going to give you six bits. It'll only take you a minute to restring that wire. But don't do her till we get this critter out of here. Give him the money, cowboy."

The hand reached in his pocket and handed down some quarters as he protested, "I don't see why it has to come out of my pocket."

Longarm said, "It sure as shit ain't coming out of *mine*." Then he nodded at the mollified Mexican and said, "Here's what we're going to do. I want you to mosey off out of sight. Then we're going to put this son of a bitch back on his feet and get him back out the gap. You can fix it later. Are we parting friends?"

The farmer smiled and said, "*Sí, Señor.* You *caballeros* are *muy simpático*, for Anglos."

Longarm said, "Hell, fair is fair. You'd best move off, though. I can't vouch for this critter's disposition once I untangle his hooves."

The farmer took off. Longarm waited until he was well clear before he removed his bandanna and tied it around the downed steer's eyes. The other rider asked what he was doing. Longarm shot him a disgusted look and asked, "Where did you learn about cows, a gal's boarding school? How the hell do you think I aim to get off, if he can see me?"

As Longarm expected, the outlaw settled down once the blindfold convinced the animal it was midnight. Longarm untied its hooves, hauled it erect by an ear as he hung onto the blindfold, and said to the cowboy, "Take care of my pony and follow me."

"You aim to *walk* that cow out of the field, straw boss?"

"Shit no, I was going to carry him in my arms like a baby. What did you think we were going to do, chase him all over this infernal beanfield? Get my mount, goddamnit."

And so, leading the rogue on foot, Longarm moved it out to the trailway. Then, as the other rider held his mount, he let go of its ear, whipped off the blindfold, and booted it in the rump to send it bawling back to the safety of numbers before it could spot a man on foot. Longarm mounted up to tell the green hand, "Chase it in and keep an eye on it. The son of a bitch knows there's food out here, and it'll take him a spell to settle down."

Longarm turned away to ride forward, not looking back to see if his order was obeyed. He saw McBride dropping back to join him. As they fell in together, McBride asked what had happened. Longarm said, "The usual. Had this been up to me, we'd have let them graze a spell before heading them out."

McBride shrugged and said, "It ain't up to you. I drive 'em hard the first couple of days. I find it settles them down and lets them know who's boss."

Longarm didn't answer, and McBride went on, "I know Captain Goodnight likely had other ideas. But I've done this before. I saw how you saved that fool Mex. You likely saved us some trouble with the sodbusters and I thank you. You have any other suggestions on how I should run this outfit, old son?"

Longarm said, "You're the boss, but if I was, I'd have a few calves along."

McBride shook his head and replied, "Not hardly. I don't like to drive bulls, cows in heat, or cows with calves. What we have us here is a uniform herd of dry cows and steers who all march to the same drummer. Calves slow a drive down."

"I know," Longarm said. "They also have a calming influence on their mamas. A cow won't stampede fast enough to matter once her baby gets left behind and starts bawling for her."

"Well, let's just not have no stampedes, then. You sure have gentle notions about beef, Long. They ain't *pets*, you know."

Longarm had McBride's number and knew it was a waste of time to argue. For all he knew, drovers like McBride were right. There were two schools of thought on driving cows, with much to be said for either. Many successful drovers pushed a herd hard and got it there fast, accepting the inevitable losses as they figured that each day saved was a day that nothing could go wrong. The way Longarm had learned was to baby the critters a mite and get them all there, even if it took longer. You spent more days on the trail with contented cows, but they tended to be less frantic, so it evened out. Old Captain Goodnight had trailed half-wild Texas longhorns all the way up to Montana along the Front Range of the Rockies, and despite blizzards and Arapaho, to say nothing of bandits or Cheyenne, he'd set a record for arriving with most of his herds.

But Longarm knew it wasn't his business to nurse-maid Uncle Sam's beef. He'd been sent to find out who was stealing it, and the more he saw, the easier it looked. McBride wasn't half as smart a drover as he thought he was, and the government agents guarding the chuckwagon were downright pitiful. He figured he just had to keep his mouth shut and his eyes open and he'd nail the first cow thief who tried. It would be a miracle if this ragtag outfit didn't just *lose* more than anyone could steal.

He didn't know it, but he was a mite overconfident, too.

Fair was fair, and Longarm saw some method in McBride's madness by the time they'd finished the first day's hard drive. The cows had been driven over thirty miles, and were too worn out to do anything but stop when McBride called a halt at the north end of the valley.

The hands were saddle-weary and tired, too, having stopped only once for a short noon meal. They, like the cows, could only think of food and rest. A frisky cowboy could be as much trouble to a trail boss as a frisky yearling.

The advance party had driven on ahead to set up camp by the time they cussed the herd in. McBride had chosen well. The first camp was by a little running creek, and there was a meadow of sun-cured grama and forbs set in a semicircle of steep hillside. The herd was driven into the natural pasture and the cows commenced to water and feed themselves. McBride said the night guard would only have to watch them on one side. Longarm made no comment. He didn't think any cow would voluntarily try to climb a steep chaparral-covered slope, either. But the hill wasn't too steep for a critter to climb with somebody driving it.

Longarm saw to his mount and left it with one of Fong's remuda hands before he moseyed over to the chuckwagon and got a tin plate of son-of-a-bitch stew and a mug of coffee. He hunkered down near the range detectives and some other hands. One of the federal men looked dubiously at the mess in his plate and asked what in the hell it was. So of course one of the hands said, "I'll be a son of a bitch if I know!" and everybody laughed. Longarm laughed too, but it was sort of sobering to think that here was a man who didn't know what son-of-a-bitch stew was, trying to match wits with professional cow thieves.

Cracker McBride came by and stopped to jaw with Longarm. He didn't hunker down, so everyone in earshot could hear him when he said, "Well, grass-roper, as you can plainly see, we got this far without losing a critter down a gopher hole. Have you any other suggestions to pass on to us poor ignorant buckaroos?"

"Nope, no suggestions, but I got a question. I noticed that Fong and his wranglers watered the remuda carefully. But haven't you let the cows inhale a mite more water than they should have?"

McBride laughed and announced, "Boys, I want you all to know that we have us an authority here who rode with Captain Goodnight." Then he said, directly to Longarm, "These are Californee cows. They're whang-leather toughened from growing up on alkali water and mustard greens. I know they'll drink themselves kettle-bellied. We've got a mean *jornada* through Las Pedregales tomorrow, with a dry night camp at the far end. They'll drive steadier, waterlogged, and they'll be less likely to go tearing off after a drink. Which is just as well. 'Cause there ain't none in Las Pedregales."

Longarm shrugged and said, "You're the boss."

McBride drifted on to hoorah somebody else. One of the range dicks came over to Longarm, hunkered down beside him, and asked, "Is it true you've ridden the Goodnight-Loving Trail?"

Longarm said, "Yep," and didn't add that he'd been working for the Justice Department at the time. They'd cleared Goodnight on that fool charge about his Texas beef, and it wasn't polite to remember suspicions that hadn't panned out. Besides, he wasn't ready to confide in a fellow lawman who looked like an asshole and might be a crook.

The range dick said his name was Scanlon and that his partner was Morgan, so Longarm said to call him Long. He knew his name had a certain reputation in law-enforcing circles, but Scanlon didn't make the connection if he'd heard it before. As the range dick went on talking, the hell of it was that Longarm knew he was being questioned. It was sort of pathetic. Scanlon kept asking things in a desperately casual, friendly tone, like he expected to trip somebody up. They'd taught him how to question a suspect pretty good, but they'd neglected to teach him shit about the cattle industry, so

Longarm didn't see how Scanlon was going to catch a slip even if somebody made one.

The range dick got tired of his charade sooner than Longarm did, who'd found it amusing. He drifted down to jaw with one of the young drag riders when Longarm got up to give his cup and tin plate to the cook's Chinese helper. He saw that some of the weary hands were already getting their bedding from the hoodlum wagon, and noticed that the evening star was out. He moved over to the remuda line at the far end of camp and asked the wrangler on guard which of the mounts he'd chosen for the drive was the best night horse. The Mexican kid pointed out a dun gelding and said, "That *bayo* has a cold mouth, but he's sure-footed and steady in the dark, Señor Segundo. Shall I saddle him up for you?"

Longarm said yes, and helped out. The wrangler didn't ask where he was going, so Longarm didn't offer the information. The kid likely thought he was off to check the nighthawks guarding the herd. Longarm forked aboard, saw that the *bayo* was settled from the long drive, and decided it might be a good idea to see who was holding the herd on the far side of the creek, and how. It was still twilight, with some red up on the chaparral-covered ridges and everything in the hollows going purple. He heard a voice singing in the middle distance as he forded the creek, and knowing how cows spooked at folks riding up on them quiet, he joined in as he approached: "I ain't got no use for a woman,/A true one can never be found./For they'll stick to a man while he's winning,/And laugh in his face when he's down."

By this time he saw the nighthawk, and as he joined him, Longarm saw that he was one of the young drag riders, the one they called Froggy. Longarm thought it was stupid as well as unfair to put a green kid who'd swallowd so much dust on night guard, but he didn't say so. Froggy stopped singing as he reined in by Longarm. He sounded pissed as he complained, "I thought we was going to stop at Mission San Fernando tonight. I hear tell there's a mission Injun gal there, named La Concha, who can screw a man to death for two bits. I've never had me one of them mission *mahalas*, have you?"

Longarm said, "Not recent. I thought you California boys cut your teeth on *mahalas* and Mex *putas*, Froggy."

"Hell, straw boss, I ain't from these parts. I hail from Canada. That's why they calls me Froggy. Me and my sidekick, Pirate, come out here to look for gold. But they told us all the gold has been found and we wound up working in the durned old stockyards."

"That do get tedious," Longarm allowed. "Is this your first cattle drive, Froggy?"

"Sort of. Me and Pirate worked on a Kansas spread one summer. That's where we met up. Digging post holes was a pain in the ass, and we decided as long as we was digging, it made more sense to dig for gold, so—"

"Say no more, old timer," Longarm cut in with a laugh. "I can see you ride tolerable and know enough to move up and down the herd soothing-like. Who else do we have on night guard?"

Froggy pointed off into the gathering darkness as he said, "A Mex called Robles is over that way. My other pard, Osage, is further down the creek. Let Osage know you're coming when you check on him, though. He's sort of snuffy about folks creeping up on him in the dark. He's from the Indian Nation, and to hear him tell it, he growed up sort of wild."

He composed a mental picture of the quartet of drag-riding kids. They were nondescript white boys in their teens, as far as he could tell. "Is Osage an Indian?" Longarm asked, and Froggy said, "Naw, he's just a good old poor white off a hardscrabble farm. He's sort of mean when he's been drinking, but he means no real harm."

"I've met his breed. Did you boys come out here together?"

"Nope. Me and Pirate met Osage and Shadow when we went to work in the yards a while back. Osage is a loner. Shadow was already there. He's a California boy, that's how I know about screwing *mahalas*. Old Shadow said he'd fix us up if we stopped near the mission, but we never, and I'm mad as hell."

Longarm said he was sorry Froggy couldn't get laid, and rode on. It was sort of odd that McBride had assigned two green kids the first night, assuming the Mex in the middle knew his ass from his elbow, but maybe McBride figured that more experienced night-hawks would be needed farther on. The thieves preying on the beef shipments had so far left the cows alone the first few days.

Longarm rode through the herd, singing softly and walking his *bayo* as he headed for the slopes. The critters were dozing and chewing their cuds, loggy with water and as contented as hogs in a wallow. He threaded through to the natural hedge of chaparral and moved along it, looking for a break. He found a steep pathway zigzagging up into the hills and heeled his mount. The *bayo* hesitated, then sighed and gingerly started up, the sharp thorns scraping hollowly on the leather *armas* and Longarm's chaps. He rode to a saddleback above the camp, dismounted, and tethered the *bayo* to a clump of scrub oak. He took his Winchester from its boot and found a big flat rock dominating the scene below. It was darker now. The hands were turning in around the campfires, and somebody was playing a mouth organ, sad and low. Somebody always was, in a cow camp. He could just make out the bedded-down herd, a hundred yards closer on his side of the creek. They were ink-black dots against the lighter darkness of the sun-cured grass. He spotted the nighthawks riding up and down the line.

It looked peaceful. Anybody out to sample some free beef would have to move down through the chaparral all around him, and he was sure he'd hear a lizard, if it stomped its feet carelessly.

Longarm hunkered on the rock for a million years, dying for a smoke. He knew he couldn't, so he took out a cheroot and put it between his teeth unlit. He'd often thought of the advantages of learning to chew or dip snuff, but somehow tobacco didn't taste right to him if it wasn't on fire.

He didn't aim to spend the night up there. He didn't really expect anyone to hit the herd so close to town; he was just trying to get the feel of how McBride's outfit must look to a self-employed cow salesman. Longarm had made some good arrests by putting himself in the other man's boots. So, as he watched the herd settle down, he studied how he'd steal it if his folks hadn't raised him honest.

He'd about decided there wasn't any sneaky way to cut a critter out, just yet, when he heard a metallic click behind him. Longarm had become an expert on metallic sounds, the hard way, and there was no mistaking the sound of a rifle cocking. So he rolled off the rock pronto as the bushwhacker fired. Landing on his side and facing upslope, he fired back at the other's muzzle flash. It couldn't be helped, but he was sorry as hell even before the man he'd hit yelped like a kicked dog and rolled toward him through the chaparral. All hell busted loose down by the creek as the echoes of the gunplay faded. The cows were up and bawling and somebody was yelling, "Hold 'em! For God's sake, hold 'em!"

Longarm muttered, "Aw, shit!" as he climbed back on the rock to watch the stampede. There wasn't anything else he could do right now.

The stampede was a pisser. Most stampedes were. Bawling, the cows tore through the camp, scattering embers as they trampled the fire and crashed into the wagons. The chuckwagon held; the hoodlum tipped over. But Longarm was more concerned with the men. The smart ones fired off their guns and waved their hats. The dumb ones would try running. He saw cows running off every which way across the flat valley, and some hands were mounting up to chase them. He sighed and headed upslope to see who he'd swapped lead with.

The dead man was lying on his gut, head down the slope and one boot hung up in a greasewood fork. His Remington had made it farther down the dusty hillside. Any friends he'd brought along were long gone. Longarm had noticed that nobody was backing his play when they shot it out.

He rolled the corpse on its side and struck a sulfur match. The man he'd shot was a Mexican. His face was a bit torn up from sliding over rocks and the Winchester round in one eye socket, but the dead man sure reminded Longarm of Doña Maria's segundo, Hernando. The match went out and Longarm said to the mortal remains, "Well, what we have here is a pure mystery, Hernando. Did Maria send you after me? Did you come on your own, out of jealousy? Or were you folks fibbing when you said you didn't know who'd been stealing Uncle Sam's cows?"

Hernando didn't answer, so Longarm got his mount and rode on down to help the boys round up the herd. He didn't think Hernando had followed him all this way on foot, but if he'd had a mount, it was long gone too. It could have been spooked by the gunplay, or it could have been led off by somebody. He'd know soon enough.

He rode down to find some hands righting the hoodlum and McBride hopping around like a chicken with its head cut off. McBride spotted him and yelled,

"Where the hell have you been, Long? Who's the dumb son of a bitch who fired them shots? I'll have his balls for this!"

"I fired the second shot," Longarm told him, "But before you grab for my balls, I'd best explain that another gent was after them. He tried to shoot me, up in the hills. I shot him instead. I'm sorry about the noise."

"Goddamnit, you ought to be! What in thunder were you doing up there getting shot at and spooking my cows?"

"Looking for owlhoots. Like I said, I ran into one."

McBride's dawning interest overcame his rage. He asked, "Jesus, did you really nail a cow thief, Long?"

"Nailed somebody," Longarm replied. "I asked him what he was doing up there, but he was dead as a turd in a milk bucket, so he didn't see fit to explain his actions."

Longarm didn't say he knew who the dead man was. He didn't want folks following red herrings if the mess had been the result of a grudge, and if Doña Maria was a cow thief, he knew where she lived and could take it up with her later, once he had more evidence.

To change the subject, he asked McBride about the scattered herd. The drover said, "The boys will outdistance 'em and turn 'em out on them open flats. We had one man hurt, but he only has a busted leg."

"It could have been worse. Who got tromped, boss?"

"That range detective, Morgan. His partner, Scanlon, is with him over by the hoodlum. Fong's splinted his fool leg. The damn fool's lucky. He ran when he should have stood his ground and parted the horns coming at him. But the hell with that. Where's this hombre you had it out with?"

Longarm said, "Up the slope where I left him. We'll drag him down for a look-see as soon as things simmer

98

down some. Might have trouble driving spooked cows past a recent death, but they'll likely remember there's water over here, after they tire of their game of tag with your riders."

McBride said that made sense, so they moseyed over to the hoodlum to see how the others were coming with the injured man. Morgan was propped up with his back to the rear wheel of the hoodlum, and his leg stuck out, wrapped in bandages, with a pick handle to keep it company. Scanlon was squatting by Fong, bitching like it was himself with the busted leg. He looked up at Longarm and McBride and said, "My partner has to go to the hospital in San Fernando. How am I supposed to guard this herd alone?"

Longarm hadn't noticed him guarding it, but he said, "You'll manage. I shot me a Mexican a few minutes ago, as you likely heard. We may be partway out of the woods, if he was one of the gents you boys were after."

The injured man, Morgan, who seemed the smarter of the two, grimaced and said, "I must have missed something, Long. You don't think one man has been stealing all those cows, do you?"

"Nope. They'd need at least a dozen riders to drive up to a third of your government beef anywhere worth mention."

"I agree. So what difference does it make if you nailed one lousy cow thief?"

Longarm noticed that he still had the unlit cheroot gripped in his teeth, so he fished out a sulfur match, lit it, and said, "The one I shot ain't invisible anymore. His friends will pull in their horns, knowing he can be identified and that you BIA agents will be looking up his known acquaintances and knocking on the doors of places he frequented."

Scanlon brightened and said, "That's right! They'll be too busy setting up alibis to trifle with this herd! I'd say you just put them out of business, Long."

The tall marshal took a long pull on his cheroot, then took it from his lips and gazed pensively at its glowing end. "We'll find out. If he was riding with the thieves, it's over. If I was just a passing fancy, it ain't."

Chapter 8

By midnight the herd had been rounded up, driven in and bedded down again, tuckered out. Most of them had been too waterlogged to run far, but Longarm still thought some calves would have steadied them, and it was sobering to think what they'd be like, dry and spooky in a thunderstorm. McBride said it hardly ever thundered in the Coast ranges. Longarm sure hoped he was right.

Once the herd was settled, they dragged the late Hernando down and spread him out by a fire. Morgan was already on his way to the nearest town to have a doc set his leg. Scanlon said he had no idea who the dead Mex was, which came as no great surprise. Longarm had mentally leafed through his files, and Hernando didn't match any wanted flyers. He didn't tell the others he knew the man; he waited to see if any of them did. But there were no takers. The other hands just said he looked like any other Mex with half his face blown off. So McBride said to bury the son of a bitch and mark the spot in case anybody ever came forward to claim him. It struck Longarm as a mite informal, but what the hell. Folks who cottoned to a decent funeral had no call pussyfooting up on others with a rifle. One of the hands said he needed a good saddle gun, so Longarm gave him the Remington. The drag rider called Shadow claimed Hernando's spurs. They were sort of fancy. Shadow was, too. Longarm figured the kid had gotten the nickname because of his pretty charro outfit. They called gussied-up hands "shadow riders" because they seemed to admire their own outlines so much as they rode. Shadow packed a nickel-plated Starr .36, and had fly tassels on his Spanish hat. He wasn't any older than the other green kids McBride had hired for the drag, but he sure was pretty. As a local boy, he seemed to have the other three convinced that he was a real California vaquero who only punched cows around the stockyards as a sideline. None of the kids noticed the amused looks on the older hands' faces. Longarm didn't comment when Shadow put on the fancy spurs, either. He'd had cowboy fever too, when he first came out west and didn't know any better. They'd grow up soon enough.

Longarm checked the cocktail guard, sang a sad song to the cows, and turned in. It had been a long day.

It seemed like he'd just closed his eyes when he heard McBride shouting, "All right, you sons of bitches. Drop your cocks and rattle your hocks. It's almost sunrise, damn it!"

Longarm opened one eye, and sure enough, the goddamned sky was light enough to see by. Others were sitting up, hawking and cussing as the cook banged on a pan. Everything on the wrong side of his sleeping bag was clammy and cold, and Longarm felt like he could sleep another year. But he'd learned that it only hurt worse if a man put it off, so he rolled out, shucked on his boots and gunbelt, and went over to the creek to wash the sleep from his eyes.

They had shit-on-a-shingle and scrambled hen fruit

for breakfast, and the cook was good, for such a morose and quiet cuss. After he'd downed two cups of Arbuckle coffee, Longarm decided he'd live after all. He carried his used tin to the chuck box on the wagon's tailgate, and selected a slate-gray grullo mare as his mount for the morning.

McBride caught up with him as he sat the grullo on the far side of the creek, cutting notches in a tally stick. McBride asked what he thought he was doing. Longarm said, "Counting. The cows are getting up, but they're quiet and spread enough to tally."

"Hell, we tallied 'em when we rounded 'em up after the stampede, remember?"

"I remember. I won't do it if you don't want me to, boss. But I wanted to make sure we're not missing any since midnight."

McBride glanced uneasily up the steep slope. "I follow your drift. But I'll be surprised to hear it if any critters goat-legged up that way."

Longarm said he would be, too, and went on cutting a notch for each hundred head. By the time he'd finished, the sun was up and so were the cows. It got harder to tally as they started grazing, but they all seemed to be there. Three thousand and twelve. McBride had said three thousand when they left L.A. Either he was given to sloppy bookkeeping or they'd picked up some extra beef in that roundup. McBride likely favored round numbers. Longarm made a mental note to watch for strange brands anyway, as they headed them out.

The wagons, camp crew and remuda left at about eight o'clock, to be waiting at eleven at the midday stop ahead. McBride said to let the cows graze and water some before they followed, which seemed reasonable. Longarm noticed the range dick, Scanlon, riding on ahead with the advance party, which seemed stupid if he was really worried about the herd. Scanlon was still upset about losing his sidekick, Morgan. Maybe he

103

felt that some coffee along the trail would settle his nerves.

Around nine o'clock, they drove the herd back across the creek and squeezed them onto the trail. A cow knocked over Hernando's marker as it walked across his trailside grave. Nobody cared. McBride took the point, with Longarm leading the right swing riders again, to keep between the cows and the hills to the east. The hills to the west were just as brushy and steep, but it hardly seemed likely that anyone would drive stolen stock toward the Pacific Ocean.

They caught up with the wagons at eleven, and had grub as the herd grazed a hillside. The forage was good enough, save for some pretty matalija poppies that the critters avoided, but there was no water handy. McBride said maybe now Longarm understood why he'd overwatered the stock, and that it got worse over the next pass.

McBride told it true. The afternoon drive through Las Pedregales was a bitch. Longarm wasn't an expert on geology, but it was obvious that something awful had happened to California north of the San Fernando Valley. The trail wound through a maze of granite boulders and sugarloaf buttes. The ground underhoof was like broken glass and smelled like mummy dust. A little cheat and cactus grew among the boulders, but there wasn't enough fodder off the trail to tempt a hungry jackrabbit.

It was a good thing that the trail was narrow and the slopes on either side too rough for a lizard to run across, for Longarm heard a pistol shot back down the line, and the critters turned wild-eyed and started dancing. He saw that the flank riders had them under control, and rode back to the drag to see what in hell was going on.

As he rode through the dust he saw Shadow, riding with a bandanna over his face. Shadow yelled, "It wasn't me, straw boss!"

104

Longarm caught the kid they called Osage putting his S&W away. He fell in beside Osage and asked, "Do you just like to watch stampedes, or did you have some reason for firing that gun, boy?"

Osage looked sheepish, which wasn't hard, since he had a head start with his goatlike face. He said, "I was just funning at that big-ass bird up there, straw boss."

Longarm followed his gaze up to see a big California condor wheeling away to the cliffs to the east. He said, "You'd play hell hitting it at this range, and I can't think of a thing you could do with it if you could. Didn't your mama ever tell you it ain't nice to shoot a gun around cows?"

Osage threw him a sullen glare and said, "You've got no call to mention my mother, mister. Them's fighting words where I come from."

Longarm said, "Well, you'll be headed back where you came from if you play a fool trick like that again. I'd fire you right now if it was up to me. But no harm's been done, so we'll say no more about it."

"I ain't afraid of you," sulked Osage.

"You probably ain't," Longarm said. "I just got through telling you that you were stupid."

Before Osage could think up a suitable retort, the boy called Pirate rode up and said, "Cool down, Osage. We told you you'd get in trouble, shooting at that buzzard. Straw boss is just doing his job."

"I don't like to be called stupid," said Osage. He was staring down morosely.

Longarm said, "I said the war was over, son. I have to move forward now. So you boys behave back here. We're depending on you to guard the rear. It's all right to shoot at cow thieves creeping down through them rocks. But let's leave the birds alone, hear?"

Osage looked a little less muley-mad, so Longarm rode off, cussing under his breath. As he passed a Mex flank rider named Pedilla, the older hand asked what had happened back there. Longarm said, "Kid stuff," and rode forward. He read brands as he passed them. He didn't see any cows without ID on their flanks. McBride just liked round numbers. It was no wonder he leaked cows. A dozen didn't sound like many, next to three thousand, but many a cow thief had swung for stealing fewer. Most of the breed were petty criminals, content to run off a few head at a time. The gang he was after seemed to be in the cattle business in a bigger way, but they weren't the only thieves in the world, and Uncle Sam had paid by the head.

Longarm pondered that thought as he fell in on the right swing. More than one dishonest foreman or trail herder had started his own herd by losing track of a cow here and a cow there. He thought back to the scene when they'd formed up the herd in the Los Angeles yards, and decided that McBride was just casual. He remembered that Carver's crew had tallied the stock and kept a record book. The government purchasing agent would have the few extra head recorded. Nobody was going to get too upset if roughly three thousand reached the yards by the Frisco Bay. It was almost a flat impossibility to finish a drive without any shrinkage at all. Some cows always got away and others just died on the trail. If they didn't get them out of this infernal rockpile soon, that condor the kids had missed figured to dine on Indian beef.

Longarm heard a shout behind him, and turned in the saddle. Robles was chasing a breakaway brindle who'd suddenly decided he was part mountain goat. Longarm whipped his mount up the slope to head off the fool cow as Robles cut it off on the far side with some damned fine riding. Longarm moved in from the near side as the brindle balked at a house-sized boulder in his path and studied a way out. Longarm boxed him in and called across, "We got him, Robles. Let's lane him back slow and easy."

The Mex nodded and they worked together, riding on each side and slapping their hats at the brute just enough to drift him downslope. "He's a mosshorn I've had trouble with all the way, Señor," Robles informed him.

Longarm nodded. "I've noticed. Pick out a steady old gent, and we'll neck this rascal until he minds his manners."

They drove the brindle back to the trail and he fell in, trying to look innocent. Robles said, "That fat chongo likes to soldier. Should I rope him?"

"You picked him. I'll handle this mosshorn."

So Robles threw a loop over the chongo's crooked horns and hauled him gently out of line as Longarm dropped his rope on the breakaway and reeled him in. The brindle didn't like it much and tried to hook Longarm's knee. Longarm whipped him hard across the eyes with the coiled end of his rope, and the brindle decided to be nice. The two riders moved the brutes together, side by side, and Robles got some pigging from his saddlebag and haltered them together with loose nooses around their necks. Longarm didn't tell the Mex to make sure the nooses wouldn't slide tight. Robles knew his trade, and the knots were square. They both recovered their throw ropes, and Robles booted the steadier chongo into the herd with a fond farewell. Longarm saw that he wasn't needed, so he waved adios and rode forward. He wouldn't have picked the chongo. Cows with droopy horns were often mixed up inside their skulls as well, but Robles sounded like he knew what he was doing, and Longarm rode with a light hand on the reins, when he could. The chongo was too fat to run far, even if the brindle talked him into it.

The cows settled down to just walking, which was enough of a problem in this rockpile. By eleven they were hanging their tongues, and Longarm was wondering where in hell the chuckwagon was.

Then they rounded a bend, and he saw that the advance had set up in a natural amphitheater gouged out of a hillside by some awful misadventure of the planet a while back.

They ran the cows up into the half-bowl, and they commenced to fall down among the rocks or sniff for something edible. The only grass was cheat, and it was summer-killed and worthless as fodder. As Longarm joined McBride near the chuckwagon, McBride spat and muttered, "Goddamn sheep."

Longarm held his cup out to the cook's helper as he said, "I don't see any sheep, boss."

"Of course you don't," McBride said. "Some son of a bitch mutton puncher has grazed off this place and moved on. There ought to be a law against sheep-herders using a public right-of-way. I figured on grazing here for an hour. We'd best just grub ourselves and move on."

Longarm sipped his Arbuckle, glanced up at the sun, and opined, "I'd let 'em siesta some, grass or no. How much more of this shit do we have ahead of us?"

McBride said, "All day and then some. They'll be hungry and thirsty as hell by the time we reach the next *vega*. All the more reason to get 'em there pronto, right?"

"You're the boss. But if you're asking for an opinion, I'd let them rest and chew their cuds while the sun makes up its mind to move. It's high noon and three times hotter than it ought to be. You say there's no bait or water for them tonight, in any case. They'll be easier to hold after dark if they're just hungry and thirsty instead of desperate."

McBride started to object. Then he shrugged and said, "You may be right, Captain Goodnight. It won't hurt us or the horses to rest up for a couple of hours. But it's still gonna be hot in here until sundown."

He moseyed off before Longarm could point out that at least one side of the trail would be shaded by the steep rocks after three or so.

The range detective, Scanlon, joined Longarm as he

hunkered in the meager shade of the hoodlum wagon's north side. "I've been looking at those rimrocks all around," Scanlon said. "This would sure be a neat place for an ambush, wouldn't it?"

"It would, if you wanted to gun somebody. It's a shitty place to steal a cow."

"How do you figure that, Long? Can't you see how easy it'd be to sneak down to the trail and cut out a few head?"

"Sure I do. But where in thunder would you drive them, afterwards? It's broad daylight, and if anyone got sassy, one of us could shinny up almost any of these buttes and see for miles. There's no water, there's no grass. A critter bigger than a cat raises a column of dust anywhere it wanders. It'd take all day to drive a stolen cow out of here, and McBride would likely get surly and come after you."

Scanlon said, "Well, maybe, but I've been studying the map. There's a big interior valley between the Coast Range and the Sierras. It's flat and grassy. I don't see why folks take the Coast route at all. The interior valley north and south is the way I'd travel."

"I asked about that," Longarm told him. "The Spanish padres had reasons when they laid out the Old Mission Trail. It twists and turns some, but it gets you up the Coast faster. Such water as there is runs free of alkali. The grass stays greener, and the nights at least are cooler. The big valley needs some engineering before it'll be the smooth pathway you picture. Right now there's a mess of alkali flats, tule swamps and such, where folks ain't living. Where it's settled, the interior valley is cut up by fences and irrigation ditches, and you know how touchy farm folk get about cows in their kitchen gardens. Rough as it looks, this Coast Range route figures to be the faster way."

"Well, I still think a man who knew the country could drive cows north and south in the interior."

"Hell, if he wanted to bad enough, he could drive

cows anywhere. Back in the old days, some Mexicans ran cows across the Chihuahua Desert and over Apache Pass. The point is that folks don't drive cows the hard way when there's an easy way."

Scanlon grumbled off, and Longarm studied on what they'd both just said. Scanlon struck him as an idiot, but there was something to his notion. He'd have to keep the big interior valley in mind. He didn't know the country that well, himself. Folks who said they did had assured him it would be a bitch to run cows over there. But the interior was fertile in spots, and there were some cattle spreads. He'd sudy more on passes over the Coast Range, and see if anything happened when they were near one. He didn't see how a big gang of thieves could have a whole mess of innocent-looking ranches up and down the whole Great Valley, unless a whole mess of county sheriffs and brand inspectors were either crooked or awesomely stupid. He remembered how one sheriff he'd arrested had been working with owlhoots, but that had only been one county. The different local governments tended to be proddy and suspicious of one another. He already knew that some counties were Republican and others Democrat. A statewide conspiracy was possible, but not likely. Anyone who had the whole state system in his hip pocket wouldn't stoop to stealing Indian beef; he'd start with the San Francisco Mint and steal a few railroads first.

No. He was after less impressive crooks. They had to have a well-organized operation to dispose of all that beef. They likely had a few crooked officials not looking too closely at the brands and keeping a false set of books somewhere. But sooner or later he'd pin it down to one locale. They had one safe outlet; all he had to do was find it. It seemed so simple. Why in hell couldn't he figure it out?

They bedded the cows for the night in a box canyon, still in Las Pedregales, and dry as a spider's sense of humor, with nothing to graze on but rocks. Longarm made a quick tally as the sun was going down, then he swore and did it all over again. It came out the same.

He went over to the wagons and hunkered down near McBride and Scanlon. He said, flatly, "We're missing twenty-one cows."

McBride's spine stiffened. "That ain't possible."

"I know," Longarm said. "They're still gone."

"I told you so!" said Scanlon. "What are we to do?"

Longarm said, "You're a detective. Maybe you'd better start by asking questions."

Scanlon just looked confused, but McBride stood up and pulled his hatbrim lower. "Let's go, Long. There's no way twenty-one cows can take off in broad daylight without anyone noticing."

But as they made the rounds and questioned the hands, it seemed there was. Robles said he'd noticed the two-necked critters drifing back, but the drag riders said they'd never seen two steers roped together. Longarm didn't see how even green hands could have tripped over the roped-together chongo and brindle without noticing either of them. But they were among the missing.

Everybody got excited and went out to have another look at the night herd. Pedilla said he didn't see a calico he'd had words with earlier in the day, and an Anglo named Creedmore said he'd noticed an apron-face he didn't see among the others now.

"God damn it to hell, this is starting to bust me up!" McBride exploded. "How in hell could you lazy no-good bastards lose that many cows in broad-ass daylight on a boxed-in trail? You was supposed to be herding them, not jacking off in the saddle!"

Nobody answered. Nobody had an answer. McBride cussed them out some more and then Longarm said, "It's my fault. I thought I was watching, but, like you said, I must have been jacking off."

McBride still looked disgusted, but he'd simmered down. "*I* was aboard a bronc, too. I tell you, boys, this is getting spooky as hell. We're going to double the night guard and put a rifle up on that rimrock. Robles, you lost the neckers. How do you feel about perching up there with your Henry?"

"I'll go," Robles said. "But they've never hit us at night, Señor."

McBride said, "Maybe. I want you shooting to kill anyhow. They never hit us this *early* before, either, and I'm so mad I could spit shit!"

One of the green hands asked, "Can't we cut sign in the morning and go after them, boss?" and Scanlon said, "Sure, that's a good idea!"

McBride looked disgusted again, and turned to Longarm and asked, "Do you want to tell 'em, or do I have to?"

Longarm said, "We have to move these cows to water. There's no time for backtracking."

McBride said, "Right, damn it. But what the hell, we've still got *almost* three thousand."

"Two thousand and ninety-one, to be exact," Longarm corrected.

McBride said, "Whatever. I'll leave the tally to you cow professors. I contracted for a rough three thousand with a ten-percent wastage allowance. I can lose three hundred before it starts to cost me, but, damn it, we got to keep a better eye on these cows, boys!"

Scanlon did some mental arithmetic and said, "We're two days out and we've lost nearly two dozen. Figure a dozen a day for thirty days and, hell, it only comes out to three-sixty. Some herds have lost over a thousand."

McBride snorted, "That's what I just said, damn it. I figured on a few head dropping in this rough stretch, but they never. They was stole. The drag would have seen any that just lay down."

He took off his hat, wiped the sweatband, and added,

"We've never been hit by the rascals in this stretch before. How do you figure her, Professor Long?"

Longarm said, "There's no natural law that says there could only be one cow thief working on the Mission Trail. The recently departed cows could have been driven off by another gang, you know."

McBride said, "No, I don't know. None of the rancheros this close to L.A. are missing any stock. The rascals who just hit us are using the same spooky tricks they've used before. If we was hit by amateur rustlers, how come none of us noticed?"

Scanlon nodded and said, "According to our records, there hasn't been much robbing going on of late on the Mission Trail. Almost all the stolen cattle have been government beef. How do you account for that?"

Longarm didn't answer. Folks sure were asking a heap of questions he couldn't answer, lately.

Chapter 9

The herd was all there, and thirsty as hell, at sunup.
They started the drive at first light to save some heat-
stroke, but a couple of cows dropped anyway before
they were out of Las Pedregales. The drag riders
noticed. Even a green kid notices a cow lying smack
in the road. Shadow rode forward each time to tell
McBride or Longarm. They rode back to see if there
was anything to be done, but there wasn't. All a drover
could do for a heat-prostrated cow that far from water
was to shoot it. Osage volunteered to do the shooting.
Longarm told him to wait until the herd had moved on
half a mile, and then catch up. It got to be routine.
They lost two in the rock country and another after
they made the coast. It was cooler as the trail cut
through an *abra* in the rimrocks and started winding
through smoother chaparral, with the Pacific winking
up the draws at them from the west. The herd got hard
as hell to hold. So while there still wasn't any water,
McBride said to let 'em move upslope and graze some.

There wasn't much moisture in the summer-browned vegetation, but it seemed to steady them.

Froggy and Pirate rode up to Longarm and asked permission to ride over to the ocean while the herd grazed. They said they wanted to go swimming. Longarm told them they couldn't; even if they didn't drown, it hardly seemed fair to the other riders. Froggy took it with good grace, but Pirate opined that Longarm was mean.

The wagons had gone on ahead to set up the midday break, so there was nothing to do but watch the damn fool cows, and Longarm felt wistful about the nearby ocean himself. He was hot and dusty, and even after he took a drag on his canteen, his mouth tasted like the bottom of a hen house. Sitting his mount, Longarm broke off a branch of trailside *cenizo* and commenced cutting tally marks with his jackknife.

McBride rode over to him with Robles, and told him, "I reckon they're about ready to move out. We've set up the noon camp in a watered *rincón* just a few miles up the trail. They'll swill like hogs, but that dry straw they're working on won't bloat 'em. What in the hell are you doing? We tallied 'em at sunup, remember?"

Longarm nodded morosely. "I remember. We're shy another seven cows. Ten, if you count the three we had to shoot."

McBride said, "That ain't possible, old son."

"I know. But we're missing seven anyway." Longarm turned to Robles and said, "We work pretty good together, Robles. You feel up to some hard riding?"

Robles nodded grimly, and Longarm said to McBride, "If you could see fit to wait up for us at the noon camp, Robles and me might cut some sign."

McBride smiled sweetly and asked, "What are you waiting for, a kiss goodbye?"

Longarm and Robles started riding back the way they'd just come. Shadow asked if he could help them. Longarm shook his head and said, "You boys are

116

needed with the herd. But while I've got you handy, I don't suppose you noticed any critters wandering off among the rocks, or maybe a sombrero peeking over one?"

Shadow shook his head and said, "No sir. Old Osage was watching, too. You told him he can't shoot his gun off, but he likes to dry-fire."

"Dry-fire?"

"You know, snap his hammer on an empty chamber at likely targets. Old Osage admires hell out of his gun, and he snaps a dry shot at anything that moves. So far I reckon he's killed a dozen buzzards, a couple of rabbits, and God knows how many lizards. He even dry-fires at yucca and cactus. So far, I've never seen him gun a rock or a bush."

Longarm nodded and led Robles off. Osage was getting to be a pain, and he'd likely get himself shot if he didn't outgrow being a gunslick before somebody took him seriously, but it seemed safe to assume that Osage and the other kids had been riding the drag with their eyes open. But the swing and flank riders had been riding wide awake, and cutting breakaways back on a regular basis. It made no sense. As they trotted along the trail, Longarm didn't notice any trapdoors in it.

They rode up to a ridge for a far look-see. The granite fangs of the pelegrades were quiet and sort of broody in the sunlight. There wasn't a hint of dust against the sharp blue California skyline.

They cut crosscountry and entered the rocky scablands by a game trail above and more or less in line with the main route. Robles agreed that any cows driven upslope to the northeast would have crossed the higher path, and while it was narrow and twisted all to hell, it was covered with wind-drifted dust. They could see that no other riders had followed it recently. Robles said, "Of course, one can always drag brush across hoofprints, no?"

But Longarm pointed at some sharp little etched

117

marks and replied, "Not along this stretch. A covey of quail ran along this path just a while ago."

Robles sighed and said, "You have good eyes." But the quail tracks he'd overlooked seemed to sharpen him up. They squeezed single-file between some boulders and Robles, in the lead, said, "Deer. A doe with a half-grown fawn left *those* tracks."

Longarm said, "Right, and deer don't move in broad daylight if they can help it. So those deer tracks were left no later than dawn, and we had those seven missing cows at dawn."

"Meaning nobody could have driven them this way and covered their sign?"

"Meaning they went some other way. This is a hell of a big scabland. How do you feel about them running the cows off the other way, to the west?"

Robles frowned. "Toward the ocean? Forgive me, Señor. We are talking about cows, not sea lions."

"I'd be surprised if they swam them anywhere, too," Longarm admitted. "But there could be another trail over there, between the Mission Trail and the sea bluffs."

Robles grinned, showing long yellow teeth. "The padres did not lay out their Camino Real through Las Pedregales because they liked to climb over rocks, Señor. There are many trails running near the ocean, but none of them go anywhere. The transverse ranges jut out to sea like fingers, and each one ends in a sheer drop. If the thieves drove our cows to the west, they would be trapped. Besides, someone would have seen them, no?"

Longarm found a path down to the main trail and started down it as he said, "We do keep getting back to that, don't we? I can't see how *one* cow could go east, west, or even straight up, in broad daylight. It gets even sillier when you make it seven!"

As they reached the main trail, Longarm spotted one of the dead cows in the distance, with a condor sitting

118

on it, pecking out its eyes. He said, "This ain't getting us anywhere. Let's ride after McBride and the others. You watch the left side for sign, and I'll watch the right."

"There is no escape route to the right, Señor."

"I'll watch it anyway. I can't see even seven head leaving much sign on this gravel, but look for a fresh turd or a rolled-over pebble."

Robles looked insulted and said frostily, "I know how to cut sign, Señor."

Maybe he did, but Robles didn't spot anything on his side, and Longarm didn't see anything, either. There didn't seem to be anything wrong with his eyes; he spotted a couple of lizards and a horny toad before they moved, and he saw a dead gopher that even the condors had missed, in the shadow of a rock. The air was clear and everything was sharply etched all the way to the jagged skyline. He noticed a gap in the menacing rimrock, and even though there were no tracks, he trotted his pony up to the break. He reined in between two sharp fangs of rock and stared morosely at more of the same, rising like chessmen in row after row as far as he could see. It was rough country, and it looked empty and dead.

He rode back down, caught up with Robles, and asked the native son if there were any known water holes in Las Pedregales.

Robles said, "If the padres had found water, they would have run the trail that way. There are many tanks after the winter rains, but they have all dried up by this time."

"Not all," Longarm amended. "Quail need water. So do deer. There's water here and there in every desert. But I'll take your word it's hard to find."

They gave up after they reached the place they'd started from. They coaxed their horses into an easy lope and caught up with the outfit in a pleasant dell of live oak and grama, with a rill of spring water running through it. The others had eaten, and the cows were shading themselves and chewing their cuds. Longarm and Robles turned their tired mounts over to the remuda hands and joined McBride and the others by the chuckwagon. The menu of the day was "Mexican strawberries," otherwise known as beans. Longarm hunkered down near McBride and started eating as he stared moodily into the cookfire. McBride knew Longarm would have said something if he'd spotted anything, so he asked the tall lawman, "What do we do now?"

Longarm told him his next move, and McBride said, "Might be worth a try. We'll be camping wet again tonight, six or eight miles on. I figure we're sixty miles out, and we've already started losing beef. Them rascals are sure getting bold. Must be 'cause nobody's ever caught 'em." He looked at Scanlon accusingly.

The range dick caught the look and said, "Damn it, if I knew how they were doing it, I'd say so."

Neither Longarm nor McBride was impolite enough to mention that he hadn't seen fit to ride out scouting for sign. It was getting obvious that Scanlon was a lawman who specialized in crooked bookkeepers, if he'd ever caught anyone worth mention. Longarm had run Scanlon through his memory and come up dry. Not that he knew every lawman working for the federal government, but he'd at least heard mention of the good ones. There weren't that many. President Hayes had been elected on a reform ticket, but a lot of federal deputies and Indian agents were still appointed by political hacks that the voters had somehow not caught with their hands in the till. Longarm favored democracy, but it tended to get out of hand, west of the Big Muddy.

Young Pirate came to the fire with an armload of brushwood and dropped it on the coals. The cook ran over from the chuckwagon and screamed, "You silly son of a bitch! I ought to take a skillet to you! And I would, if the boss wasn't watching!"

Pirate looked surprised and hurt. He asked, "What's wrong, cooky?"

The cook advanced on the nonplussed cowhand, poking an insistent finger into his chest. "That fucking fire is *mine,* goddamn your eyes! You had no call to put wood on it! Did I ask you to put wood on it?"

"I only meant to help," Pirate stammered helplessly. "The durned old fire was about to go out and—"

"Of course it was about to go out, you ignorant little son of a bitch! Fires is supposed to go out when nobody's using them no more! It's high noon, damn it! What in thunder do I want with a big fire like that, with the sun hot enough to melt hell's hinges? You just leave my fire alone, hear?"

Pirate looked around for someone to back him. There were no takers. Pirate had not only broken a strict cow camp rule against even stirring the coals of a cook's fire; he'd dumped green *cenizo* branches in the fire, and while it smelled nice, it smoked like hell. McBride said, "You do that again and I'll fire you, boy. If I'd hired you as a cooking hand, I wouldn't have you riding drag."

Pirate looked like he was about to cry. Longarm smiled at him and said, "We know you aimed to help, but never offer to help the cook crew, and if you're asked, make sure it's dry wood."

Scanlon sniffed and asked, "What is that stuff? It smells like a drugstore on fire."

McBride said, "We call it *cenizo* or *chamis*. Had he brung in creosote brush, you'd have really smelled something and I'd have fired him sure. Go fill your hat and put that fire out, boy."

Then McBride noticed the cook still glaring and added quickly, "If it's all right with the chuckwagon boss, that is."

The cook shrugged and said, "Hell, I don't care if he *pisses* it out. But not till we're ready to move on. My

Chinee has pans to wash, once it dies down to a white man's coals."

Longarm got up and ambled over to the tailgate to get rid of his plate and fork. He went to the remuda and had the wrangler unhobble a zorrilla gelding to saddle up. The little black pony speckled with white dots looked like he could run if he had to, but Longarm had noticed that he was a quiet, sober critter, the kind he had in mind for the ploy he'd discussed with Mc-Bride.

Longarm rode out to the northwest along the trail to the next stop, hoping that anyone watching from a distance would assume he was scouting ahead for a campsite. He rode until the trail passed through a tight *abra,* reined in, and made sure he wasn't being followed. Then he busted brush upslope to the ridge line, moved over it to keep from being silhouetted against the sky, and dismounted. He led the zorrilla through the chaparral on the far slope, picking their way and raising no dust as he kept his eyes peeled. He got to the saddleback he'd chosen in advance, and tied the reins to a clump of live oak. Then he took the Winchester from its boot and Apached through the brush of the saddle until he could see the cow camp and the herd. His position dominated the *rincón* and the trail below. He found some shade and waited. The others had already started to drift the cows down to the trail and form them up, but it still seemed to take forever. The wagons left, and a million years later the herd started moving out. He waited and watched the drag move out of sight, and sure enough, young Osage had his gun out and was pointing it at a hawk wheeling overhead. Then they were gone, the dust was starting to settle, and life got tedious.

Longarm hated stakeout work. Every lawman did, but it formed a good part of their time on the job. He sometimes wondered how many years of his life had been wasted sweating out a stake. He was sure he'd spent more actual time like this than loving up a pretty gal. His boss, Marshal Billy Vail, had once told him that he'd get tired of women if he had nothing else to do. Longarm had always wanted to give that notion a try. He wondered what it would be like to come home night after night to the same woman, getting all the home cooking and loving he could use up. One gal might not be a fair test. He'd lived with some long enough to know that one gal could get to be just work, once she got used to a man and started telling him about all the bad habits she hadn't noticed when she first threw herself at him. To find out if Billy was right, a man would have to be a Mormon or an A-rab, with, oh, a hundred women or so in his remuda. How long would it be before he got tired of it, Longarm wondered as he fished out a smoke and stuck it between his teeth, unlit. He decided he'd likely last a good ten years and die with a smile on his face, weighing maybe sixty pounds.

His present plan, of course, was to see who, if anybody, was following them. McBride was an independent cuss who didn't run his cows on a timetable. It seemed more likely that the cow thieves were ghosting them than it did that they were laying for the herd somewhere ahead. Anybody tailing McBride on trail or ridgeline should be along any time now.

He spotted movement on the trail, but it was an old Mex leading a string of burros, the wrong way. Longarm knew the others had met him further up the trail. The burros were toting packsaddles, not cows. Their passing gave Longarm something to look at until they too were gone. The birds began to twitter and the lizards began to skitter as the chaparral around him got used to him and came back to life. He knew the critters would fall silent again, should anybody try and creep in on him, but he kept his eyes open anyway.

About an hour later, a mud wagon drawn by a four-mule team came north along the Old Mission Trail.

Longarm couldn't see the passengers in the California answer to a Concord coach, but he knew that at the rate they were going they'd soon overtake the herd, and the riders would tell him who'd been riding in the mud wagon, once he rejoined them. He'd never met a cow thief who worked out of a public conveyance, anyhow.

The sun was in his eyes now. Longarm lowered the brim of his Stetson and lit his cheroot. Anybody in the valley to his rear would be too dazzled to notice the little smoke he aimed to blow, and he could see anybody coming the other way for over a mile in three directions.

He smoked that cheroot and two more after it, before he decided he was ruining his health and chewed a grass stem as the sun kept sinking and not a damned thing happened.

Nobody seemed to be trailing the herd close enough to matter. They could be waiting for dark. But whenever they moved, they seemed to steal in broad daylight.

Longarm studied on that. The herds were bunched and under guard at night. Not wanting to swap shots with the nighthawks figured. But why, then, did they risk cutting cows out on the trail with everybody watching? It would be easier to sneak in after dark and throw a community loop. The nighthawks sang and soothed as they circled the night herd. A thief coyoting in could hear them coming and move out of the way easily. The Sioux stole horses at night. Apache stole anything that wasn't nailed down at night. Was this infernal gang afraid of the dark?

They're using some trick that only works with the lights on, he told himself. So far, so good, but that was where he ran out of ideas. Try as he would, Longarm couldn't think of a sneaky way to steal that didn't work better in the dark. He knew the gang wasn't worried about the drovers being more alert at night. Everybody on both sides knew the herd was being watched hard, every step of the way. It was common knowledge that McBride expected to get hit in daylight. It was as if the gang were openly taunting McBride or . . . But the cows didn't belong to Cracker McBride; they belonged to Uncle Sam. Could there be a *political* motive to what was going on? Longarm had met Mexicans before who were still a mite pissed about *los Americanos* taking over half the continent without their permission. What if the game wasn't beef at all?

He spit out the grass stem and told himself, *If I was an unreconstructed Mexican and wanted to just make the* gringos *look foolish, I wouldn't have to sell his damned beef! I'd just run it off and lose it someplace. You could shoot a cow up any of these canyons, and nobody but the condors would be the wiser!*

There was only one thing wrong with the notion. Alive or dead, the missing cows had vanished from a guarded herd in sight of God and everyone. He'd worry about how they were disposing of the beef after he figured out how they were stealing it.

After a while it was evening, and he knew he'd miss supper if he didn't move on down the road. So he went back to his patient zorrilla, forked himself aboard, and rode after the outfit. He was getting hungry, as well as angry. He knew McBride was going to josh him about his fruitless game of cops and robbers. That worthless range dick, Scanlon, was starting to make sense. Chasing invisible owlhoots seemed to be a profitless chore after all.

Chapter 10

It was after dark when Longarm rode in. The cook gave him a tongue-lashing as well as more coffee and beans, saying, "I ain't running an all-night kitchen, goddamn-it."

McBride joined him as he ate, and asked if he'd spotted anything. Longarm said, "Not hardly. Did you boys check out that mud wagon that I saw passing?"

"Sure. It was on it's way to Santa Bob, full of Mexicans. There was one tolerable *señorita* in the bunch, but when I howdied her she just stuck her nose up prissy. There's nothing more stuck-up than a *señorita* that's mostly white."

Longarm chewed thoughtfully and asked, "Do you know Doña Maria Verdugo y Alverado, boss?"

"It wasn't her. I've seen that twitch-ass Doña Maria. She brung some cows in and tried to screw old Carver on the price. How come you ask? I didn't know you was a social climber, Long."

"I met up with her, out riding one day."

"Well, you know what she is, then. A real bucket of ice. The gal in the mud wagon was younger and prettier, but just as snooty. Sometimes I don't think they know who won the war back in '48."

Longarm lost interest in the *señorita,* since a grand idea had just been stepped on again. "I don't suppose you tallied before you bedded down the cows," he said.

"Wrong, Professor Goodnight," McBride answered. "I tallied myself, and surprise, they're all still with us. Now, if you'll be good enough to tell me what that means, I'll turn in and get some shut-eye."

Longarm shrugged. "It just means nobody run up behind you and stole a cow. Since I was watching for them to do it, it's not as big a surprise as all that. I'd say that if they ain't ghosting us, they're circling wide and laying in wait."

"Maybe. They wasn't waiting for us here."

"I know. How far up the trail did you say that next town is?"

"Oh, eight or ten miles. We'll pass through her tomorrow. Why?"

Longarm said, "I'm riding on ahead, if it's all right with you."

McBride frowned. "I'll let you, but I wish you'd tell me why."

"It's early," Longarm said. "The cantinas will be open. Who knows who a man might see in a trail-town cantina if he moseys in alone and a herd's not due in for a while?"

"Makes sense," McBride replied. "I reckon I can spare you on the morning drive. You better take along a couple of the boys. It's a mean little Mex town and you'll want somebody keeping an eye on your back."

Longarm declined the offer. "I'd feel safer alone. The trouble with having a sidekick watching your back is that *you* have to watch *his* back, neither one of you sees a damn thing."

"That makes sense," McBride admitted. "But I'd still feel a hell of a lot better if you had somebody backing your play. What about Scanlon? He's a lawman, and ought to be able to handle hisself."

Longarm glanced around and saw Scanlon down the line, jawing with some hands, and said, "Not hardly. He seems to be in over his head. If the BIA hired him, they must have checked his credentials. But I suspect that his teammate, Morgan, brought him along to have somebody to take dictation. Since Morgan got stove up, Scanlon hasn't detected a cow flop."

McBride sighed and said, "I wondered if that was just my own surly notion. You noticed it too, huh?"

"Scanlon ain't a man you notice much," Longarm agreed. "He'll be safer here in camp. Meanwhile, I'll drift on ahead and see if I can pick up any gossip."

Longarm took his tin to the spring and washed it with sand to save the chuckwagon crew the trouble. When he turned it in, the cook was fussing with some other gear on the folded-down chuck box. He asked Longarm why he'd washed his tin. Longarm said he'd done it because he'd ridden in late. The cook told him not to do it anymore, anyway. But he only called Longarm a son of a bitch once, so Longarm knew he was secretly pleased.

Longarm picked the zorrilla from the remuda again for his night riding. He hadn't ridden the gelding hard that afternoon, and there were advantages to a black horse at night. The moon was rising and the Old Mission Trail was a silver ribbon. As always, it was cool and damp along the coast after dark, in marked contrast to the dryness of the country by daylight. The chaparral likely depended on the night mists for water, and some had to sink into the soil before the morning sun burned it off. He knew it didn't rain for nine months of the year out here, yet there were more little springs and even running rills than he'd have allowed for. Back

in the deeper canyons to the east, there'd be shaded
rincónes with standing water. There were probably hun-
dreds of little pockets too small to claim as a homestead or cattle spread, but large enough to shelter a
stolen cow for a time. But the finances didn't add up
if the gang only had a cow here and a cow there. The
cattle industry depended on a balance between the cost
of keeping a cow and its selling price on the market.
An outfit paid a few men to watch a lot of cows. An
outlaw expected to make more money than an honest
hand, so a gang of cow thieves as big as everyone
imagined would lose money on the deal. The price of
beef was going up, but it wasn't going up enough to pay
an outfit using a couple of hands for every half-dozen
or so scrub cows. They had to be consolidating them
into a big holding herd that a couple of riders could
tend. He figured that three to six riders could cut out a
dozen or so at a time and run them to the hideout. If
only he knew how they made themselves invisible. The
gang wasn't as big as McBride's corrida or any of the
other crews they'd hit. Why shilly-shally with an outfit
you outnumber and have the drop on? If there were
more than thirty in the mysterious gang, they'd just
jump the strung-out drovers on the trail and take the
whole herd and the chuckwagon too!

The town was called Stover's Wells. That meant
Spanish-speaking folks were still running things. Longarm had noticed that as soon as Anglos took control of
the local government, they gave the town a fancy Spanish name. He didn't know whether California Anglos
felt guilty, or just wanted folks to think they'd been
there since Coronado's time. They'd take a stage stop
or gold camp with a perfectly sensible name, like
Jenny's Crossing or Stinkweed Camp, and rename it
to sound Spanish. Mariposas and Alamedas were
sprouting all over the map out here, although no

Spaniard in recorded history had ever named a real town after a butterfly or a cottonwood tree.

He'd almost reached Stover's Wells when he spotted the mud wagon he'd seen earlier, under a valley oak by the side of the trail. It was standing at a crazy angle, and as he rode in, he saw that it had a busted rear wheel and that the team had been unhitched and driven off. He dismounted, tethered his mount, and moved in with his Winchester. The mud wagon was empty. The baggage rack on top was empty, too. There wasn't any real mud on the sides, this time of the year. He knew the open coaches were called mud wagons because they splashed mud all over their passengers in the rainy season. Even rich folks rode them in the summer. They were a cool and cheap means of transportation. But whoever had been aboard this one was long gone.

He moved up the trail, hunkered down, and struck a match. There were footprints in the dust. Some of them had been left by high heels. He shook out the light and went back to get his mount. If he read the sign right, the wagon had just broken down and the passengers and crew had walked on into town. They'd be there by now, so it was no concern of his.

The town was half an hour on up the trail. And the trail, in these parts, was turning into a real road. The coast hills crowded close to the sea, and the fences and hedges crowded closer to the trail. Like most Hispanics, the local farmers preferred to live close together and mosey out to their fields, instead of living spread out among them like Anglos. So Longarm passed no houses at first. A nightbird kikiwhimpered at him. He heard the gurgle of water and smelled wet fertilizer, so he knew they were irrigating their crops. Some of the fencing was little more than piled brush. Herding cows past all that wet greenery was likely to prove a task. He found a side lane leading toward the ocean, and trotted over that way for a look-see. The path ended at the beach sands.

The moonlight illuminated long lines of breakers rolling up on the beach, and it was right pretty. But Longarm saw a black fang of bedrock jutting out to the north and blocking the far end of the pocket beach. Running the cows along the strand was out. The more he saw of the Old Mission Trail, the more respect he had for the padres who'd laid it out. They had purely picked the best, and perhaps the only way to get from here to there up the coast.

He got back on the main *camino* and rode on into town. Stover's Wells was little more than a wide spot in the road. He passed the stage station that gave the place its name. The station was a low adobe with a long veranda, and he noticed some unhappy-looking folk sitting there. A man hailed him and he rode over. They were the passengers from the broken-down mud wagon. Their driver had ridden on to the next station to fetch another vehicle, and for some reason they thought Longarm might know when he'd get back. Longarm said he didn't know. One of the passengers was the pretty gal McBride had mentioned. She was snooty, all right. She never looked his way, and a formidable *dueña* tried to block Longarm's view of her charge as he jawed with the others. But he'd already seen enough of her to know he'd never seen her before, so what the hell. The *dueña* had no call to stare at him so mean. He wasn't after the snooty little gal she was guarding. She was pretty, but she wasn't *that* pretty. The *dueña* was taking her job too seriously. Longarm was tempted to tell her to relax, but he didn't. She was sort of ornery-looking. He could see that she'd been pretty too, a while back. In her day she'd likely given her own *dueña* a hard time. It was ironic, he reflected, that once folks got a mite long in the tooth for flirting, they just busted a gut to spoil it for anyone younger.

He left the passengers to their fate and rode on to the center of town, which lay within rock-throwing distance. There was a smithy, closed for the night. There

132

was a general store *cum* post office, ditto. The one and only cantina was open and selling drinks two for a quarter. It was crowded anyway. Longarm noticed that the townies were mostly Mexicans dressed sort of Anglo, and Anglos dressed sort of Mex. He couldn't get to the bar without shoving, but there was an empty table against the back wall, so he went to it and sat down. A colored gal came over and asked what his pleasure was. He asked for Maryland rye and she said they didn't have any, so he ordered a jug of beer. When she brought it, it was warm and flat, but he didn't fuss at her. He knew she only worked there, and he was more interested in the conversation than in what he was drinking. He had a good view of the proceedings, although not as good a chance to hear the bar talk. He sipped his beer as he sized up the crowd. They were strangers to him, but they all seemed to know each other. One gent in a fancy charro outfit adjusted his gunbelt, and nobody flinched. This meant not only that he knew the crowd, but that they all knew him. The sudden move had made Longarm stiffen in his chair, but nobody else had paid it any mind. An outlaw on the prod would have jumped a country mile and come down with iron in his fist. The fancy-dressed farm boy had a lot to learn, but he was safe in his own backyard, among friends.

Longarm was halfway through his beer when another man came over and sat down across from him, uninvited. Longarm noticed that the intruder wore a brass star on his vest, so he nodded politely and said, "My name is Long. I'm riding segundo for the Indian agency herd. I rode in ahead to scout."

The man with the badge was obviously part Anglo and part Mex; he was a sticklike, walleyed individual who introduced himself with a humorless smile. "I'm Constable Carillo. I'm sure glad you rode in ahead, polite. You see, we just passed a herd law here in

133

Stover's Wells. You can't drive your cows through here."

Longarm took a sip of beer and put down the mug before he said, "I'm afraid we have to. There's no way along the beach, and the hills to the east are gulleyed past common sense."

Carillo shrugged and said, "I know. The law wasn't my notion. I just enforce such laws as the town council sees fit to pass. You see, the last couple of herds through here tore the hell out of things, and some harsh words and bullets were passed. The folks around here don't want any more cows tear-assing off with laundry draped over their horns. It's rough on you, but easier on us."

Longarm caught the colored girl's eye and pointed at his almost-empty mug and then at the town law. As she went to the end of the bar to fetch their drinks, he told Carillo, "What we have us here is a problem. We'll work with you if you'll work with us."

"Friend, we don't have to work with you. The herd law says you can't come through here."

Longarm said patiently, "I'm sorry, but it don't. You folks are straddled on a public right-of-way. The State of California could pass a law forbidding cattle drives up the Old Mission Trail, but they haven't done so. Like I said, we're going to have to work something peaceful out."

Carillo said, "It won't be peaceful at all if you try to shove those cows through us. You can jaw all you want about public highways, but you still ain't coming through unless you want a war."

The girl brought their drinks. Longarm waited until she left before he spoke again. "All right, let's talk about that. McBride has close to thirty guns backing his play, counting the wagon and remuda crews. I'm going to be surprised as hell if your budget calls for more than five or six deputies."

Carillo looked uncomfortable and said, "I can always deputize some farm boys."

"Sure you can, and it's possible, just possible, that you'll win. But a lot of folks will have to be buried at the town's expense, and let's not forget that we're talking about stopping a herd bought and paid for by the federal government. After you console the local widow women, what are you fixing to tell the army of U.S. deputies they'll send down here to arrest you all?"

Carillo bristled. "Nobody can arrest me. I'm the law."

"You mean you pack a mail-order badge bestowed by an unincorporated township, friend. McBride has a federal lawman riding shotgun on that Indian beef. If he gets gunned in the general confusion, I wouldn't be surprised if your town council stretched some hemp at your side to keep you company."

He saw that he had the small-town lawman reconsidering his options, so he smiled and said, "I can see *your* problem, too. You can't just knuckle under without looking like a sissy. But I suspicion we can work it out so that you wind up looking modestly firm and nobody gets hurt."

Carillo looked downright relieved, but still confused. So Longarm explained, "You deputize some locals to help us. Only you don't put it that way, see? You tell everybody that we've posted a behavior bond, and that you and your boys have gotten us to agree to behave. With your riders holding the flanks, we can squeeze the cows through four abreast and moving gentle. McBride can be reasonable about damage money, if it's his fault, and since it's a government herd, you can always sue Uncle Sam if there's any dispute."

Carillo sipped his own beer and finally said, "I don't know. The boys won't like it. I have to put up at least a token show of force."

Longarm said, "Token gunplay can get a man killed just as dead as if he meant it. I'm talking sense to you

135

because I am a civilized gent who'd rather talk than fight. But if push comes to shove, I'm still riding segundo, and come hell or high water, we are purely coming through with those cows. Start a fight with us, and aside from the usual gunplay, you'll have close to three thousand spooked critters stampeding every which way. My riders will be too busy killing your men to worry about your fucking clotheslines and kitchen gardens. So by the time we round them up amid the debris—"

"You do have a convincing way with words," Carillo cut in, adding, "I can see meeting you halfway as the lesser of two evils. Is it all right if I bawl you out some for the benefit of my constituents?"

"Sure. I'll clear it with McBride. You warn the hell out of us, and then we'll all work together to drift the cows through without stomping a petunia."

Carillo nodded and swallowed some more of the awful beer. Longarm said, "As long as we're jawing about cows, I've got some other questions. Am I right in assuming you folks here are mostly farm folk?"

Carillo nodded and said, "You are. Aside from beans and kitchen truck, we've put in apricots and almonds. The trees are young and easily damaged. Livestock running wild around here tends to get shot up. There's a sheep outfit over to the east. They stay there. The only critters close enough to matter are the usual milking goats, burros, horses, and fowl. We used to have some hogs until we laid in the fruit trees. But now we have a swine law, too."

"So, in other words, you'd notice if anyone else was herding cows within a day's ride of here, eh?"

"We'd notice and we'd get testy as hell. Why do you ask?"

"We've been getting hit by cow thieves. My main reason for scouting on ahead was to try and get a line on the who and how of it."

Carillo asked, "Are you a range detective?"

"Nope," Longarm said. It was the truth, in a way.

Then he said, "I've chased cow thieves some, before. They tend to be unemployed cowhands. So when they ain't stealing, they drink and whore like everyone else. I was hoping I might not be the only stranger here in town tonight. But I can see that your only visitors are those stranded passengers over at the station. I didn't see any cows on the veranda with them, though."

Carillo smiled and said, "Yeah, they're stuck for the night for sure. One of 'em was asking me if we had us a hotel, ain't that a bitch?"

"Well, I can see how they'd think they needed one. Where do you reckon they're to bed down if their driver doesn't get back soon?"

Carillo shrugged and said, "Beats me. I don't expect another mud wagon before morning. The driver rode off drunk. The way I hear it, he was swinging wide and fast with a skinful of booze, and ran into a tree. He may reach the next stage tonight. He may be sleeping it off under a tree in the moonlight. It's hard to get good help these days."

Longarm consulted his watch. He saw that it was past ten and he wasn't going to learn much more here. They'd be rolling up the sidewalks soon. He discussed some technicalities of the next day's drive through Carillo's edgy community and said adios for now.

He went out and untethered his zorrilla, and remounted and headed back to camp. As he passed the woebegone passengers seated outside the station, he told himself their misfortune was none of his business.

Then he reined in and trotted over to them, counting noses. There were six of them. Three men, an Indian gal, the snooty *señorita* and her *dueña*. He told them what Carillo had said about their driver and nobody seemed surprised. One of the men said, "I asked if any of the folks here would bed us for the night. We offered to pay, but this is one unfriendly little town."

137

Longarm said, "I noticed. I'm the segundo of that trail herd you must have noticed in passing. We're camped about a three hours' walk from here. If you folks are up to legging it, we could spare you some blankets and tarps by the fire, and we've plenty of coffee. Come morning, we'll be headed back this way and you could ride bareback on the spares from the remuda. The town constable tells me the company won't send another wagon any sooner."

The *señorita* asked, "Can't you fetch us some mounts and let us ride both ways, my good man?"

Longarm said, "I could, ma'am, but I don't aim to. I don't own the outfit, and if I did, I was only being neighborly. If you want room service, you'll have to find a hotel. Have to pay, too. The offer I just made was for free rough shelter, like you'd find in any cow camp."

The girl stood up and said, "You'll have to ride me pillion, then. I can't walk that far in these heels."

Her *dueña* gasped, "Lolita, have you gone mad? We have not been introduced to this *caballero*. Even if we had, it is unthinkable for you to be alone with a man!"

Longarm was tempted. The gal was a nasty little stuck-up thing he wouldn't ordinarily mess with, but the *dueña* had no call to say he wasn't a gent to be trusted. The girl stepped off the veranda and said, "Don't be absurd, Tia Rosa! I can look out for myself."

She raised her hand imperiously to Longarm. He shrugged and took it. Lolita put her right foot in the left stirrup, pinching hell out of his booted ankle, and swung up sidesaddle behind him with the grace of a woman born to make horses, men, and other critters do just as she told them to. The *dueña* wailed "Jesus Maria! You cannot do this to me!"

Lolita said, "Nonsense, hand me up my bag, unless you want to carry it for me. I will meet you at this *caballero*'s camp."

Protesting, the *dueña* held up a carpetbag. Longarm took it and hooked the handle over his saddle horn as the older woman sobbed, "I cannot allow this, Lolita. What will your parents say?"

Lolita shrugged willfully and replied, "I don't care. I am not about to spend the night sitting like a bump on a log in the sea mists. Ride on, my good man."

So Longarm did, as the other passengers picked up their gear and began to follow. He saw no reason to dally at their pace, so he clicked his tongue at the *zorrilla* and they trotted off. He figured bouncing her sassy ass on his saddle skirt was as close to the spanking Lolita deserved as he was allowed to administer.

She rode lightly, with a hand gripping his gunbelt and her ankles crossed on the left, one toe wedged in with his foot in the stirrup. She was a good rider, sidesaddle or no. As they left the others behind, she said, "My father is Don Pedro Castro Pico y Vallejo, and if you rape me he will have you killed in a most horrid fashion, Señor."

"I'm particular who I rape, ma'am, so let's say no more about it."

"Just so you know your place. Can't you gallop? I don't like to trot."

"In a minute you'll wind up walking. I can see how you might have gotten the notion that your shit don't stink, ma'am. But you have piss-poor manners for a guest."

Lolita sucked in her breath and said, "Nobody talks to me like that, my good man!"

He growled, "I just did. I ain't your good man or even your pussycat. I am a freeborn citizen of these United States and I ought to have my head examined for messing with you in the first place. I'd leave you sitting in some cactus, but there are outlaws skulking about and I don't mean to have to explain your where-abouts, come morning. But if you aim to get along with me and the boys up ahead, you'll stuff a sock in that pretty mouth of yours."

Naturally, Lolita didn't take his advice. It got tedious as hell, listening to her fuss at him about his manners all the way back to the cow camp. By the time the fires were in sight ahead, she'd started to repeat herself. He didn't envy the poor brute who'd have to marry her some day. Next to a nagging woman, there was nothing worse than one with no imagination to her bitching. She hadn't contributed one original complaint about Longarm. He'd been told before that he was arrogant, boorish, brutal, mean, and just like all men. He *knew* he was just like all men; what he couldn't figure out was why women bothered with men at all, if they hated them so much.

He rode in to find everyone bedded down, but of course McBride and a couple of the others crawled out of their rolls when they heard a gal cussing and hoofbeats coming in at a trot.

McBride joined them at the remuda line as they dismounted. Longarm introduced him to Lolita and explained. McBride nodded and told a hand to rustle up some groundcloth and extra blankets.

They went to the night fire and hunkered down. There was a night pot of Arbuckle's simmering on its trivet. McBride hadn't said to wake the cook, but the cook came over anyway, muttering things about their mothers that could have gotten him killed if anyone had taken his suggestions seriously. He asked how many freeloaders were expected, and when Longarm told him, the cook opened his chuck box and started slicing off some bacon, complaining to himself. They knew he was secretly pleased to show off with bacon and eggs. He bitched a steady stream as he started dicing onions to fry with the hen fruit and "overland trout." He wouldn't put it on until the others got there, of course, so while they coffeed and waited, Longarm drew pictures in the dust with a stick as he filled Mc-Bride in on the plan to get the herd through the bottle-neck. The gal, Lolita, was staring daggers at him across the fire, but the deal he'd made with the town was more important, so he paid her no mind and that seemed to make her even madder at him.

McBride agreed that it was a good plan, but he said, "I don't understand why they've gotten so touchy all of a sudden. We've never had anyone trying to bar our path before."

Longarm said, "Law tells me they had trouble with the last drovers. Were you them?"

"I thought I was," McBride said. "They don't make that many drives up the Mission Trail these days. I dis-remember having trouble here before, though. This far north I generally have the cows moving steady, and I can't think of incident one."

"Might have been another outfit. Carillo said they moved rough and exchanged unkind words and gun-shots."

McBride said, "Hmm, drovers in a hurry and on the prod don't sound like professionals. They study like a wild bunch who might not have had a bill of sale for every critter in the herd. Did you ask that lawman about brands?"

"No. He's a farmboy who's too spooked by cows to be interested in the fine print. But cow thieves looking for trouble on the main route sound sort of dumb. They're already in trouble. Why look for more?"

McBride helped himself to some coffee as he opined, "A cowhand who turns rogue tends to have a high opinion of his gun hand, and you say the folks ahead are mostly greasers."

Longarm didn't look at the girl across the fire as he said, "I call 'em Mexicans. I know some Anglos have poor manners in these parts, but Carillo was packing a Colt Lightning in a sensible cross-draw rig, with a plain

141

waxed holster. Some of the others looked sort of like they knew their business, too. They ain't a bunch to be ridden over lightly by anyone with brains, owlhoots or not. We know the outfit robbing us is slick. They're shy of gunplay, too. Anybody ready to tangle with a whole town would have just come down out of the hills by now to tell us we didn't own these cows anymore."

"Makes sense," McBride agreed. "But I was sure I drove the last bought-and-paid-for herd through here. Somebody is telling fibs."

"You reckon the town council is just being mule-headed?"

"Don't know what to think. I've never given them trouble, and like I said, I suspect I'd know about other drovers running herds up the coast. It ain't like they don't have beef up north, you know. With the price of prime beef at thirty to sixty a head back East, a nine-hundred-pound steer would fetch twenty or more right now in Frisco."

Longarm whistled softly and said, "I didn't know we had so much *dinero* on the hoof."

McBride said, "We don't. There ain't a scrub cow in the herd that tips the scales at nine hundred pounds. The BIA has been getting 'em for ten dollars or less, and they're still losing on the deal because of the wastage and all this infernal stealing. I don't expect to be in business down here long, no matter how it all comes out in the wash. I contracted to deliver and I mean to, but if I was running the Interior Department, I'd buy the durned beef closer to the Indians and spoil 'em with good Valley-bred Durham crosses."

Longarm looked around and saw that the detective, Scanlon, hadn't seen fit to crawl out of his warm roll, and said, "I've been wondering about that, too. I don't reckon the thieves are in business for the exercise, but they're not stealing good cows, as many as they've stole. Can you think of anybody dumber than Uncle

Sam who'd be in the market for so much inferior beef? Figuring they must have stolen at least five or six thousand head by now, where in thunder could they unload them?"

"Beats me," McBride said. "Even the Mex rancheros have started breeding up their herds with imported stock. Old Mexico, maybe? They call anything a cow, south of Tijuana."

Longarm shook his head and said, "They don't raise much beef in the Baja, direct south. Herding stolen cows through the Yaqui country of the Sierra Madre sounds like a scaly way to sell 'em at a discount over in the Mex cattle country. Nobody along the Rio Grande would give you five dollars a head for scrubs, bill of sale or no."

"Couldn't they drive 'em up into Texas?"

Longarm couldn't mention what he'd learned from investigating the notorious Laredo Loop, but he shook his head anyway and said, "Hell, why stop at Texas, if you aim to cruise halfway around the world with a ten-dollar cow? Why not drive 'em direct to New York City? It would only be twice as far. Folks in Texas would laugh at the dog meat the BIA has grazing over yonder. Then they'd notice the big ID brands and ask mean questions. No, the thieves are unloading closer to home."

"Maybe. But we're talking in a circle. I've never seen cow one with a government brand in the L.A. basin, and I get about."

"Scanlon mentioned some fair-sized cow outfits over in the big valley to the east."

McBride sighed deeply. "I know. He's been chewing my ear off about it. I know the cattlemen over that way. Know the brand inspectors, too. I'm not saying more than one old boy never got his start in the business by mavericking or even stealing a few head. But we're talking about almost worthless scrub cows with Uncle

143

Sam's brand on 'em. Nobody with a lick of sense would touch 'em with a ten-foot pole."

The cook had been listening. He stared down at the onions he was chopping as he said, "Cannery."

McBride said, "Come again?"

"Cannery," the cook repeated. "Have you got wax in your ears? You can hide all the brands you want in a can of corned beef. If them owlhoots are working for a cannery, the stole cows are hiding out in tin. Nobody ever asks a cannery where they bought the stuff they can."

He saw that he was holding their interest, so he cackled and recited:

"A canner exceedingly canny
One day did remark to his granny
A canner can can anything he can can
But a canner can't can a can, can he?"

Everybody but the sulky Lolita laughed. McBride said, "It's a new suspicion, at least. I'll tell Scanlon about it if he ever wakes up, and he can go pester any canning outfits around here."

Longarm asked if McBride knew of any. The drover shrugged and said, "There's a couple near the L.A. railyards. Couple more up near Monterey, but they mostly can fish and produce from the Salinas valley."

"Nothing this side of Monterey? That's pretty far."

"I know. By the time you drive a stole cow to Monterey, you may as well take her on to Frisco. But I disremember any canneries between here and there."

The cook said, "Secret cannery." Then he went back to his chores.

Longarm considered the notion before dismissing it. He'd learned not to ignore a stump before he sniffed it some. But a cannery had to be near a railroad, and he'd never heard of a secret cannery. A secret moonshine still was risky enough, and a lot more profitable.

They'd run out of ideas about the cow thieves, and couldn't swap dirty stories in front of the Mex girl, so they made small talk until after a while the other passengers staggered in and flopped down around the fire, footsore and weary.

Tia Rosa ran over and slobbered all over Lolita as she asked her in Spanish if she'd been gang-raped. Longarm understood enough of the lingo to know that Lolita was assuring her *dueña* that she was still pure, god-damnit. Longarm looked away, wondering if he'd passed up anything. Was Tia Rosa just a silly old gal, or did she have her reasons for being so worried about Lolita being alone for a few minutes with a stranger wearing pants? Now that she'd stopped fussing at him, Lolita was a pretty little thing. It seemed a shame that he'd never know if she was bawdy as well as bitchy.

The cook dished out the grub and just grunted when the refugees complimented him on his cooking. He stomped around like he was mad as hell, but he opened some canned peaches for dessert and handed them out, growling. One of the male passengers reached in his pocket, but McBride shot him a warning look and said, "Don't do it. Do you want to get scalded?" So the man put his money away.

Having grubbed them and taught them cow camp manners, McBride and his hands issued groundcloths and blankets. When Lolita demanded to know where they intended her to sleep, McBride just looked confused. So Longarm said, "Just pick yourself a soft spot, miss. I'm sorry as hell this ain't the Palace in Frisco, but that's the way life is."

"You expect me to sleep on the *ground?*"

"Honey, you can sleep in a tree like a hoot owl, if you've a mind to. But you'll be more comfortable if you spread out your groundcloth on some grass and get under the tarp and blankets like us mortal folk."

"This is disgusting! I'm not used to sleeping on the earth like a dirty Indian."

145

Longarm noticed the Indian *mahala* trying to ignore her on the far side of the fire. He said, "I'm sorry I invited you, too. You just do what you aim to. I'm off to my own roll, and I can't think of a thing to say to you that's fit for female ears."

"I need help with my bedding!" she protested as he walked away, not answering or looking back. He figured she needed a birch rod on her bare ass more than she needed anything else, but thinking about bare asses wasn't a good way to go to bed, and he knew she'd manage. How complicated was it to spread out some bedding and just lie down?

It was after midnight now, and he knew he had a long day ahead, so Longarm sat on his roll, shucked out of his duds, and turned in to sleep the sleep of the just. Despite the last few days on the trail and his generally good condition, Longarm hadn't herded recently and he was really tired, so he dropped off to sleep with no further discussion.

He was having an interesting dream about a big cannery where naked ladies were stuffing bawling cows in tin cans. One of them smiled and grabbed him by the pecker. He didn't want his pecker canned, so he woke up.

Somebody still had him by the pecker, and it was hard as hell. He stared without much success at the woman in his bedroll with him in the dark and said, "Howdy. What you're doing is sort of embarrassing if you just dropped over to borrow a cup of sugar, ma'am."

She placed a finger against his lips and whispered urgently, "Hush, *caballero!* We must not let any of the others hear us!"

He whispered back, "That sounds reasonable," and took her in his arms. She was wearing nothing but a thin silk chemise with nothing under it. He ran his free hand exploringly down her flank as he kissed her, and she sure kissed back friendly. So he hauled her chemise up under her warm, firm breasts and slid his calloused hand down her quivering belly. She tongued him and giggled, "Naughty boy!" as he parted the thatch between her legs and slid two fingers into her moist cleft. She was built more loosely than he'd expected, but she clamped down on his fingers like an expert and started squirming as she sighed, "Oh, don't tease me. *Do* it!"

So he did. He was still a little mad at her, but as long as she aimed to make up so nicely, he forgave the hell out of her and pounded her some, too. She got her thighs up to help him as she hugged his hips and started bouncing him. He ran a hand down under her naked rump to protect her tailbone from the ground on the down strokes, but he saw that she was well-padded. Funny, but he'd thought she was skinnier than this. Lolita had been wearing a flouncy skirt, and he remembered that she'd sat pillion at the trot comfortably, too. But somehow he hadn't pictured her this chunky with her duds off. Her breasts felt nice against him, even before he shucked the chemise off over her head and tossed it aside. Her nipples were big and hard as they rubbed against his chest, and he knew she was as hot as a firecracker even before she stiffened in his arms and moaned deep in her throat. But she came as quietly as a mouse and he knew she was used to stolen moments within earshot of her *dueña*. It was no wonder poor Tia Rosa was so worried about her. Lolita was a man-hungry little bitch who did this every chance she got.

He came himself, and she felt it and whispered, "Please don't stop."

He whispered back, "I don't aim to. You're as bad as I am, Lolita."

The woman in his arms suppressed a giggle and the penny dropped. He frowned down at her in the pitch blackness and said, "You *are* Lolita, ain't you, ma'am?"

Tia Rosa giggled again and said, "Don't be an ass.

The girl is a virgin, and I've promised my brother and his wife I would keep her that way. I have sacrificed myself in her place to protect her from your advances. I saw the way you were looking at her by the fire."

He chuckled softly and said, "I can see how you just suffered. I sure admire your devotion to duty. Do I get to call you Rosa, or do you aim to be my *tia*, too?"

She moved her hips suggestively and said, "Call me what you wish, alone. But we shall have to be more formal before the others in the morning, no?"

"Say no more, honey. I have rounded this curve before, although seldom in such strange company."

He started to pump some more and she said, "I don't do this sort of thing with every man who admires my ward."

"Just the ones you can get alone, right?"

"Don't be nasty. You don't do it like an innocent *muchacho,* either, you know.

"You're right. Fair is fair. Powder River and let her buck, with no questions asked and no strings attached."

She wrapped herself around him and moaned, "Oh God, you really are so nice and understanding. I feel young again in your arms."

Longarm didn't answer as he pleasured her. He'd never met anyone under thirty who did it that good, but he knew she didn't want to hear that. Her face was sort of going to seed, but her body was still fine, and he thought it was a crying shame how time treated folks, leaving all the good looks to kids who didn't know what to do with them. Then you sagged and grayed up just as you were getting the hang of things. Tia Rosa was getting to be a dirty old lady, and he supposed someday he'd be a dirty old man. He sure hoped he'd meet up with gals like this when the time came. Dirty old folks had a hell of a time getting laid, which was likely what made 'em so dirty.

He came again and kept going, in that twilight stage of sex between enjoying it and just showing off. It was no effort with Tia Rosa, for she did her share and the night was cool. He caught himself wondering how a gent could get himself a pretty sixteen-year-old with the ability of a forty-year-old widow woman in love. He'd never in this world planned on spending a night with a grim-faced *dueña* with a mustache, which just went to prove that Lady Luck knew more about such things than he did.

Tia Rosa sensed that he was getting tired, so she suggested that he roll over on his back. When he did, she started kissing him down the chest and belly to arouse him again, and when she started to give him the best French lesson he'd had in a month of Sundays, Longarm smiled up at the stars and murmured, "Why, thank you, Lady Luck. You've been considerate as hell this evening."

Chapter 11

The nicest way to wake up in the cold gray sea mists with an old gray gal was for her to be in her own bed-roll someplace else, and since that was how it turned out, Longarm rolled out bright-eyed and bushy-tailed. He rode over to the herd and tallied as the camp slowly came to life. The other hands were rousted early, but the passengers and the lazy Scanlon lay slugabed until breakfast time.

Longarm found that they hadn't lost any beef during the night, but they had a long day ahead. By this time, McBride was ready to send the camp crew and wagons ahead to set up the noon camp on the far side of Stover's Wells, so Longarm nodded adios to the stranded passengers as they rode off in the hoodlum. Lolita still looked peeved at the world. Tia Rosa looked like she'd had a restful night. Neither of them waved back at him when he tipped his hat.

They grazed the herd for an hour to steady them, and to let Carillo and his deputies get used to the idea that they were coming through. Then they drifted them

151

onto the trail, squeezed them into a long skinny line, and got them moving at a slow walk. It took until after ten before they met Carillo, looking stern as he guarded a privet fence with his life and some shotgun deputies. McBride was primed and listened politely as the town law told him all the dreadful things that would happen if they ran a cow through anybody's flower bed. Then, having run for reelection, Carillo fell in with them and they led the strung-out herd into town. Other deputies and some kids were lining the street like it was a circus parade. But nothing exciting happened. The drovers had the cows under control, and the cows didn't seem interested in goring any outhouses or trotting through clotheslines. Longarm spied something he'd missed the night before in the dark. It was a sign over the door of the general store, and it read:

ANYTHING AND EVERYTHING FROM A PAPER OF PINS TO A CONESTOGA WAGON. PROVISIONS FOR YOUR HOUSE, CAMP, FARM OR RANCH! BOOTS, HATS, HARDWARE, GUNS AND CLOTHING: A GENUINE CALIFORNIA OR TEXAS SADDLE COMPLETE WITH HARNESS! A NOBBY SIDESADDLE FOR YOUR PRETTY GAL! ASK TO SEE OUR GENUINE GOLD RINGS AND SILVER-MOUNTED SPURS! DON'T GO TO STRANGERS, COWBOY! WE GOT IT ALL RIGHT HERE!

Longarm didn't mention it to McBride until they made the far side and had the cows heading out peaceably. When he did, McBride said, "I saw it. What about it?"

Longarm said, "It strikes me as odd that a trail town has suddenly gotten so proddy about folks in our business. That store is losing money, with trail hands barred from town."

Carillo had dropped off to one side to supervise their

exit, so McBride couldn't ask him about it, but he said, "I follow your drift, Long. I've never passed this way without dropping some money in their pockets. But this time they purely gave us the bum's rush. Do you reckon they're hiding something?"

Longarm shrugged and said, "Don't know. If they ain't, they're dumb, or somebody's put a bug in their ear. Farmers don't like our breed, with some reason. I've seldom seen a trail-town merchant who didn't welcome free-spending cowhands. Farm folks ain't such big fools about watered drinks and expensive play-pretties. Carillo said the town council voted that new herd law. The local merchants usually control such meetings. It doesn't make much sense."

McBride said, "Well, we're near the starting end of the trail. Few drovers would have been paid off by the time they got this far. They may just reckon we ain't worth the usual busted glass and noise."

Longarm let the subject drop and took the swing to make sure the herd stayed polite as it wound on out of Stover's Wells. Despite all the war talk, it had gone as smooth as silk.

Once they were out in open country again, they bunched the cows up a mite and drove them harder. They caught up with the wagons just a few miles beyond, and ran the cows up a draw for the noon break.

They tallied, found everything in order, and headed out again, the wagons moving faster and the cows following slowly until once more the two parties were separated. The afternoon was a dull repetition of the ones before. The country was rolling, open park land with oaks spangled up the tawny slopes of grass. McBride complained that the range was grazed short by sheep, but the cows tended to stay on the trail when there was nothing green to beckon them away. They were falling into the routine, too. They caught up with the wagons near sundown, off the trail to the west, above an open stretch of sea beach with a fine bowl of grazing, rimmed by steeper, brushier ridges.

McBride and Longarm approved of the night camp, but they were surprised to see the little Indian *mahala* tending the fire. The cook followed them over as they put their mounts in the remuda, explaining, "I ain't turned squaw man. The kid was treated mean and we come upon her crying by the road."

McBride asked, "What happened?"

The cook said, "Near as me and the Chinee can make out, she got in a fight with that snooty Spanish gal. They'd started earlier than us from Stover's Wells this morning. Anyway, they got into a hair-pulling contest on the trail, and being an Injun, she was voted out of the wagon and left to walk to Santa Bob." He spat and added, "I wasted good grub on them no-account sons of bitches, too. The way I see it, if two gals want to have a fight, the gentlemanly thing to do is just to stand aside and let 'em have it. The kid says the snooty gal's daddy is a big hoorah up the coast, so the relief driver took her side. I took the liberty of saying she could ride the chuckwagon till she gets closer to home, if she behaves herself. She said she hardly ever tries to scratch anyone's eyes out unless they call her a mission pig. That's what the Spanish gal called her, a mission pig. Ain't that a bitch?"

McBride said, "I knew that Lolita was a bitch before you told me. But I don't like gals on a cattle drive." He turned to Longarm and asked, "What do you think, segundo? Shall we let her ride with us a spell, or give her a pony and tell her to git?"

Longarm said, "It's a hard choice either way. You could lose a pony or have the boys fighting over her. I vote to let her stay as long as Cooky can use her. We might need friends up the trail, and Indians who know the country make the best kind."

McBride told the cook, "All right. But you keep an eye on her, and if you get to screwing her, don't let the others know. We got us enough trouble. Let's coffee up and run another tally."

The *mahala* served the coffee, and everyone agreed she was an improvement on the Chinese who usually did it. The rough good humor seemed to confuse the Indian girl, but she soon figured out that they meant to treat her like a lady, and she had a pretty smile. She was no great beauty, but her round little face had nothing wrong with it, and her petite figure was downright disconcerting when she bent over to pour. Longarm admired the shape of her ass as he eyed it over the rim of his cup. So he began to reconsider his voting to let her stay. She was one of those gals a man had to look at twice before he considered fighting over her. He'd been lucky on the trail. Some of the other hands were young enough to jerk off twice a day, and they'd ask a sheep to marry them, if they thought it wouldn't give in any other way. Longarm knew himself well enough to question his own motives. So he did, and pleaded innocent. He hadn't had country thoughts about the little Indian gal when he voted to let her tag along; he'd just been asleep at the switch, and now it was too late. It would cause even more trouble if they chased her off.

He put the *mahala* out of his mind as he left to tally. He double-checked, swore, and circled the herd, trying to cut sign. He found no sign. The cows they'd herded in to graze the hillside were all there. But they'd lost thirteen more since the last tally, and Uncle Sam was out a rough hundred and thirty dollars more. Uncle Sam pissed a lot more than that away every minute, but it still made Longarm sore. They were starting to make him look downright foolish. How in hell was he going to write this up for Billy Vail? A letter composed itself in his mind: *Dear Boss: Regret to inform you that as I was staring at a squaw's behind, some cows got stolen by person or persons unknown.*

He wasn't being fair to himself. The cows had been

155

stolen before he'd seen the *mahala* working for the cook. But Longarm tended to be as hard on himself as he was on any other idiot wearing a badge. It didn't soothe his feelings that Scanlon was a bigger idiot who never even tried. They were getting the same results. Scanlon just seemed to be along for the ride, while he was tear-assing all over the place, but neither of them knew what in thunder was going on!

He rode back, intending to tell McBride. But he decided not to, for the moment. So far, only he knew they were missing any cattle. It might be interesting to see how the others reacted if he kept it to himself.

McBride asked if he'd tallied, and Longarm said he had, which was the unadorned truth. They grazed the cows another hour, and headed them up the trail after the vanishing wagons.

Longarm thought about the wagon crews as he rode right swing. There was of course no way for the advance party to cut out a cow from a herd far behind it. But a confederate of the owlhoots riding with the advance was in a good position to signal folks skulking on a far ridge.

He ran that through again and decided it was a poor lead. Cow thieves scouting them from the hills had a better view of the herd than they did. They never seemed to hit the herd at a trail stop, so knowing where the outfit meant to stop wouldn't be worth paying for. Any everybody involved in the operation had to be paid; nobody risked a hanging just for the hell of it. He did some mental arithmetic. Even if you cut out a thousand scrub cows, you were talking about less than ten thousand dollars for a month-long operation. Nobody but Uncle Sam was about to pay anywhere near that much for skinny scrub stock. So, saying the boss owlhoot kept at least half for himself, that left less than five thousand to share out among his thieving help. An honest cowhand could collect thirty to sixty a month; a rogue would expect at least double that for hazard wages. So the puppet master couldn't have more than two dozen strings to pull. Less, if he was bribing any officials to look the other way. A crooked brand inspector would expect at least five hundred or so. A crooked lawman would come even higher. A sheriff or federal deputy couldn't be bought for less than a thousand. It started getting expensive as hell when you put all the folks you could suspect on the owlhoot's payroll. So Longarm started scratching folks off his list of suspects.

One of the flank riders caught up with him on a quiet stretch. He was a soft-spoken young Mex they called Blanco. Longarm asked Blanco what was up. Blanco said, "I seem to be missing an old friend, segundo. A breakaway yearling grullo with black stockings has been trying to get past me since we left Los Angeles. I have not seen him this afternoon. Forgive me, I mean no disrespect, but was that last tally a rough count?"

Longarm considered this silently, then he said, "I doubt like hell that a vaquero would report a missing cow he had anything to do with misplacing, so I'll level with you to keep you from yelling your head off to the others about it. We're missing a baker's dozen. But keep it under your hat."

Blanco sucked in his breath and said, "I don't understand, segundo."

Longarm said, "Neither do I, if you're asking how they done it. We could bunch the herd and run all over, yelling and cussing. But as you may have noticed, it don't do any good and the thieves must be hugging themselves for being so infernal smart. My plan, half-assed as it sounds, is to just ignore the latest loss for now, and see what happens."

"But what do you expect to happen, segundo?"

"Beats the shit out of me. If I knew their next move, we'd be set up to stop it. You ever play chess, Blanco?"

"A little. I am not very good at it," the young Mex admitted shyly.

"Well, I find it tedious, too. But sometimes you get snowed in. An old chess master showed me a trick one time. You make a meaningless random move when you can't think up a good one. It can throw the other player off as he tries to figure why you failed to jump a pawn you could have, or sent your bishop off in a corner for no sensible reason."

"Ah, I see," Blanco said, his black eyes narrowing. "If they are watching us, they must be wondering if we have noticed the missing cows and why we are not looking for them, no?"

"Right. It makes them bolder. As we know, they've been pulling some slick thieving, up to now. If we could get them to think we're even dumber than they've made us look, they might get greedy. Why steal a dozen when you may as well try for two dozen? Meanwhile, I want you back in position. We don't want to lose any cows by accident."

Blanco dropped back. Longarm had confided more than some might have approved, but he'd found that if you told folks anything, it was best to tell them all. Blanco seemed honest and sharp-eyed. Arming him with inside savvy couldn't hurt, and it might help if he spotted something odd. The boy was shy and wouldn't report anything unless he thought it was important. Now that he knew he could talk to the segundo, it gave Longarm an extra pair of eyes.

It was getting on toward evening, and everyone was riding bored and hungry when a couple of shots rang out down near the drag.

Longarm swung wide, pulled his mount around, and headed for the commotion at a dead run, yelling, "Hold them, damn it, hold them!" He saw that the hands were controlling the herd, and he swore as another shot rang out. He followed the sound with his eyes and saw two cows and a Mexican tear-assing up the slope through the trees. The Mex had lost interest in the cows and was just riding for his life, with Shadow and Osage in hot pursuit.

Both of the kids had their guns out as they chased the Mex. As Longarm cut left to head him off, Osage opened up again at impossible range. Longarm swore, but to his surprise, and likely to Osage's as well, the fugitive's pony went ass over teakettle and spilled its rider in the dry grass. As the Mex struggled to rise, Shadow closed in, shaking his pistol at him, so the Mex slapped leather. Shadow rained in, took aim, and fired. He hit the Mex in the thigh and knocked him down. By the time he sat up and tried to draw again, it was all over. Longarm had moved in, shaking out a loop, and roped the wounded man, pinning his elbows to his side and dragging him just enough to tighten the noose. Shadow dismounted, ran over, and kicked the Mex flat to disarm him as he covered him with the gun in his free hand.

Osage came up the slope, yelling, "I got him! Sweet Jesus, I got him!" Longarm thought at first that the kid was bragging about the Mex he and Shadow had just civilized. Then he glanced down the slope and saw the dark form of another man laying facedown in the grass. Osage pointed back at him with his smoking six-gun and repeated, "I killed the son of a bitch neat as a whistle. Who ever would have thought it!"

Longarm was a mite surprised himself. He dismounted, walked over to the wounded man at Shadow's feet, and said, "Well, amigo, you seem to be in a fix and that's a fact."

The wounded man spat and said, "Fuck your sister, *gringo*."

Shadow said, "We spotted him and his sidekick sneaking a couple of head out between some bushes down yonder. They likely didn't think we'd notice in all that infernal dust."

"Good work, boys," Longarm said. "But let's congratulate each other later, after this gent tells us about it."

The Mex said, "I tell nothing. Your mothers are all *putas*."

McBride and some other riders rode up slope to join them. McBride took in the scene and said, "You fellers just earned a bonus we'll discuss at the end of the drive. How many head did we lose?"

Longarm pointed at the cows grazing in the middle distance under a live oak and said, "None. Osage, why don't you run them critters back and tuck them in? What happened to Froggy and Pirate?"

Shadow said, "They're holding the drag, like I told 'em. It was Froggy who spotted this greaser. I was on the uphill side, so I said I'd chase 'em."

"I helped, damn it," Osage protested. Longarm nodded and pointed at the strays. So Osage went to round them up, still bragging to himself.

McBride sat his horse, staring hard-eyed at the wounded cow thief. He said, "I can see by your outfit that you're a California rider. So you know the local customs, amigo. You want to spill some beans for us?"

"Fuck your sister and your mother, too. I am not afraid."

McBride shrugged and said, simply and flatly, "Hang him."

Longarm and Shadow hauled the wounded man to his feet. "It ain't too late to make friends, old son," Longarm told him. "A judge wouldn't give you more'n twenty years if we saw fit to bring you in alive. Why don't we talk about it? What's your name, and who was that other gent you were riding with?"

The Mex tried to spit in Longarm's face, but his mouth was too dry. He said, "I tell you nothing. I spit in your mother's milk. Get it over with. My leg is starting to hurt."

So they hanged him.

Longarm didn't do it. Robles and Creedmore were the ones who put the cow thief's own rope around his neck and strung him from a live oak branch. Longarm had to watch, but he didn't like it much. He knew that as a federal agent he wasn't supposed to let things like that happen. But he didn't want to tip his hand and he knew the California lawmen took a casual view of such rough justice.

It was sort of unsettling to watch a man twitching and shitting his britches on the end of a rope, but the hardcased cuss had as much as begged for what he got. Folks had no call stealing stock if they didn't know the penalty for getting caught.

They found a running iron but no identification in the dead men's possibles when they searched them. The pony of the one Osage had shot had gotten away. Robles and Creedmore suggested trying to trail it, as it might be headed for home. Longarm glanced up at the sun and said not to. McBride agreed. The hanging had put him in a good mood, and he said it was time to catch up with the night camp crew. Trailing through grass was hard enough in broad daylight, and it wasn't like the runaway pony was packing anybody important.

So they left the dead owlhoots for the condors or their friends, whoever found them first, and moved on up the trail.

Night camp had been set up near another pocket beach where the trail ran close to the sea. The bedding grounds were a grassy flat surrounded by a ramada of prickly pear and greasewood. There was no water, but the cows could lick the sea mists off the grass after the winds shifted in off the ocean after dark. California couldn't seem to make up its mind whether it wanted to be hot and dry or cold and clammy. For a High Plains rider like Longarm, it took some getting used to. The others seemed to find it natural. McBride was so pleased that evening that he looked like he was fixing to walk on his hands. As he hunkered down next to Longarm with a steaming cup of coffee, he said, "The gang is Mex, and we've knocked off at least three of the rascals, counting the one who tried to gun you back in the valley. I'd say it's about over, wouldn't you?"

Longarm shrugged and said, "It'll be over when those cows are in the BIA corrals by Frisco Bay, boss. The three we accounted for could have been independent thinkers. A herd this size could tempt more than one gang of thieves, you know."

"Hell," McBride said, "I was just beginning to enjoy the evening. You sure do like to pour cold water on everything, Professor."

Longarm said, "Maybe. That Mex you strung up was hairy-chested, but a mite less slick than most. He and his partner got spotted by green kids, and they'd only cut out a couple of head when they got caught."

"They were sneaking 'em in brush, though. I talked to Froggy, the lad who caught 'em doing it. He said they worked down close to the trail where the brush growed close and——"

"I talked to the kids, too," Longarm cut in. "It was an old and risky play. The boys we're really after have been cutting out a dozen or so at a time, and they ain't been getting caught at it."

"Hell, old son, that gent who kept spitting in my mother's milk had a running iron in his saddlebag!"

"I know. I never said he wasn't a cow thief; I said he wasn't a very good one. I've been thinking about that running iron. I don't think the gents we're after use one."

"You don't, huh? What do they use to change the brands, then?"

"I'm still working on that. There's no way to doctor that big ID that a canny brand inspector wouldn't spot. Uncle Sam has flyers out on his lost beef. There's not a lawman on this coast who isn't watching for a mark that could have read ID at one time. Big simple brands are a bitch to blot, and those two letters stand out no matter how you fancy them up, once you know they might be there."

McBride poured the dregs of his cup on the fire and said peevishly, "I wish you hadn't said that. I was planning on a good night's sleep for a change. If you're so damned smart, old timer, how would you go about running them government brands?"

Longarm said, "When I figure that out, I'll have a better idea where they're selling your stolen stock."

"God damn it, son. Every time I think you're on the trail, you go back to the starting place."

"I know. It's tedious, ain't it?" Longarm said sympathetically.

"It sure is," McBride agreed. "I'm off to my bedroll. You just study all you want."

He left Longarm musing by the fire. Others were starting to turn in now, but Longarm was too puzzled to drop it. He stared into the dying embers, running over every cow thief's trick he'd ever heard of, as he had himself a good-night smoke.

He heard a commotion on the far side of the chuck-wagon. It sounded ugly, so he got up and went to see what was going on.

As he rounded the wagon, he saw the tangle silhouetted against the moonlit sea beyond. The cook and Robles were holding Blanco; Shadow and Pirate had Osage struggling between them. As Longarm approached, Osage yelled, "Turn me loose, damn it! That greaser struck a white man, and I aim to clean his plough!"

Longarm asked the cook what had happened. The cook answered breathlessly, "Beats me. They just lit into each other while my back was turned."

Longarm stared hard at Blanco, whose face was a study in stubbornness as he said, "It was personal, segundo."

Osage yelled, "He started it! He hit me, and I am gonna kill the son of a bitch as soon as I get loose!"

Longarm glanced around and saw that everyone else looked too puzzled to take sides. The little *mahala* was peeking around the wagon, looking scared. Longarm got between the two kids and said, "I want everybody to listen sharp. You boys are on the outfit's time, and no fighting is allowed in camp, as any grown man knows. I am going to tell everybody to turn everybody else loose. And then I am going to fire the first dumb son of a bitch who starts up again."

He paused to let it sink in. Then he nodded and everybody let go of the two antagonists. Blanco stood his ground but made no move. Osage took one step toward him, and Longarm's voice whipcracked, "I said the war is over, Osage. You're a hero tonight, but don't bank on using that to defy a direct order."

"He had no call to swing at me," Osage protested.

Longarm said, "He won't hit you no more. If you boys start up again, I'll personally kick the shit out of you both, and then I'll fire you so that you can work it out for yourselves off the payroll. There'll be no fighting in camp while I'm segundo."

"What about later, after we get to Frisco?" Osage asked.

Longarm shrugged and said, "You'll be on your own time."

Osage glared at Blanco and hissed, "Later, greaser!"

Blanco stared back and said, "I'll be there, *leparo!*"

Longarm nodded at Shadow and said, "Take Osage down to your end of the camp and tuck him in. Blanco, saddle up. You just made night guard."

Then Longarm walked over to the Indian girl, took

her by the arm, and led her off toward the ocean. As they walked across the sand, she asked, "Are you going to throw me in the sea, Señor?"

"No," he answered gently. "I want to talk to you alone. You saw the fight. What was it about?"

"Me, Señor. The *gringo* tried for to kiss me. The Mexican boy pulled him off me and knocked him down with his fist."

Somehow, this came as no great surprise to Longarm. He stopped by a driftwood log, silvery in the moonlight, and put a boot up on it as he said, "I thought it was something like that. What are you called, Señorita?"

"*Por favor,* I am called Catalina, but I am no *señorita.* I am Indian."

"Let's not worry about your place in California society, Catalina. What do you think we ought to do about this problem?"

Catalina sat down on the driftwood and stared miserably at her sandals as she said, "You will have to leave me behind, no?"

He said, "That would be sensible, but it doesn't sound Christian. Don't you have any friends this side of Mission Santa Barbara?"

"No, Señor. I may not even have friends *there.* I have been very wicked."

"Oh? Are you saying Osage may have had good reason to think he could trifle with you, Catalina?"

"Oh no, Señor! He came up behind me and tried to put his hands on my breasts. I did nothing to encourage any of your men. Señor Cooky told me not to. The wicked thing I did was for to run away. My father wished for me to marry a man I did not like. I had heard there were many jobs in Pueblo de Los Angeles and so I went there. But the only jobs I was offered were very nasty, even for an Indian girl to think of.

It is bad enough to marry a man you don't like. To work as a *puta* on Bunker Hill is worse, I think."

He nodded understandingly and said, "So you had enough of the wicked city and you're going home to take your medicine, eh?"

"*Sí*. I was raped in Los Angeles and I did not like it. I think I had better marry Carlos after all. He has bad teeth and a fat belly, but I may have a baby now. There are worse things, after all, than marriage."

Longarm couldn't think of one. "We'll be in Santa Barbara soon. Do you think you can stay out of trouble for the next few nights?" he asked her.

"I will try, Señor. Do you wish for to sleep with me? Nobody would bother me if they knew I was your *mahala*."

Longarm said, "They might bother *me*, though. It's share and share alike on the trail, and I don't think you'd enjoy being passed with the coffeepot."

She stared up at him, sincerely frightened. He nodded grimly and said, "That's what happens to wicked girls who can't behave. I want you to stay close to the cook and keep your eyes polite. I'm not saying you gave Osage a sensible reason for thinking he could feel you up, but if it happens again, I'll have to leave you lovebirds by the side of the trail to sort it out."

He left her there and walked back to the fire. The others were gone. The cook shot him a funny look, so Longarm said, "No. I never. I want her bedded down close to you. I won't insult you by discussing how close that should be."

The cook looked disgusted and said, "Shit, she's young enough to be my daughter."

Longarm ambled on. Either the older man would treat Catalina like a daughter, or, if he didn't, nobody would ever know.

He went to his roll and sat down to shuck his duds. The night wind off the ocean was giving him goosebumps by the time he snuggled into his blankets. He was bone-tired and wondered why he had a hard-on all of a sudden. He knew he didn't have to piss. Hard-ons were funny that way. A man just had no way of knowing when he was fixing to get one. He couldn't think of a reason that made any sense.

Chapter 12

Nothing happened on the trail the next day. They moved in away from the sea coast, following the Old Mission Trail, and the country became convoluted, with a lot of cover all around and a mess of canyons that any sensible owlhoot might have admired. But that evening the herd tallied right, and McBride was sure they'd discouraged the gang who'd been preying on them.

Longarm kept an eye peeled for more fighting in the camp, but that didn't go wrong, either. The fight had knocked some sense into the other hands, and when they noticed the quiet little Indian gal at all, they bent over backwards to treat her with respect.

It had settled into the usual cattle drive. Boring as hell. The trail-broken herd was well-behaved. There was plenty of fodder and water. They just kept going, slow mile after mile, until one afternoon they got to the outskirts of Santa Barbara and made night camp in a flat-bottomed canyon.

The cook's Chinese helper put Catalina in the hood-lum to run her over to the nearby mission. Longarm wasn't sorry to see her go. Maybe now he and the others could go to sleep soft-peckered of an evening.

The sun was setting and the Chinese hadn't yet returned with the wagon when a trio of riders came in. They said they were county brand inspectors, so Longarm took them over to the herd. They weren't interested in the big ID trail brands. They had some other marks on their clipboards and wanted to make sure the government hadn't bought any shady beef at bargain prices. As the two assistant inspectors did most of the tally, Longarm got to talking with the head inspector, who showed him the brands they had in mind. Longarm took the board and studied it for a time before he handed it back and said, "I've had to chase most of these critters once or twice since we left Los Angeles. I disremember seeing any wearing any of these brands you got here. The paper says you're talking about cows stolen to the north of here. Carver, the Indian agent, told me he'd bought close to the L.A. basin."

The brand inspector said, "We're just doing our job. I know Uncle Sam wouldn't pay for stolen beef on purpose. The boys who used to own the missing stock have discussed the possibility that some rascal might have run them south, since they sure as hell never turned up in the north."

Longarm nodded and said, "I hear there's an inland route, over to the east in the big valley. How do you boys feel about that?"

"It's possible to herd cows to the south over there, but it ain't as easy as the coast road. Lots of tule marsh and arroyos. You'd have to know the country good, and besides, we have folks checking over there. There's a stretch called the Grapevine where you have to almost boost the critters one at a time. State police have it patrolled."

"Couldn't cow thieves slip by them, looking innocent, if they had a bill of sale and properly registered
brands?"

"Hell, of course they could. But do we look like
blind-ass greenhorns? We're paid to *inspect* brands,
damn it. We don't look at them through the wrong end
of a telescope!"

"You'd notice an ID changed to a TB huh?"

"You bet your saddle, cowboy. We caught an old
boy a month ago trying to slip a Rocking-I changed to
a Circle-Seven past us. He's doing time in state prison
at the moment, feeling surprised, no doubt. I've been at
this awhile. I've caught 'em hair-branding, counter-
branding, balding and scalping. Scalping works the
best, if it's a small brand to start with, but you lose
cows to infection that way."

Longarm nodded. "That's where you cut out the
whole patch of skin, pull up the slack, and brand over
the stitching, right?"

"Yeah, it's mostly done by horse thieves. Takes
time for the critter to heal, and a cow can't hardly be
resold for enough to make the surgery worthwhile."

Longarm stared at a grullo grazing nearby and considered the big government brand before he said,
"Nope. Wouldn't work. It'd leave a hell of a wound,
and a scar that'd show on that thin flank hair."

"That's what I just said."

The other inspectors rode up to join them. One said,
"Light's going bad, but I'm voting for a clean bill of
health, chief. We've never spotted a stolen cow in these
government herds, anyhow."

The headman nodded and they all rode down to the
fire to coffee up. Before they left, they gave McBride a
certificate saying that his herd had been inspected by
the county.

So it came as a surprise, the next afternoon, when they

171

were stopped by a line of grim-faced riders fifteen miles beyond the county seat, near the old mission.

The wagons had been sent on ahead, but Longarm saw them drawn over to the side of the trail as he rode forward to join McBride and the point riders as they argued with the men across the road.

As he fell in beside McBride, the boss drover turned to him and said, "These damn fools say we can't go through here."

A man facing them on a dapple gray stud said, "You heard us right, goddamnit. We have posted us a quarantine, and that's the end of it."

Longarm said, "Maybe. We were just inspected by Santa Barbara County, friend. Are you saying we're already over the line into San Luis? I must have been asleep the last few miles."

The leader of the vigilantes said, "Where you are ain't no never-mind. We don't want you driving them infected cows through our lands."

"What are they supposed to be infected with?" Longarm asked. "And while we're on the subject, if you boys are riding with the California health department, I'd like to see your identification."

"We're packing all the identification we need on our hips, cowboy. We heard tell there's Texas fever down by L.A., and them cows you got ain't gonna give it to ours!"

"Oh, hell," McBride snorted in disgust. "Hang some roses on your hat. Your brain just died and your hat's in mourning! Who ever heard of Texas fever in a California herd?"

The man on the gray said, "We did. Some gents rode through saying cows are dropping like flies on the banks of the Los Angeles, and we aim to keep it down yonder where it belongs!"

Longarm said, "Mister, I'll set aside the fact that you are blocking a public thoroughfare with neither

172

badge nor warrant. Let's talk about Texas fever. I've never had it, but I've shot many a cow that did. It's a tick-borne infection that cows pick up in the swamps along the Gulf of Mexico."

"So what? Every damn cow has a few ticks on it."

"They do indeed. But the ticks that give Texas fever are a fancy breed you don't get anywhere else. They generally drop off or die before Texas cows make it as far north as the Indian Nation. Sometimes a sick cow makes it as far as Dodge, but without the ticks, he can't pass it on. The reason I'm explaining this is because I've seen dumb wars like this before. A couple of thriving trail towns have put themselves out of business by barring Texas drovers who took their trade somewhere else. You boys look sensible, so now that I've explained it polite—"

"Goddamnit, you are not driving them cows another step!" the head bully shouted. The others must have agreed, for they shouted like Confederate cavalry fixing to charge.

McBride looked at Longarm and said, "Shit, let's take 'em."

Longarm said, "Not yet. We'll spook the cows. I'd say our best bet would be to vamoose back the way we just came."

McBride caught his meaning and shouted over to the cook by the side of the road, "We're bedding in that *rincón* a mile back. You follow us for a change."

Robles, Creedmore and a hand named Thayer had been close enough to hear it all. So when McBride nodded to them, they turned the point into a drag as Robles rode down the line to tell the others why the cows were switching ends.

The vigilantes jeered as the herd crawfished back down the trail. McBride said, "I'm going to get me that son of a bitch on the gray." But Longarm said, "Simmer down, boss. Let's bed the cows well out of range and get 'em all."

He didn't mean it. Billy Vail hadn't sent him all the way out here to fight a war. But he had to keep the two sides from killing each other until he could figure out what was going on. Meanwhile, it soothed the enraged McBride to agree with his plans for blood and slaughter.

They bedded the herd under double guard, out of harm's way. McBride was for going back up the road right away for a showdown. Longarm suggested they set up camp first, and study on it over grub. He pointed out that the self-appointed protectors of the suddenly sacred cows were all tensed up and braced for a fight at suppertime. "Let them sweat and tire their mounts while we sit in comfort, inhaling coffee and beans. The defending side has the advantage of being set up better for a coming fight. The attacking side's advantage is that it's up to them when and if they come."

McBride asked, "What do you mean, *if?* Sooner or later, we have to shove them sons of bitches out of our way. My contract calls for these cows by Frisco Bay, not chomping petunias south of Point Concepcion!"

Longarm unfolded the map he'd taken from his saddlebag and spread it out on the ground as they hunkered side by side. He said, "In the first place, we're not *south* of Point Concepcion. We're due east. The coastline zags way off to the west in these parts. Whoever built this Coast Range sure did things complicated. Most of the ridge lines run in line with the seacoast, but the Lord must have felt like playing tic-tac-toe the day he made California. See how your so-called transverse ranges cut across the grain like ladder rungs?"

McBride said, "Shit, go home and teach your granny to suck eggs. I reckon I know well enough how fucked-up the mountains have always been. Why else would the Mission Trail hug the coast like it does?"

Longarm stabbed a finger at the map and said,

"We're about here. Those vigilantes have blocked the trail as it runs way the hell west and cuts north again. But look here. There's this Santa Ynez River running east and west almost in line with us. It empties into the ocean well north of Point Concepcion, on the far side of those unfriendly rascals."

"You keep telling me things I already know, damn it. In case you hadn't noticed, there's a mountain range running east and west between us and the Santa Ynez. That's likely why the trail runs around the point. I see your plan, but it ain't no good. We can't cut due north over the mountains to move down the Santa Ynez Valley."

"Why not?"

"Shit! Just stare due north and you can see why not! The padres would have run the Old Mission Trail the short way from Santa Bob to the Santa Ynez if there was a way over the ridges."

Longarm took out a cheroot, lit it with a twig from the cookfire, and said, "There's always a way over, boss."

"Maybe," McBride agreed, "if we was herding mountain goats. I ain't about to drive a herd of cows through all them cliffs and canyons. I'd feel safer having it out man-to-man with them coyotes up the trail."

Longarm said, "Later. Let them cool off, too. It'll soon be cold and dark. Let them waste a night staked out in the sea mists and sweating us out."

"I thought our play was to bed the herd down safe and then ride back to hit 'em in the dark," McBride said.

Longarm puffed at his cheroot patiently before answering, "That's what they're expecting and hoping for. The men on the trail were just a brag. Didn't you spot any of the riflemen forted up on the hillsides back there?"

McBride looked sheepish as well as surprised. Longarm nodded grimly and continued, "They're dug in for a war of their choosing, on their own ground. They have us outnumbered. We're going to take some losses if we tangle with them head-on. Assuming you don't like your riders all that much, how many can you afford to lose if you aim to drive the herd anywhere important? We're not even a third of the way to Frisco yet."

McBride didn't answer. That was a good sign. Long-arm knew he was starting to think. Men who went for their guns without thinking made him nervous.

He was doing some thinking himself. He didn't want to do it, but it looked like it was time that he flashed his badge. He'd already been a reluctant party to an informal hanging, but he couldn't take part in a range dispute as a federal officer, undercover or no. He was supposed to be a peace officer; The taxpayers hadn't put him on their payroll to make war. The frightened cattlemen up ahead had been sold a scare by a trouble-maker, but they were taxpayers, too. If they were half-way law-abiding, they'd back down to a federal badge before they'd crawfish from a fight with civilian drovers. He'd get Scanlon to back his play, they'd pin on their badges, and—

Suddenly he stood up, pushed his Stetson back from his forehead, and scanned the camp all around them. Then he took his cheroot from between his lips, and asked McBride, "Where's Scanlon?"

McBride stood up, too, took a moment to look around, and called out the same question to the cook, who replied, "Beats me. I ain't seen him since Santa Bob. We thought he rode out with you boys."

McBride and Longarm exchanged glances. McBride said, "I thought he was with the wagons, didn't you?"

Longarm nodded and said, "I noticed he was fond of coffee. If he didn't fall down a gopher hole, he must have stayed at the first town he came to after losing his sidekick. I don't reckon his mama raised her boy to be a trail rider."

"I hope they fire the shiftless skunk," McBride growled. "But they likely won't. The government hires boobs and idiots as a matter of policy."

Longarm knew McBride didn't know he was a federal man, so he didn't get sore. He had enough on his plate as it was. Two badges would have been better than one, but one would have to do. He held off dropping his cover for the moment. The night was young, and Longarm had learned that it was wise to hold your cards close to the vest and hope somebody else made a poor draw when the cards you had weren't the ones you wanted.

The sun was a red ball on the horizon and they'd finished eating when Robles came to the fire and said some folks were coming in from the east on burros.

McBride said, "Let 'em come. It's a public right-of-way. Maybe they'll shoot it out with them other rascals who can't seem to savvy that."

But the crew was edgy, and more than one had a casual hand on his gun butt as a half-dozen men riding burros and wearing big straw sombreros single-filed past the bedded herd an dstopped near the wagons. They looked like Indians dressed as Mexicans. The middle-aged man on the leading burro took off his hat and asked if they were the McBride outfit. McBride said, "We are, and I'm McBride. What's your pleasure, amigo?"

The older man smiled and said, "I am called Alejandro. I am *casique* of *los Indios de Santa Barbara*. I am in your debt, Señores."

"You are? I can't for the life of me see why. But if you boys want to be friendly, climb down and coffee up."

Alejandro dismounted and one of his followers jumped off to take the bridle rope he dropped casually. Alejandro was dressed raggedly and didn't look important, but the Indians must have thought he was.

The cook handed him a cup and he squatted down

near McBride and Longarm before he explained, "A woman of my people was treated with great consideration by you and your men, Señor McBride. She was my granddaughter."

McBride laughed and said, "Catalina? Hell, we didn't do all that much. We found her stranded along the trail and gave her a lift, that's all."

"That is *not* all, Señor. Catalina tells us she was treated with the utmost respect and that you called her *señorita*."

"Hell, ain't that what your girls are generally called?"

"No. Many years ago the padres came and made us into *cristianos*. But the people who followed did not treat us like *cristianos*. They call us *leparos*. They call us *pobrecitos*. They never call us *señor* or *señorita*. My granddaughter was thrown off a coach after she had paid for her passage because she dared to defend herself against a Spanish girl who treated her with contempt. You *caballeros* rescued her from her plight and treated her with respect."

"Aw, hell, let's not blubber up about it. We made her wash some dishes. I'm glad she got safely home. She was a nice little gal and we liked her. But you didn't have to ride all the way out here to thank us."

Alejandro said, "I followed you for to warn you and your men, Señor. We have heard that some men are waiting in ambush up the trail."

McBride said, "Oh, we already met up with them. We was just fixing to have a war with 'em as soon as it gets good and dark."

Alejandro turned, muttered something in his own dialect, and his followers dismounted, grim-faced, to start hauling guns out of their innocent-looking saddle covers. Alejandro turned back to Longarm and McBride, and said, "We are ready to fight at your side, Señores."

178

McBride grinned and said, "Hot damn!"

Longarm spoke up to ask, "Are you familiar with the mountains all around, Don Alejandro?"

The Indian looked pleased as well as startled by the title of respect. He nodded and said, "Of course. I have hunted in them since I was a boy."

"Could you lead us and our cows across the transverse ranges to the Santa Ynez, in the dark?"

Alejandro thought before he replied, "I know a way. It will be difficult but not impossible. I will get more men to help. We can lead them single file behind my *madrina*. She is as tame as a dog and trained to voice commands."

Longarm looked puzzled, so McBride explained, "A *madrina* is what we call a Judas cow. These folks lead cows through rough country with an old she-critter who packs a bell and moos like a mama leading her kids home from school." But then McBride said, "I don't know, gents. Taking the herd over the hills in the dark sounds risky."

"So does a firefight with persons unknown," Longarm observed. "Cutting through the hills not only saves us a war, it saves us that big swing out to the west. Once we hit the Santa Ynez, it's clear sailing along grassy bottomland for a whole day's drive. There's another angle you missed, too, boss."

"I did? What are you talking about, Professor?"

"The cow thieves. If they aim to hit us again, they won't know about our cutoff. We'll not only avoid a fight with honest but mule-headed ranchers, we'll confuse the shit out of anybody else laying in wait up the trail."

McBride said, "You know, you just went and convinced me? But you sure are a spoilsport, Long. I was sort of looking forward to that gunfight."

Chapter 13

So the herd went over the mountains. It took some doing, and they'd never have made it without the help of the mission Indians. The moon helped, too. Alejandro's route wasn't simply a path up and over a pass; it snaked through the tangle of busted-up country like a kite string tangled in a tree. The canyons were choked with laurel and the ridges were hogbacks of treacherous sandstone carved by time and patient rainwater. Everything else was covered with oak and chaparral, and they'd have skinned the critters alive if they'd just tried to bull through in anything like a straight line. But old Alejandro and his Indians were as patient as erosion, and though there were times when it seemed impossible, the sun rose again to see them down to the rolling parklands by the Santa Ynez. Alejandro guided them to a ford and got them to the north side of the river before they parted company with handshakes and some beans and coffee for the Indians to carry home. McBride offered Alejandro a bottle of redeye he'd been saving in case of snakebite. But the old man declined

181

it with thanks. He said the government didn't allow him to drink, since he wasn't grown up yet or something.

McBride was more familiar with the Santa Ynez Valley than Longarm was, but he'd never driven a herd down it, and the right-of-way was sort of complicated. Much of it was open range, but new homestead claims and old Spanish grants, honored by the peace treaty of '48, extended in places from the riverside to the ridges to the north. Most freeholders tended to be reasonable about a well-behaved herd crossing their land, if they were asked politely. It beat being asked impolitely, and the cowshit improved the pasturage more than a few hooves hurt it.

But McBride ordered Longarm to ride forward with the advance crew for now. Longarm was more diplomatic than the surly cook, and meaner-looking if diplomacy failed.

So, as the herd rested up from its night drive over the mountains, Longarm headed toward the seacoast trail, mounted on a pinto barb and just ahead of the lead wagon.

Things went smoothly at first. He'd spot a spread, lope on ahead, and state his name and business to the ranchero who came out to meet him. Some were a mite moody, but not of a mind to have a war, so they just told Longarm to keep his damned cows near the river, and that they'd be disappointed as hell to meet a cow in their hen run. Others were more friendly and said they'd sell eggs and produce if the outfit needed any. At Longarm's suggestion, the cook bought a basket of eggs here and a bucket of fruit there. It made for goodwill, and the hands would be cheered by fresh vittles on the trail.

They were looking for a place to make the noon camp when things got more complicated. The cook pointed out a nice hedged-in *vega* of grama and mustard, sloping up from the running water. So Longarm headed for a nearby ranch house to ask permission.

Two women met him on the veranda. One was little and cute, if a man admired pigtails and sort of buck teeth. The taller one was prettier, if you ignored the fact that she was flat-chested and a trifle boney. They both had dishwater-blonde hair and identical calico dresses. They both had shotguns in their hands. Longarm sat his barb as he tipped his hat and told them who he was and what he wanted. The taller gal said they were the Ashton sisters, and that they owned the homestead, including the *vega* where the outfit wanted to camp and graze. The younger gal said she saw no reason why they couldn't, but her taller and tighter-mouthed sister said, "Our hands ain't here. They drove some stock to town to sell. I don't know as I feel safe, alone like this, with a cattle outfit in my front yard."

Longarm said, "The cows are trail-broke and steady, ma'am. I can promise you they won't get out of line."

"Can you promise the same for your cowboys? My sister, here, is only seventeen and I don't fancy getting raped all that much myself."

Longarm blinked and said, "Ma'am, we're drovers, not banditos. If that's all that's fretting you, I can post a guard here by the house, and we'll tell the boys not to come anywhere near you."

"Really? Who's going to guard these guards?"

Longarm sighed and said, "I hope you won't take this as an insult, ma'am, but you ain't really as tempting as you may feel. I'm riding with grown white men who hardly ever go crazy at the sight of a skirt. I will also promise to shoot any who do. Slavering sex maniacs ain't safe to leave near female cows."

The little one laughed a bit saucily. The tall one got sort of red in the face, but she stood her ground. She said, "I can see you mean to use our grass whether I agree to it or no. If my husband was still alive, he'd run you off. But as you see, we are defenseless and at your mercy. If I agree, will you take it on yourself to protect us, personal?"

"You look like a real gent," the younger one chimed in.

Longarm said, "Ladies, we'll only be here a couple of hours. If you'll get me a rocking chair, I'll set right on that veranda with a Winchester across my knees and defend you from hell and high water until the last dogie is out of sight."

The two girls looked at one another. Then the tall widowed one said, "All right. But keep your cows and your hands the hell away from me and mine."

Longarm told them he'd ride back and tell the cook to start setting up, then he'd come back and guard hell out of them after he had coffee and grub ahead of the others. The widowed sister said they'd give him coffee and cake, and not to tarry.

So Longarm rode to the wagons and explained. He told the cook to tell McBride and the others not to go near the house. He said he'd catch up as the outfit moved out. The cook said female notions were a pain in the ass, but it saved washing a plate, so what the hell.

Longarm rode back, dismounted, and tethered the barb to the veranda rail. The tall one was inside. The little one had put her shotgun away and told Longarm to step into the kitchen and join them at the table, so he did.

They seemed in a better mood, now that they'd laid down the law to a man and gotten him to do as they demanded. They put tolerable coffee and some too-sweet pastry in front of him. He noticed that the cast-iron range was cold. Maybe they thought it was too hot for cooking, or maybe they thought everybody lived on sweets. He asked permission to smoke, and when they gave it, he lit a cheroot. It helped to cut the cloying taste in his mouth. He thanked them for a swell feed and allowed that he'd sit out front. The older sister

184

said, "Let's go into the front parlor. You can see just as well from there, and the south side of the house is hot at noon."

It wasn't noon yet, but it was getting there, and he had noticed that the door yard was baked hard and dusty. They led him to an overstuffed sofa covered with a buffalo robe and sat him down between them. It left him with a hand on each of his own knees, feeling awkward. He stared out the window. In the distance, he saw that McBride's point had reached the wagons. He said, "I'll get my rifle from the saddle boot. I'd better move the pony around to the shady side, while I'm at it."

The little saucy one got up and said, "I'll do it. You just sit here and protect poor Nancy." Then she scampered out before he could agree or not, leaving him alone with the tall one. Longarm noticed that Nan was breathing hard, as if she'd been running. She was looking at him funny, too.

He cleared his throat and said, "Well, as you can see out the window, the herd's halted a quarter-mile off and nobody is headed this way with fire and sword."

"Wouldn't you be more comfortable if you hung up that gunbelt and your hat?" she asked.

Then, before he could answer, she plucked off his hat, skimmed it into a chair across the room, and started fumbling with the buckle just above his fly. He put his hands down to help, saying, "I'd best do that, ma'am. You seem a mite confused. I don't use buttons to hold my sixgun in place. He unbuckled the rig and rebuttoned the top button of his pants. This left Nan's hands with nothing to do in his lap. So she put them around his neck and kissed him hungrily and started groping at his crotch some more. He enjoyed it for a moment. But when they came up for air, he shot a glance at the window, saw that the pony was out of sight, and said, "Your kid sister likely saw what

185

we just did. She'll be popping back in at us directly, too."

Nan said, "I know. We'd better go in the bedroom."

She rose, holding Longarm by one hand, and started tugging him as he clutched at his unbuckled gun rig to keep it from falling off. He was too confused to do more than follow. Nan led him into a smaller, darker room, but it was light enough to see the four-poster bed. The little sister was lying on it, naked as a jaybird. She grinned up at them and said, "Me first, Nan. You still have your clothes on."

Longarm smiled wryly down at her and said, "You ladies sure are sort of forward, considering all that talk about your fears."

The little one lay back and parted her thighs in invitation as she said, "My name is Pat, and I'm not scared of you at all."

Behind him, the older gal was shucking herself like an ear of corn, and Longarm didn't want to be insulting, so he took off his shirt.

Pat sighed, "Oh, you have a lovely body. What's your name, cowboy?"

Longarm sat down to remove his boots as he said it was Long. By this time, both of them were stripped. Nan dropped to her naked knees on the floor, and as Pat sat up and started kissing Longarm's spine, she hauled off his pants and longjohns and said, "Oh, you *are* long, aren't you?"

Longarm muttered, "Help, I think I'm being ravaged by fair maidens!" as Pat hauled him backward across the bed and started kissing him. His rump was on the edge and his legs were stretched out, with his heels on the rug, when Nan slid up and mounted him with her knees on the bed. Pat looked up from kissing him and said, "That was sneaky, Sis. I started first."

Nan started moving up and down on Longarm's extended shaft as she laughed and said, "You started with

186

the wrong end. But don't you fret. This one has enough for everybody."

Longarm found it exciting but a little unsettling to be treated like a side of beef with a hard-on. Most folks were a mite more romantic. These saucy gals had *seduced* him! They'd planned it between them before they'd even asked his name. It was downright degrading, and he'd have gotten as sore as hell if it hadn't felt so good.

He kissed and teased Pat's nipple while Nan slid up and down on him in long, teasing strokes.

"Hurry, damn it!" Pat protested. "I can see it and I want it in me. Why do you always take so long, Sis?"

Nan screwed down tight, contracted, and purred, "It feels better if you make it last. Don't you think so, cowboy?"

Longarm growled, "All right, as long as you ladies brought it up, let's do it right." Then he half rose, rolled Nan off and over, and got on top as she protested that she liked to do it her way. He said, "I noticed," as he got in the saddle with his feet on the floor and her skinny tail half off the edge of the bed. Then he proceeded to pound her as the kid sister bounced up and down on her knees, yelling, "Whee! Give it to her good and then give it to me!"

Longarm grinned and came fast. Two could play at selfish pleasure. As a matter of fact, three could. Nan climaxed as he slammed her a couple of times for luck and to keep it up. Then he rolled off her, grabbed the saucy, bouncy little Pat, and said, "All right, missy. You've been asking for it and now you're going to purely get it!"

Pat had last-minute hesitation in her eyes as he mounted her. But then she gasped, "Oh, Jesus, yes!" as he pinned her to the mattress and began to do the same for her as he had done for her sister. The novelty aroused him, and it felt like starting for the first time. Pat's petite body was more padded, and the important parts between her plump thighs felt different. Nan had more internal control; Pat was a mite tighter. They both took a man at a different angle, so that new things rubbed the right way. The day was getting as interesting as hell, and it wasn't yet high noon. If any of the others moseyed over to the house, he had no idea what on earth he was going to say, unless he invited them in to join the party. He was beginning to suspect that the sisters weren't as worried about gang rape as they'd let on.

Nan was sitting up now, watching, and it was her turn to urge them to hurry. She was still hot, and it showed. She forked a thigh over Longarm's back and started rubbing her open crotch against his bouncing hip as she moved her kid sister's thigh higher, out of the way. Pat protested, "Damn it, you're splitting me, Nan! It goes too deep as it is!"

"I want to do it some more," Nan panted, rubbing and squirming. Then she suddenly swapped ends, bracing a knee on either side of Longarm's shoulders with his and the younger gal's heads between her thighs. She leaned forward, rubbing her small boyish breasts across Longarm's shoulder blades. Her belly was against the back of his head as she pleaded, "Eat me!"

Longarm said, "I'm as courteous as the next gent, but I can't, in this crazy position."

Then he saw that Pat had tipped her head back, her throat and chin just visible in the shadows of her big sister's groin, and knew Nan hadn't meant him. Little Pat was pleasuring Nan with her tongue as he pleasured Pat more in a more old-fashioned way, and his head was sandwiched between them. The view was stimulating, and he knew he was fixing to come, but the girls saw that they were going at it wrong, and Nan suddenly rose and swung around to shove her rump in Longarm's startled face as she settled back on her kid sister's mouth. Longarm rose on his elbows and the next few minutes were sort of crazy. The bed gave way as all three of them were coming, and they finished in a tangle on the floor. By the time Longarm recovered his senses enough to wonder who was doing what, with what, to whom, he noticed that he was on his side, giving it from the rear to Nan while she ate her baby sister. He knew the three of them ought to be ashamed of themselves, but he kept going, and when he got his breath back a mite he rose to his knees, hauling Nan's skinny but rollicking rump up into a good solid dog-style, while she went on committing crimes against nature. Pat lay spread-eagled on the far side, eyes closed and smiling like an angel, as Nan tongued and fingered her. He felt Nan stiffen and contract as she climaxed again on his questing shaft. So, fair being fair, he rolled Nan to one side and fell forward on little Pat. Pat gasped, "Don't stop! I'm almost there!" Then, as Longarm entered her, she opened her eyes in surprise and said, "Oh God, I *am* there! Oh . . . Jeeeezusss!"

So, having gotten acquainted, the three of them settled down for a nice long orgy. The sisters were inventive as hell. Longarm figured they must have gotten that way from being alone so much, with nothing better to do. When they got to the stage of quiet conversational screwing, Nan explained that they had to think of their reputations, so they never trifled with their hired Mex help. Pat stopped kissing Longarm's rump as she said he likely didn't believe them. He did believe them. It was clear enough that they hadn't had a man for a time, and as a lawman, he knew more about what went on behind closed doors than most folks. Queen Victoria's odd notions about sex had produced more lesbian gals than Her Majesty had intended by acting so strict, and any lawman could tell you incest was one crime whose reported rate of incidence didn't square with the facts. He felt sort of sorry for them, but what the hell, *he* hadn't done anything all that queer. He knew he'd have been sort of cooled off by watching two young brothers acting this way, but watching two pretty gals act silly in the nude seemed to stimulate him. He suspected he had a dirty mind. But they said they wouldn't tell on him if he didn't tell on them.

He felt downright wistful when it came time to leave and ride on after the herd. But as he mounted up outside, he decided it was just as well. Another hour of that would have left him a cripple.

Chapter 14

They got the herd back on the Old Mission Trail, and nothing happened for a full two days of the drive. That is, nothing happened except that they tallied one evening and found they were missing thirty-seven head.

McBride threw his hat on the ground and stomped it before he said, "Goddamnit! I thought we hung the bastard as was doing it! We took 'em over mountains in the dark. We run 'em through unfriendly nesters. We led 'em past them sea cliffs yesterday, and we never lost one head. Now, after a day's drive through easy country . . . All right. Let's gather all the hands together and see who saw what."

Longarm tossed his tally stick aside and said morosely, "Why waste time jawing? If anyone had seen thirty-seven head leaving without permission, don't you reckon he'd have mentioned it by now?"

McBride said, "Yeah, you're right," as he gazed at the guarded herd grazing upslope. They were on open range with no nearby spreads. It was rolling grass and oak savannah. There was little chance of their spotting

191

sign, and nobody was living nearby who might have noticed anything or anybody. The sun was low. The cows, wherever they were, were long gone. Apparently, as usual, they'd simply dematerialized from amid the herd, with riders watching from all sides.

"Funny," Longarm said, "the last place they hit us was country like this."

McBride shrugged and said, "Hell, most of the Coast Range country is like this. Besides, we caught that Mex and killed him and his sidekick."

Longarm said, "Those tinhorns were on their own, or part of another gang. They acted bold and dumb enough to be spotted by kids you picked up punching in the stockyards. The point I'm making is that they did try where the grass grows thick near the trail, and there's still enough cover to matter. This oak country is made for stealing stock. No bare trails through chaparral to leave a hoofmark behind, and any number of unmapped, watered canyons over to the northeast."

"Hell, I don't care where they hide the durned cows, once they steal 'em. It's the stealing part that has me so mixed up. There is no way a man can lift a cow straight up in the sky, and even if there was, we would have noticed. Are you sure you tallied right?"

Longarm said, "Yep. Two comes after one, and three comes after two. I've been a tolerable counter since I was old enough to spell 'cat'."

"Don't get snotty, Professor," McBride said. "I'm already sore enough to punch my mother in the nose. I'll take your word we lost thirty-seven more head. We're only about a quarter of the way, and from here north, the country gets emptier and meaner. We've lost most along the middle stretch, up to now. The sons of bitches have dented us good—and early. I sure wish there was another way to herd 'em, but there ain't. Let's coffee up and study this. I can't afford these losses. The purchasing and contracting agent, Carver, tells me Uncle Sam is getting fed up, too. He says the BIA hasn't saved the money it expected by buying cheap cows far and losing them getting them near."

They went over to the chuckwagon and got some Arbuckle's before they found a place to squat. Longarm said, "I've been wondering about that all along. You and the other drovers have insured delivery, right?"

McBride said, "Sure. But nobody insures stock for full value. The insurance on a thousand lost head wouldn't buy three hundred."

"Who gets it, boss, you?" Longarm asked.

"Hell, no, the BIA insures the beef. I'm only paid to deliver it. I collect a flat fee, with a penalty for any more than a ten-percent wastage. Expenses come out of my pocket. I just about break even when I get the whole herd through. I've lost money on the last two drives, and it looks like I'm about to repeat the sad experience."

Longarm sipped his coffee and asked, "Why do you bother, then?"

McBride answered, "I don't aim to after this. I told Carver this would be my last job for him. I ain't in this business to see the scenery. He promised me a bonus if we could punch on through with less than a twenty-percent wastage this time. We ain't halfway there, and it already looks like I can kiss my bonus goodbye."

Longarm figured in his head and said, "You can afford to lose three hundred head, counting the ones that have already been stolen. If the country to the north is empty, I'd say our best bet would be to bunch 'em thicker so the riders could stay closer together."

McBride spat and said, "I sure wish you'd tell me something I don't know, Professor. Last trip, I had 'em packed like sardines, crossing the Salinas. That's where I lost close to a hundred at one crack. Crossing a shallow river with riders all around and the sun shining straight damn down!"

Longarm whistled softly. "That sounds pretty wild, boss. Are you sure none of 'em slid under the water?"

"Under *what* water, damn it? The Salinas is only six inches deep at that ford, in summer. I was riding the downstream flank. I might have missed a dead fish floating past me, but I'd have spotted a hundred cows, dead or otherwise. How do you reckon you and Captain Goodnight would have handled that crossing?"

Longarm chewed thoughtfully on the edge of his mustache, and squinted into the distance. "Can't say. Did you tally that other herd in the middle of the stream?"

"Of course not. We missed 'em later, when we made camp for the night."

"How do you know you lost 'em crossing the river, then? You could have lost 'em on dry land, on either side."

McBride said, "You don't know the Salinas Valley, son. It's dead flat, and open on both sides of the river. The grass all around was as overgrazed as a drawing room carpet. A cow would have to stray a mile or more in plain sight before it could get to cover."

Longarm said, "I wasn't there, but I'll take your word for it."

"Is that meant suspicious, cowboy?" McBride asked, bristling slightly.

"I don't reckon so, boss. I've heard tales of contract drovers losing other folks' cows on purpose. But they tell me these government herds were getting robbed before you took cow one up this trail."

Mollified, McBride said, "You're damned right. I can prove I was over in Arizona when they started robbing these BIA herds. You can check it out by wire when we come to the next town, if you want to."

Longarm spilled his coffee grounds on the fire with a thoughtful frown before he asked cautiously, "Why would I want to do that, boss?"

McBride snorted and said, "Don't shit your elders,

194

son. I've known for some time that you're a federal man."

"Oh? Who told you a fool thing like that?"

"Nobody had to tell me. Carver and his boys promised me there'd be some feds along this trip to help us catch the thieves. Morgan got hurt, and Scanlon couldn't catch a cold setting wet in his underwear, even if he was still riding with us. Uncle Sam would have sent a replacement by now if Scanlon had been the last of you boys. Only they never. So I knowed I still had at least one of you aboard. It was easy to figure out who it was. You're the only decent cowhand I have that I've never rode with before."

Longarm didn't answer. McBride chuckled and said, "I ain't as dumb as you took me for, huh? I put the name together, once I started thinking. I remembered hearing tell of a U.S. deputy named Long. They call you Longarm, 'cause you are said to extend the long arm of the law pretty far and pretty good. But, just between us, do you have any idea at all what the hell is going on?"

Longarm said, "I'm working on it. Have you told anyone else that you know I'm law?"

"Shit, do I look *that* dumb? I've been playing detective, too, and I long ago learned the advantages of letting other folks read their own cards."

Longarm took out a smoke and lit up as he digested what McBride had just revealed. He'd about decided McBride was innocent. The admission almost cinched it. Almost, but not quite.

A crook who'd spotted an undercover lawman would be stupid to let the lawman know about it, unless he was too damned clever to be let out of the house unleashed. McBride didn't strike him as a man who played three-dimensional chess as a hobby, but the thieves Uncle Sam was interested in were a cut above average. He'd established that they didn't just ride down the hill with a loop in one hand and a running iron in the other. They were sneaky as hell. Sometimes the sneakiest thing you could do to a lawman was to slap him on the back and call him pard.

So Longarm didn't admit anything or deny anything. He said, "We have another settlement to drive through tomorrow. What say I ride on ahead and set it up, boss?"

McBride said, "Good idea. I'll ride in with you."

Longarm had been afraid he'd say that. There was no way in hell for him to wire Billy Vail without admitting everything.

The town up the trail was another Anglo settlement with a silly Spanish name. Longarm and Cracker McBride found the only saloon, tethered their mounts, and went in to wet their whistles. A loudmouthed man in a checkered suit was holding forth at the far end. He hadn't paid them any mind when they bellied up to the bar, but since he was spouting off about cattle, they listened with considerable quiet interest.

The man in the noisy suit looked like a dude, but his fancy duds were muted a trifle by the worn grips and well-broken-in leather of the sensible sixgun rig he wore under his open coat. So the local rancheros were paying polite attention to him, too.

He said he was a cattle buyer from Frisco, which seemed legal and civilized enough. Then he said something else that wasn't:

"This may be your last chance to unload your beef at a fair price, boys. If that Texas fever spreads any further north, you won't be able to give your cows away."

McBride put his glass on the bar with ominous calm. Longarm grabbed his arm and murmured. "Don't do it yet. Let's size this up a mite."

But McBride shook Longarm off and was walking stiff-legged down the bar, like a pit dog too old and ornery to bother with growling. Men who'd been standing between him and the loudmouth just naturally got out of McBride's way without having to be asked. The cattle buyer saw him coming and read the expression on his face. He smiled and stepped clear of the mahogany, dropping his gun hand out to the side as he nodded and said, "Howdy. You look like a man with something stuck in his craw. Do I know you, friend?"

McBride just kept walking as he answered, "Nothing is stuck in my craw, you son of a bitch. I'm telling you right out that you are a fucking liar!"

The locals dove out of the line of fire, knocking over tables as well as chairs. Longarm had crabbed clear of the bar to cover the angry McBride's play, but McBride didn't need help with the cattle buyer. The buyer went for his gun, a bad move for a man who moved so slow. McBride just walked into him swinging, and the buyer's gun went flying as McBride started slapping him silly. A taller, quiet gent in a black frock coat lined up on McBride as he went for his own gun. Longarm had expected a man so free with his mouth to have at least one bodyguard, so he shot the man in the frock coat, shattering his right elbow and putting him on the floor. Longarm shouted, for the world to hear, "Everybody freeze and stay out of it!"

Nobody argued and nobody moved as McBride shoved the cattle buyer into a corner, holding him up with one hand, and hammering his face to chopped meat with the other. The gunslick on the floor sat up, groaning, and said, "I'm gonna kill somebody as soon as I can figure out what's going on."

Longarm stepped over to him, kicked him flat on his back, and said, "Just you hush, sonny. You're so lucky to be alive that your mama owes me a drink."

He noticed that McBride seemed to be killing the one he was working on, so he called out, "He's had enough, boss. You're just wasting effort on a gent who can't hear you no more."

McBride hit the unconscious liar another good lick

for luck, and let him slide down the wall like a wrung-out dishrag. But he was still worked up a mite. Turning around, he asked in a dangerously calm voice, "Does anybody else in here want to talk about Texas fever?"

Nobody answered for a minute. Then a runty old-timer with a grogblossom-sprinkled nose laughed and said, "If I follow your drift, stranger, you're trying to tell us there ain't no Texas fever headed this way, right?"

McBride said, "Damned right! My handle is Mc-Bride, and I just brought a herd from L.A. to right outside of town. A couple of days ago we nearly had to shoot some ignorant boys that these sons of bitches lied to about my cows. Can't you see what they was doing? They was trying to scare you into selling cheap by making up a tale of mortal terror."

Another local said, "You do have a way with words, mister. You don't have to kill us to convince us. It ain't like anyone here wants Texas fever. Once you point it out, anyone can see what they were doing, and why. Let's get us some ropes and string 'em up."

McBride looked like he thought that was a fine idea, but Longarm said, "Hanging folks is fun, but it's over almost before you start. I vote for starving these gents to death."

Another of the townies said, "Well, you've got a gun in your hand, so I'm listening polite. But your notion sounds sort of complicated, stranger. How do you figure we can starve them to death? We don't have no jail. Do we put 'em in a barrel or what?"

Longarm said, "No, that's too much trouble. Do you folks have a newspaper in town?"

A man in a business suit and a derby said, "I work for the *Weekly Sentinel*, cowboy. I've already started taking notes. But what's the deal about starving these fellers?"

Longarm said, "You put their names in your paper

and tell folks what they've been pulling. They'll be out of business long before their bruises heal."

The reporter grinned and said, "Hot damn! You're right! No other broker will touch 'em with a ten-foot pole, and a lot of cattlemen they slickered will be gunning for 'em high and low."

Most of the others agreed, but McBride grumbled, "Hell, I still say we ought to finish the rascals off."

Longarm said, "Let somebody else do it for us, boss. You've had your fun and these boys have some running to do."

He stepped over to the man he'd wounded, who was at least awake enough to listen. Longarm holstered his .44 and smiled down at the man at his feet. He said, "As soon as your boss wakes up, I want the two of you aboard your broncs and moving sudden. You can stop at the nearest doc and let him fix that arm, for I'm an agreeable cuss. Just don't be around me a couple of hours from now."

The wounded gunslick sat up, so Longarm bent and helped him to his feet. The man growled, "I'm going to kill somebody for this, cowboy."

"No you ain't," Longarm said. "You're upset and not thinking straight. But we both know I was too good for you even *before* you got hurt. Go set and have a beer on me while we put your friend on his feet."

Longarm started walking toward the corner where the fibbing cattle buyer was propped up on one elbow, muttering to himself. Suddenly McBride yelled, "Longarm!"

Since he'd half expected it, Longarm was to one side and drawing as he balanced on one knee when the injured gunslick fired the derringer in his left hand. His bullet parted the air where Longarm had just been, and since the hired gun hadn't aimed too well, left-handed, the bullet tore the top of his semi-conscious employer's skull off. Longarm's return fire put the gunslick down a second time, staring at the ceiling with a puzzled smile, a big red blossom of blood in the center of his shirt front. "Some boys sure are hard to convince," Longarm sighed.

McBride said, "I told you they needed killing. Let's get back to the outfit."

But Longarm waited, and sure enough, a shaking, ashen-faced townie cleared his throat and said, "I hope you boys won't take this personal. But this is getting sort of serious."

Longarm asked, "Are you the town law, mister?"

"Sort of," the worried man replied. "I'm a county deputy. I left my badge at home. It's sort of an honorary position and I'm really in the business of raising horses, only—"

"Say no more," Longarm cut in, putting his gun away a second time.

McBride frowned and asked, "Are you aiming to arrest us, little feller?"

The deputy looked like he wanted to throw up. Longarm said, "He's got a job to do, boss. He ain't arresting us, he just wants us to fill out forms and such for the county coroner. Ain't that right, deputy?"

The deputy said, "Sort of. I ain't sure *what* we're supposed to do. But it seems sort of sloppy to just leave them strangers laying there."

McBride nudged Longarm and said, "Hell, you know the form. Tell him how it's done and let's get her over with."

Longarm said, "You ride on back to the outfit, boss. I'll clean things up here. Me and the deputy will mosey over to the coroner and tell him what happened. Is that jake with you, deputy?"

"Sure. I just want to do things right. I'll witness for you that the skunks sort of committed suicide after you tried to be nice."

One of the others said, "We all will. But there's a problem. Doc Hollis, the coroner, ain't in town. He rode out to the Double W to certify a Mex who took a bad fall. I doubt he'll be back before sunup."

Longarm shrugged and told McBride, "You go on ahead and I'll catch up when I can. I don't mind spending the night in town."

McBride hesitated, then said, "Well, the boys will be worried, and I'm not a man for all the jawing and paperwork I see ahead of us here. If they don't turn you loose by the time we're ready to move on, I'll come back and bail you out or shoot somebody or whatever."

He left. Longarm turned to the bemused deputy and said, "Let's have us a drink before we study on getting these boys on ice and such. Do you folks have a hotel here in town?"

The deputy said, "No. But we'll work that part out with no trouble. I've never handled a shooting before, but you seem to know what you're doing."

"I do," Longarm said wearily. "Shooting folks is a chore I like to avoid. It ain't the noise I mind as much as straightening up afterwards. Even when it's open-and-shut self-defense, it can be a bother."

Chapter 15

The combined estates of the recently departed came to twenty-nine dollars in cash and a checkbook drawing on a San Francisco bank. The liveryman said he'd go on boarding their horses for thirty days and then auction them off if nobody came to claim them. The deputy said he'd like to put his bid in early, but Longarm agreed with the liveryman that his haste was a mite unseemly.

The local undertaker carted the bodies off so the swamper could clean up. But he said they had to stay above ground until the coroner's jury agreed on a verdict of manslaughter and suicide, the cattle buyer having been manslaughtered and the gunslick having acted suicidal.

By the time they had all this settled, the party-time deputy was treating Longarm as his mentor, even though the federal man hadn't shown him his own badge. The deputy seemed as pleased as punch when Longarm explained that the deputy was holding him as a material witness on his own recognizance. But he said he didn't know what recognizance meant, so Longarm said, "It's like you deputized me to watch myself and see that I show up for the coroner's hearing in the morning." The deputy said that sounded neighborly as well as reasonable, and that he had to get home to his wife and kids.

The reporter told Longarm of a widow woman who sometimes rented rooms. Longarm said he'd look into a place to stay later. Then he went to the Western Union office down the street, alone.

He sent a night letter to the Denver home address of Marshall Vail, collect. Billy Vail would be sore, but it saved having anyone in town gossiping about a strange cowhand sending wires to the U.S. Justice Department. He just reassured his boss that he was still alive and told him his present whereabouts. Much of what he wrote was meaningless, and the rest was in code. He thought about some inquiries he might have sent to other lawmen, but he decided not to. If any of the folks he'd met were wanted by the law in other parts, they weren't using names known to the law. He remembered that Carver, the purchasing agent in L.A., had made up a list of all the riders in McBride's outfit, and that Morgan and Scanlon had checked them out for the BIA, too.

He told the Western Union clerk he'd be back in the morning to see if there was any reply from his Uncle Billy. It was getting late enough in a one-horse town to study on a place to bed down.

He went to the frame house the reporter had told him about, and gave the doorbell a crank. A woman came to the door. It was a mite dark to size her up, but she allowed that she was the widow Donlevy and that bed and breakfast would cost him a dollar. It was steep, but she had him at her mercy.

Longarm took out a cartwheel and paid in advance,

so the gal sounded friendlier as she led him down the dark hallway to her kitchen. She said, "I was having coffee and cake before I turned in. I won't charge you extra. Sit down."

He did. The woman had her back to him most of the time as she got the fixings from her sideboard. When she turned around, Longarm was pleasantly surprised. All gals looked pretty much the same from the back, in a man's bathrobe and bunned-up hair. The widow Donlevy was a handsome woman in her middle thirties. Her Black Irish face was fighting a double chin, and he noticed that she was a trifle hefty under the robe, but her eyes were big blue pools that a man wouldn't mind diving into, if only they'd been a mite more inviting. She put his cup and a plate of cheesecake in front of him, bending forward as she did so, and though he kept his own eyes polite, she must have thought he was peering down inside her robe. She pulled it closer at the neck as she sat down across from him. He lowered his eyes and sipped some coffee. It wasn't his fault if a woman went about her house bare-assed under an oversized robe.

California gals sure baked sweet cakes, but the widow's coffee was downright good. They small-talked about who he was and where he'd come from. She said she'd heard the gunfire, but hadn't paid it much mind; she was a woman who minded her own business and didn't jaw with nosy neighbors. She said, "You know how they talk about a woman living alone."

He did, but he just nodded politely, so she elaborated, "I run a respectable boardinghouse. I have never rented rooms to anyone with a sassy dance hall gal in tow, or to a Mex of any description. But I have to watch my step. You see, my late husband died in disgrace."

Longarm didn't know how to reply to this, so he just said, "Oh?" and looked at her questioningly, to which she said, "Yes. He was killed up the coast on a cattle drive."

"I may be prejudiced, ma'am, but I fail to see how getting run over by a herd or taking a bad fall could be considered a disgrace."

"Call me Billie. What my husband died of so disgracefully was lead poisoning. He was fighting in a house of ill repute and they told me later that it was over a fancy lady. I just about cried my eyes out for a week or more."

"Well, I can see how that could put a lady off her feed, uh . . . Billie."

She sighed and said, "It did. But that was only the half of it. I know how you men are away from home. I could understand my late husband's natural feelings, since God knows he sure showed them around me when he was in off the range. But the way he got himself killed reflected on me, to certain neighbors."

"That hardly seems fair, since you were here and he was there at the time, Billie."

She nodded and said, "I know, but I might as well have been working in that place, to hear the way some women carry on. Not to my face, of course. That Mabel Grogan knows I'd snatch her baldheaded if she ever dared say anything to my face. But I know how they talk behind my back."

He sipped some more coffee and said, "They might not be as hard on you as you suspicion, Billie. How do you know what they say about you if you don't get to listen in?"

He didn't really care. He was just being polite until the woman got around to showing him to his room. But Billie was wound up the way folks get, living alone. She said, "I see the looks they give me."

He didn't know if she was right or not. He knew small town gossip could be cruel and heedless. He knew folks with a guilty conscience sometimes saw mean looks when none were intended. But unless she stole cows as well as charging too much, it was no never-mind of his.

Suddenly she said, "Have some more cake. Do you play games?"

Longarm blinked and answered, "Games? What sort of games, Billie?"

"Hell, I don't care. It's too early to turn in. I thought you'd keep me company for a spell. I hate it when it's dark and crickety out, this time of night. My man and me used to play games before we went to bed. I like to play games. By the way, what's your name, cowboy?"

"Uh, you can call me Custis. I don't like it all that much, but that's the name my folks gave me. I'll play you a game of stud for matchsticks, if that's your pleasure, Billie."

She said, "I'm no good at cards. What other games do you know?"

"Well, I learned a fair game of chess, one winter when I was snowed in with an oldtimer who taught it to me. Do you have a board and a set?"

Billie sighed and said, "No. We used to have a domino set, but a boarder ran off with it. Are you any good at tic-tac-toe?"

Longarm laughed and said, "Tolerable." He knew anybody was good at that fool kid's game. It sounded boring already, but the poor gal was so lonesome-looking that it seemed mean to laugh at her.

She got up with a girlish giggle and fetched a pad and a stub of a pencil. She moved around to his side of the table and drew the cross-hatching on the pad between them, saying, "You can go first, this time."

Longarm politely drew a circle in one corner, since he'd about decided she'd have trouble with an X. Billie frowned in concentration as she took the pencil back and drew an X in the opposite corner.

Longarm saw that she didn't know this game either, but it had been her notion to play. He drew his second circle in another corner and said, "Game's over."

She said, "Not so fast. What if I just block you like this?"

He drew a circle in the remaining corner and said, "It's still over. As you can see, you only get to block me with one X. I can put my third circle here or I can put it there. Either way, you lose."

She tore off the sheet and drew again, saying, "All right. This time I get to start!" She put her X in the middle square.

Longarm took the same corner. Billie picked another corner for reasons best known to herself, and Longarm had her again. She asked, "Are you cheating?"

"Don't have to," he said. "Everybody knows that you start with the outside corners or you lose."

He saw that she was confused, so he drew a diagram and explained, "Look, there's only nine squares to start with. That leaves eight for the second move, seven for the third and so on. It's a pretty simple game, Billie."

"Then how come you keep beating me?"

"You're playing wrong. Just pay attention and I'll have you a master or at least a cat in twenty minutes."

She raised an eyebrow and demanded, "What do you mean a cat? Are you funning me?"

"No. When neither side can win, they call it a cat's game and you draw a big C across it, like so. It means there's no sense going on with it. Two folks who know the first two or three moves can't beat each other, and it's a waste of time to fill up every square."

He drew another diagram and said, "Here, start in this corner."

She did. He put a circle in the center square and said, "Now you put your next X on the far side." She did and he said, "There you go. Now, if I take any corner, you just take the opposite one and you've got me. You're set to line up three in a row no matter what I do."

She still looked uncertain. So he deliberately put his circle in the wrong place and traced his finger two ways for her. Billie squealed with delight and said, "Oh, I see it! I've got you! It's a good thing we're not playing for money or clothes or whatever."

He shot her a thoughtful look and redrew the banal diagram. This time he beat her again to teach her a lesson. She complained, "That's not fair. You moved a different way."

He said, "Heck, there are only nine moves to the whole infernal game, Billie. It's so simple, once you just study the game."

Then his jaw dropped and he said, "Jesus H. Christ! That's it!"

"Don't you swear at me!" she protested, adding, "It ain't my fault I don't know this game!"

He laughed and said, "I'm not swearing at you. I'm swearing at me. I've been pounding my head against a brick wall trying to figure out a slick game of chess, and all the time we've been playing a dumb old game as simple as tic-tac-toe!" He laughed again. "I got the answers now. I'm so tickled I could kiss you, Billie!"

Her eyes went sort of sultry as she leaned back, her moist lips parted, and asked, "Hell, can't you do better than that, cowboy?"

He'd been right about Billie being a mite plump under her late husband's bathrobe, but she was a man-eater in bed and her neighbors were likely right about her. No woman had ever learned to love so nicely without a heap of practice.

But he was in no position to make a moral judgment on the lonesome widow woman as they helped each other destroy her bed springs. Her junoesque body was covered with hide as soft to the touch as a baby's rump.

She climaxed twice ahead of him, and he didn't take as long as usual. As he rested aboard her well-upholstered torso, Billie sighed and said, "Oh, I needed that. Is there more where that came from?"

He said, "Lord, yes, just let me catch my wind. You're a hell of a woman, Billie."

"Well, I'm a mite tuckered, too, for which I thank you. What should we do now?" she asked.

"Do you reckon the neighbors would talk if we just lay aboard the bed and had a smoke?"

She laughed and popped him off, and ran to the dresser and got them a damp washrag to clean off with as he reached for a smoke.

As she cleaned him and kissed his limp tool, Billie said, "You sure teach nice games. What was that you were saying about games when we suddenly went crazy in the kitchen?"

He said, "I'm going to wait until we ride clear of this town before I confront anybody. But we've been having outlaw trouble. It came to me as we were flirting that I've been slickering myself by looking for all sorts of complicated tricks when the one they've been pulling is so old it's hardly used anymore."

She took his cheroot from his mouth, puffed it, and put it back between his lips as she giggled, "Were you flirting all the time we were playing tic-tac-toe?"

"Sure I was. Weren't you?"

"Yes indeed. Those men you had it out with over in the saloon were cow thieves, huh?"

"No, just unscrupulous businessmen. The owlhoots who've been robbing the herds are another bunch entirely."

She kissed him on the chest and said, "Oh, tell me all about it."

But he didn't. A gal who couldn't savvy tic-tac-toe might find the game the cow thieves had been playing a mite complicated, as simple as it was. So he kissed her back, shoved his smoke in an ashtray, and said he had his second wind. He had some hard riding ahead, and there was no telling when he'd get anything this good again.

Chapter 16

Longarm awoke with the chickens, eased his bare shoulder out from under a tousled female head, and fled for his life. He hadn't gotten much sleep. He knew, now, why Billie's husband had died in a whorehouse; he'd been trying to get some peace and quiet.

He got his mount and rode out to McBride's camp for breakfast and to assure them that he was all right. He didn't tell McBride he knew how the thieves were stealing his cows. McBride was an excitable cuss, and Longarm wanted to get clear of the local coroner's jurisdiction before anybody else got hurt. He told McBride he'd make his statement and such and catch up with the outfit at the noon camp.

He got back to town at about eight o'clock, and went to the Western Union office. Thanks to the time difference between Denver and the Coast, Billy Vail had wired him from the marshal's office in the Denver Federal Building. Longarm was annoyed at his boss for not going along with his code, but as he read Billy's wire, he could see how the chief marshal could have been excited when he sent it. It read:

WHAT IN SAM HILL ARE YOU DOING STOP SPECIAL AGENT EDWARD SCANLON FOUND DEAD OF SHOTGUN WOUNDS NEAR SANTA BARBARA STOP ARE YOU DOING ANYTHING AT ALL ABOUT THIS AND WHY NOT QUESTION MARK . . .

The wire went on chewing him out at length, but Longarm didn't find that as upsetting as the silent apology he owed poor Scanlon. He'd assumed that the BIA man was a total idiot, but Scanlon had been playing a game he'd played himself. He'd been onto them fairly early, and he'd been playing dumb. But they'd known that Scanlon knew. Scanlon had dropped out of the drive to fetch help, and that was when they'd gunned him.

Longarm balled up the wire and threw it in the wastebasket. It was too late to fret that Scanlon hadn't come to him; the man had had no way of knowing that Longarm was a federal man like himself. Scanlon had been killed before he could pass his suspicions on, so Longarm knew he was on his own.

He went to the deputy's house and got him. Then they went over to see the coroner. The coroner had heard about the shootout upon his arrival at home late the night before, so he had his papers already made out, and all Longarm had to do was sign in triplicate. The coroner said he saw no need to convene a jury, since the whole town knew what had happened and nobody was making a fuss about the two dead skunks.

By this time it was after nine. The herd had passed through and was just up the trail. Longarm didn't feel like herding, so he rode out the other end of town and headed up into the hills. He wasn't having a morning canter for fun. He thought it might be interesting to see if any other early-morning riders were riding the ridges above the Old Mission Trail as McBride's cows poked along it.

He topped a rise and reined in between a couple of manzanita bushes. He could see the long dusty line of the outfit from up here. They looked like ants herding aphids along a dry grapevine. Save for the dust. Even one hoof raised some dust on the dry and unpaved trail; the hooves of almost three thousand cows tended to overdo things. He could barely see the rear of the herd and the drag riders, and it was still early. By afternoon the trail would be even drier.

Longarm scouted another saddleback in the hills to his north, and decided to make for it. It dominated a bend in the trail, and from up there he knew he could see both ends of the herd as it hairpinned. McBride had claimed that he'd lost cows on open flats, but Longarm knew he tallied rough and wasn't the smartest old boy in the world. Longarm was pretty sure they were losing cows going around corners, where the flank riders lost sight of one another. He sure hoped he could catch them in the act. For even though he knew, now, how they were working it, he was going to have one bitch of a time proving it in court unless he could catch them red-handed.

Longarm had sworn to uphold the U.S. Constitution, and he agreed with most of it, but trial by jury could be a pain in the ass. A juror who'd never herded cows was going to have a chore keeping up with his testimony, and he could already see them yawning. The rough justice meted out to cow thieves with a handy rope and informal tree was wrong, he knew, but he understood why cattlemen did it. A slick lawyer could sure make a running iron or a "stray cow" sound innocent as hell to a jury of farmers and druggists.

Longarm reined his mount to the right to avoid sky-lining himself as he made for the far saddle. The gunman out to ambush him that morning was thrown off by the unexpected move, and later, Longarm would realize that he'd moved in the nick of time. A shotgun roared, followed by rapid fire from a handgun somewhere. He didn't take time to look for the source. As his mount spooked at the shotgun blast, Longarm went with the throw and snagged his Winchester from its boot as he fell off and rolled down the slope through the chaparral. He wound up on his gut, facing upslope with the rifle trained on the skyline, as dust and broken twigs that smelled like medicine settled all around. Nobody was dumb enough to pop over the ridge to see if they'd done it right. He heard hoofbeats. His own mount had stopped a hundred yards away, upslope, and while it still looked spooked, it wasn't running. Longarm sighed, "Aw, shit," and scrambled to his feet. He legged it up the hill with the rifle at port arms, went over the ridge in a low running crouch, and dropped behind some greasewood on the far side. Way the hell off, he saw a dust cloud moving fast in the general direction of Mexico. He nodded and said to himself, *One bushwhacker, working alone. The others are just stealing for a living. That bastard was the troubleshooter who nailed Scanlon, and now he's on to me.*

He gave it up for the moment and went after his own mount. It took a little doing. The barb was still skittish and didn't want to know Longarm anymore. But he finally cornered it against some cactus and a big rock, and it seemed to soothe the critter when Longarm said he'd shoot it if it didn't hold still.

He forked himself aboard and rode on. There was little sense in playing hide-and-seek up here, now. The other side knew he was up here, and it hardly seemed likely that they'd steal any cows with him watching. So he cut down the slopes at an angle and fell in with the point as he rejoined the drive.

McBride called him over and asked how things had gone back in town. Longarm said he'd had no trouble. "Heard some shots a few minutes ago," McBride said. "Sounded like someone hunting over in them hills."

"I heard 'em, too," Longarm replied casually. "There are some deer to be found in them hills, I understand."

McBride said, "Too late in the morning to be hunting deer. I heard a shotgun, so I figured it might be a dove hunter, but then I heard pistol shots. Who on earth hunts doves with a pistol?"

Longarm shrugged and tried to look bored. "Kids, maybe. Sometimes, when a fool kid misses with his scattergun he gets so mad he opens up with his sidearm. But nobody's shot us or any cows. How far up is the noon camp?"

"About six or eight miles. I'm pushing a little hard today. We're behind schedule and I aim to move slow and thoughtful through the dangerous middle stretch ahead."

Longarm said he'd drop back and ride flank to make sure the noon tally came out right. He didn't expect the thieves to hit again until he'd been eliminated, so he spent more time watching trailside brush than he did the cows. How in the hell had they caught onto him? Old Scanlon hadn't known, and it had taken McBride a spell . . . "Of course." He was disgusted with himself for thinking tricky about simple moves again. He'd started to worry about leaving that wire from Billy Vail in that wastebasket, but they'd known all along. This decision to bushwhack him hadn't been a spur-of-the-moment notion; they'd planned it from the beginning. They knew they had plenty of time, or thought they did. They'd taken Scanlon out when opportunity offered Scanlon alone on a silver platter. They didn't aim to shoot anybody in full view of the outfit. A federal officer murdered in front of witnesses meant a full investigation, with all witnesses questioned and

217

checked out as they signed their statements. The gang meant to gun him away from the herd whenever the chance presented itself, as it had a few minutes ago. Longarm found himself growing fonder of the cows and other riders all around. He waved his hat cheerfully at a mosshorn trying to bust out, and as the critter fell back into line he said, "You just git along and it'll soon be over. Now that we know the rules of this dumb game, it's easy enough to play her. There are only so many moves anyone can make. I have made my mark in the right corner and it don't matter where they draw the next X. Don't tell anybody, cow, but if I don't get killed today, we've *got* the sons of bitches."

Longarm could have made his play at the noon stop, but he didn't. They were too close to that last coroner. He knew the coroner would be reasonable in the end, but he'd be sure to convene a full jury this time, and Longarm had some loose ends to tie up that called for riding far and fast. He decided to wait until they camped for the night. It was hard to bushwhack a man riding through chaparral in the dark, and he might just get lucky. He was still puzzling over how to prove his charges. Catching folks red-handed in front of witnesses beat just accusing them.

But the gang must have decided not to steal any more cows until they got rid of him, now that they'd shown him that opening bid with the shotgun ambush.

Any cattle drive was tedious at best, but that afternoon took forever and the sons of bitches never stole cow one.

McBride seemed happy about this as he tallied up that evening. The wagons were waiting on a broad *vega* of summer-cured grama with running water. Longarm sat his mount, staring morosely at the ridge lines all around. The theater was set up nicely for his raising of the curtain. Nobody could climb down from the balcony to get into the act if they didn't fancy his lines. So he took his barb to the remuda and told Fong to saddle another mount. He said he wanted a good night horse. Fong asked if he meant to do some scouting, and he said that was close enough to what he had in mind.

Longarm went to the fire by the chuckwagon. Some hands were guarding the herd over to the east. Fong's men were tending the remuda. The cook's helpers were down by the creek, washing dishes. But everyone he wanted to talk to was near at hand, so Longarm walked around the fire, to face the semicircle of hunkered riders with his back to the chuckwagon. Then he said, "Boys, I want you all to listen up. McBride already knows, but some of you may not have guessed that I am a deputy U.S. marshal, and that your Uncle Sam sent me out here to arrest the gents who've been stealing his Indian beef."

There was a collective murmur of surprise, which seemed reasonable, and the young drag rider, Shadow, went for his gun, which didn't. So Longarm shot him.

Shadow went over backwards, his gun still holstered, and Froggy leaped to his feet, hands reaching for the sky as he pleaded, "Don't kill me, sheriff! I never wanted to do it but they made me!"

Longarm covered Pirate and Osage as he said, "You two had best stand up, too. Unbuckle your belts and leave 'em right there on the ground."

Pirate did as he was told, looking sad and sheepish. Osage hesitated, then he started to cry as he unbuckled his gun rig and got up to stand with the other survivors. McBride was standing, too, and he said, "By God, let's get a rope!"

Longarm said, "Sit down, McBride. As I was saying before I was so rudely interrupted, I was sent to put a stop to this thieving. As your segundo, it was my notion to just fire these little rascals and send you safe on your way. I didn't expect Shadow to confess like that, but as he did, the rest of you may remember he was pretty good for a green hand riding drag when those unfortunate Mexicans hit us."

Robles said, "That's right. But these boys *saved* the cows that time!"

Longarm grinned crookedly as he said, "Sure they did. They saved them for their own gang. I was as dumb as the rest of you, at first. I thought Shadow was just dressed like a top hand because he read Wild West magazines. But he *was* a top hand. He signed on with the outfit to help his sidekicks rob it."

McBride had hunkered down as he'd been told, but he shook his head and said, "I'm missing something, Longarm. How in thunder were these kids stealing my cows? They was riding with *us!* They never drove no cows off into the chaparral, goddamnit!"

Longarm said, "I know. Tell them how you did it, Froggy."

Froggy licked his lips and said, "We met Shadow working in the stockyards. He told us it was an easy chance to make some money. We never meant to do no harm, mister."

Longarm looked disgusted and said, "He's already starting to build his defense, the little shit. All right, I'll spell it out for the rest of you. Nobody pays attention to the ass end of the herd, as the drag is supposed to be back there watching it. Most rogue cows spook out the flanks, and so the rest of you boys were watching for that. You were watching the hills on all sides for owlhoots you expected to see, waiting for a chance to cut out a few head. But nobody watches the drag riders. Nobody can hardly see them in all that dust. The vanishing cows seemed too tricky to be possible, when every rider said he hadn't seen anything. It's kid-simple once you study on how easy it is to just tell a fib."

Robles smacked a palm against his own forehead

and said, *"Ay, Maria!* It was so simple it sounds *estupido!* They let stragglers drop behind! That was all! When a cow dropped back, they just forgot to drive it forward. The tired stragglers drifted off the trail to graze, and their *compadres* just came along and rounded them up as we passed out of sight!"

McBride started to object. Then he said, "Oh my God, it works! Now that I study on it, I had strange stockyard kids riding my *last* couple of drags. Nobody hardly ever looks at a rank beginner, as long as he seems to be trying. Them wild shots and smoky fires we took for foolish were signals!"

Longarm agreed, "That's about the size of it. These innocent lads have been leaving a trail of misplaced beef for their friends to round up at their pleasure. They've run them over to holding herds in the Coast Range. The reason you've lost most along the middle stretch is because the cows start dropping back more as the trail gets longer. The game is to pond 'em in the hills until their brands fade and—"

McBride cut in, "Hold on! What do you mean about them brands? Brands don't fade."

Longarm said, "Sure they do, when they're *hair* brands. Take a closer look at those big IDs the next time one passes you in sunlight. Shadow's pals set that up back in the Los Angeles yards. Some innocent useless kids were using a stamp brand in the chutes. Who pays attention, right?"

The rider named Thayer said, "I remember hearing about hair branding. You do her with a cooled-off iron. The stamp is hot enough to burn the hair and maybe blister the skin a mite, but it's not hot enough to leave a permanent scar!"

"Son of a bitch!" McBride exploded. "It only takes a few weeks for new hair to grow, and the goddamned brand ain't there no more! I do remember hair branding now, but it's such an old trick nobody's used it for years!"

Longarm said, "Don't feel bad. I was playing chess when the game was tic-tac-toe, too. These kids have been pulling tricks so old that most grown cowhands have forgot 'em. We were looking for someone slick and professional because of the numbers they've been stealing. But now Froggy and his pals are going to tell us who they work for. Ain't that right, Froggy?"

The frightened boy said, "Honest, this is the first time we rode with Shadow. Shadow was the one behind it all. We came out here to pan for gold, only there wasn't no gold and them infernal Mex rancheros wouldn't hire us and he said we could get rich and——"

"Aw, stuff a sock in it," Longarm cut in. He stared pensively down at Shadow's cooling corpse and said, "I'm inclined to buy that tale, dumb as it sounds. You contract drovers would have noticed if they always used the same green kids to slicker you. Shadow couldn't have been too high on the totem pole, either, or the gang wouldn't have sent him on this drive. What we have here is a mess of dumb young sneak thieves. The *real* rascals are the men who've been fencing so much stolen beef. That was the slick part. Any fool can steal a cow. Selling the same for cold hard cash gets complicated."

McBride said, "Well, we've got these little shits dead to rights. What are you fixing to do with them, Longarm?"

Longarm stared hard and thoughtfully at the frightened boys. Then he said, "You do whatever you've a mind to, as long as you don't murder them. You won't lose any more cows between here and Frisco. If you feel up to all the paperwork, you could drop 'em off with the next county law you run into. If it was up to me, I'd boot 'em in the ass and send 'em on their way, on foot."

"You're joshing! We can't just let them go, can we?"

"Well, Shadow won't go far, and I don't think these

222

little skunks are worth room and board at the tax-payers' expense. They'll never steal another cow from you. They'll get killed by the gang if the gang can get at them to shut them up forever. So I imagine if you turn them loose they'll do a heap of running home to mama. But like I say, it's up to you. I've cleaned things up at this end. I've got some riding to do."

"Riding? Where the hell are you going, Longarm?"

"To arrest the son of a bitch behind it all, of course. They gunned a fellow peace officer, and I'm feeling sort of testy about it."

"I can see how that might do it. But do you know who you're after?"

Longarm started to thumb a fresh round into his Colt as he said, "Oh sure, I had that figured days ago. I just didn't know how the bastard was stealing your beef. But now I do. So I'd best say adios and go pick him up."

Chapter 17

It didn't take Longarm nearly as long getting back to Pueblo de Los Angeles as it had creeping north with cows. He wired ahead in Santa Bob for a backup to meet him, of course. The job just didn't pay enough for him to engage in needless heroics. So the afternoon he rode in, some other federal agents and a squad of deputy sheriffs from Los Angeles County were ready to back his play. He'd noticed an interesting poster near the railroad depot as he rode by it on the way to the Federal Building on Main Street, so he explained things to the hands assembled in the L.A. marshal's office and said, "We may as well get cracking. There's still some sun left and there's an opera here in town that I missed in Denver. I'd sure like to see what all the fuss was about before I leave town."

They went out the back way and mounted up. A deputy riding with Longarm said his wife had made him see the opera. He hadn't liked the singing much, but he hadn't seen so many gals' ankles all together since that time the whorehouse burned down. He said,

"It takes place in Ancient Somewhere and folks back then didn't wear much in the way of clothes. The gal they call Ida in the opera is a real looker, and her legs is cruelty to animals, the way she shows 'em all the way up. They say she's a white gal playing a colored princess, so she likely had brown tights on. But, do Jesus, she looked just like she was prancing about up there half naked."

As they threaded through the back alleyways, Longarm saw others cutting right and left to hit the yards on all sides, as he'd told them.

He set a deliberately slow pace for himself and the riders around him. It was tedious chasing folks all over hell; that was why somebody must have invented the notion of surrounding them.

He led his immediate posse down the gentle slope to the stockyards. As they rode out into the open, some of the hands working there must have noticed them coming. As they approached the front gates, Longarm heard a distant shot. The men closer to him looked puzzled as they stopped what they were doing. Longarm nodded down at a man in bib overalls and said, "Howdy. We came to arrest Carver. Where's he at?"

The yard hand said, "He ain't here today. The Indian agency ain't buying. I just work here, but the way I understand it, the BIA wired him not to buy no more beef."

Longarm muttered, "Shit." He knew the crooked buyer had gotten so greedy because he'd seen that coming.

He turned to one of the federal men with him and said, "Ride over and make sure he hasn't left on the train. Pick up some L.A. coppers if you need them."

As the other rode off, the yard hand asked Longarm what in the hell was going on. Longarm said, "Carver is a crook."

"Gee, thanks," the hand replied sarcastically. "I

never would have figured that out. What I asked was what you lawmen want with him."

Longarm said, "He steals cows. Then he sells them to the government and steals them back some more. I'll ask him when I find him how many times he's sold the same cow to the government and pocketed the difference. Nobody else in California was in Carver's position to sell large quantities of beef without a bill of sale."

A couple of sheriff's deputies rounded the yards and came to join Longarm. One of them said, "We just shot a feller who didn't listen good when we told him to stop. Some folks on the far side of the yard say he works here. He runs the branding chute."

Longarm said, "We heard the shot. He must not have wanted to talk to us about the private deal he had with Carver to hair-brand certain clients' beef. We can round up his helpers in our own good time. A few older Fagans seem to have tempted a mess of wandering youth into a life of petty crime. The ones we really want are Carver and his hired gun, the one called Boomer."

The yard man in the bib overalls gasped, "Hell, you don't mean to say old Boomer is a crook, too! He ain't been around all week!"

Longarm said, "I know. He's been leading the gang of kids he picked up around here. He fired that big Le Mat at me the other day. Sent the buckshot by my ear and tried to finish me off with the revolver slugs. It was sort of dumb. I knew when I saw it was only one rider that it had to be him. I'd bet my last chip he killed a lawman named Scanlon with that funny gun, too."

Other riders were drifting in. Longarm waved them closer and called out, "I'm sorry as hell, boys. But save for that crooked brand boss, we seem to have missed the big fish here."

The man who'd admired the opera singer's legs asked what Longarm aimed to do next. Longarm looked up at the sun and said, "Ain't sure. I doubt like hell I'll meet up with those two rascals at the opera."

By sundown, Longarm and the other lawmen he'd recruited had Pueblo de Los Angeles bottled tight. It was a small town with a big police force for its size, thanks to the city fathers' concern about the Mex minority being close to a majority, and the way the Chinese Riots of the seventies had almost torn the place apart. So once the feds let the local constabulary in on the case, men with guns who knew the area fanned out to seal off all the exits. The L.A. Basin was big and empty. There were only so many trails a man could take, with a full moon shining down.

Longarm didn't expect Carver or Boomer to ride the owlhoot trail by the light of the silvery moon. He'd had time to check them both out by wire. Carver was a slick political hack who'd survived President Hayes's cleanup of the old Indian Ring left over from Grant's administration. He'd never been caught with his hand in the till before. Boomer had no criminal record, either. Longarm knew he was a killer, so that meant he was a clever one. Clever crooks didn't cut and run across open semidesert. They'd lay low like Br'er Rabbit and try to sneak out later, mixed with the more innocent folks just going about their business. So as Longarm searched for them, he tried to walk in their boots. How would he get himself out of town with everyone watching the rail depot and Cahuenga Pass and such?

Carver had a modest bank account, consistent with his government salary. Longarm knew he'd stolen enough real cash to just let it lie. He wouldn't go to the staked-out bank for getaway money. He and Boomer had furnished rooms on Olvera Street, near the hotel Longarm had used his first few nights in town. Naturally, neither of the rascals had gone back to their own digs once they'd learned the law was looking for them.

But the address gave Longarm some ideas. He knew they knew the neighborhood. He moved down Olvera in the semidarkness, peering in windows. He spotted Trixie spinning her Wheel of Fortune at the same old stand. The Mex waitress, Pepita, was serving in the same saloon. She didn't spot him watching her through the dirty glass. Neither Carver nor Boomer were among her current customers, but Longarm hadn't expected them to be.

He didn't know where Trixie stayed when they weren't sicking her on strangers. But he knew where Pepita lived, so what the hell, it was a fifty-fifty shot. He knew she wouldn't get off until late, and that she lived alone. He put himself in the place of the men he was hunting, and the more he studied, the more he liked the notion. He studied on it some more as he walked up the hill through the Mex quarter. They'd sent Pepita to him with that made-up story in order to have a chance to search his hotel room while he was busy getting pleasured. They hadn't found anything, but the point was that they knew Pepita pretty well.

He retraced the way to Pepita's. There was a light in her bottle-glass window. Longarm doubted that she'd left it for him. The narrow, dark hillside street was deserted. He drew his .44 and eased up to the thick oak door. He knew better than to try the latch. He remembered that it was barred on the inside, and he hadn't brought a battering ram. He just put his ear to the oak and had a listen.

He heard male voices, two of them, talking too low for him to make out the words. He moved over to the window, checked to make sure the moon wouldn't outline his head, and peered through what had once been the bottom of a pint of beer. The distorted bullseye of brown glass didn't offer much in the way of a view. He could dimly make out one man seated at a table and another sitting on Pepita's bed.

As he looked around for something heavy, he spied

a clothesline between two shacks across the way. He eased over, unpinned a couple of pairs of pants and a bed sheet, and folded them neatly before setting them aside. Then he took out his jackknife and cut the line free, coiling it as he recrossed the street. He found a drainpipe two doors down from Pepita's, and shinnied up it to the flat rooftops. He walked across the roofs on the balls of his feet, and as he had expected, he found a stovepipe growing out of Pepita's roof. He tied one end of the stolen clothesline to the pipe, tested the knot and the tensile strength of the rope with a couple of hard, quiet snaps, and moved over to the edge.

Holding his gun in one hand, Longarm stood on the adobe edge with his back to the street, leaned out against the taut line, took a deep breath, and kicked himself out and away. He swung down, feet first, and crashed through the window as his boot heels sent discs of glass flying like scattered poker chips. His feet-first swing dropped him smack in Pepita's bed as the man seated on it sprang off with a yell of surprise. The bedsprings gave way and Longarm wound up on the floor, atop the mattress and under a shower of glass. Then it started to get noisy.

Boomer's Le Mat roared and tore a pie-plate-sized chunk of adobe from the wall above the bed as Longarm stayed flat, firing back from under the bedrail at the four legs he could see running every which way. Carver fell, his shin shattered, facing Longarm as he lay on his side, waving a derringer. So Longarm put a bullet in his cheekbone. The hydrostatic shock blew one of Carver's eyes out to the end of its bloody stalk, but since Carver was dead it didn't upset him. Longarm heard the door open, so he sat up and threw a parting shot at Boomer's vanishing form. But he missed. So he rolled to his feet, tripped over the bedrail, jumped over Carver's body, and snuffed the light before he tore through the door after Boomer.

Longarm crossed the street in a running crouch and

dropped prudently to one knee as he got his bearings. He couldn't see Boomer, but he heard somebody's boots clattering downhill like a son of a bitch, so he jumped up and followed.

Longarm's noisy entrance had likely rattled Boomer, for he'd stopped running cautiously and was just plain running in his high heels, trying to lay some distance between them before he made any further plans. Longarm heard the *ting* of brass on stone and knew that Boomer had ejected the spent shell to reload the shotgun barrel of his big Le Mat. He kept after Boomer anyway. Boomer had missed him twice with that fool gun; there was always a chance he'd miss again. Longarm's only real problem at the moment was to *see* the noisy bastard. The moonlight didn't shine straight down, and the shadows they were weaving through were ink-like. The slope started to level under Longarm as he ran, and he knew they were off the hill and in the back alleyways of the town itself now. Boomer liked back alleys. He knew the law would be patrolling under the streetlamps everywhere else. Longarm was getting turned around in the strange town, but he could tell he was gaining, so it didn't matter where the other cuss thought he was headed.

An orange square of light appeared ahead, and Longarm saw that Boomer had opened a back door and ducked in. He'd left the door open, so Longarm charged it at a flat run and bored on through it. He saw folks trying to get out of his way, yelling crazily. He didn't see Boomer, so he just kept going. He'd figure out what sort of a place it was later. It looked like a whorehouse having a Halloween party. Half-naked gals and gents in funny hats were staring at him, thunderstruck, and there was a narrow slit of an exit on the far side of the space. He heard screaming and figured Boomer had run that way, so he followed.

Longarm ran out into the middle of the stage of the Los Angeles Opera House, which looked like Ancient

Egypt, except that Boomer was two-thirds of the way across, drawing a bead on him with that Le Mat. Longarm crabbed sideways and Boomer blew the head off a papier-maché sphinx as people dressed like folks in the Good Book scattered every damned way. Longarm saw that a lady in brown tights was in his line of fire, so he shoved her on her ass as he fired back at Boomer. The killer turned to the startled audience, took a deep bow, and fell forward into the orchestra pit.

There was a moment of total silence, then some fool in the balcony shouted, "Encore!" and everybody started to clap their hands. It made Longarm feel a trifle foolish.

The lady he'd knocked down got up, sort of glassy-eyed, as a policeman in the crowd shouted out, "It's all right, folks, he's the law!"

The girl playing Aida took Longarm's hand and said, "Bravo! You've brought down the house."

He said, "I'm sorry, ma'am. You folks can sing some more in a minute, just as soon as we get that rascal out of here."

The opera gal laughed and asked, "Are you serious? We're not about to try and top that act! Ring down the curtain, Charlie!"

But folks started to boo and hiss as the asbestos curtain was lowered, so a man dressed like the king of Egypt stepped over to the footlights and called out that the show would go on as soon as they could find a new kettle drum to replace the one Boomer had landed in.

The gal in the brown tights led Longarm to the footlights, too, and they got another round of applause. Longarm saw men in blue uniforms moving down the aisles, so he said, "We'll be out of your hair directly, ma'am."

She said, "Call me Lola. I am Lola La Rue."

"The famous opera star?"

"Yes. Thanks to you, I'll be even more famous by the time the morning papers come out. We couldn't have bought a publicity stunt like this for any kind of money! I want you to stick around, honey. We're having a cast party after the show and you're invited. You're sort of cute, and I'd like a chance to thank you properly."

Longarm stared down at her. Her eyes were sending smoke signals, and her lung capacity was astonishing inside those brass cups she wore on her chest.

So Longarm wrapped up the case and he thought he'd done right well. He didn't understand why Billy Vail chewed him out so when he finally reported into the office back in Denver. What the hell, he only got home a week or so late.

Chapter 1

Longarm stuck a fresh cheroot into his mouth and lit it. Then he tipped his head back to get a better look at the enormous skeleton. Through the clouds of pungent smoke that billowed above his head, he peered with narrowed eyes at the tiny skull, after which he followed the great swooping neck to the high, rounded backbone, until his gaze reached at last the powerful, incredibly long tail.

He had heard about these dinosaurs, and had read accounts of this exhibition in the Denver newspaper, but seeing them was something else again. He didn't know which was more flabbergasting, the height of the critter or its length. One thing was for sure: when this oversized dragon was up and about, all dressed proper in muscles and skin, it would have taken a damn sight more than his .44 to stop it.

Longarm's rapt observation was rudely interrupted when someone grabbed his arm from behind and pulled him around. Longarm found himself looking down at a very unhappy little man.

"Sir!" the fellow cried. "Must you smoke that noxious weed in here? This is a closed hall. We must keep it so to preserve the specimens and allow the plaster to harden properly. There is no way to vent that foul-smelling smoke issuing from your person!"

Longarm removed the cheroot from his mouth, mildly amused. The little man glaring up at him was in his late forties, he figured—a bone-hard, wiry man with fierce, intense eyes that seemed as dark as obsidian. As the agitated little fellow rocked back and forth on his heels before Longarm, the tall lawman thought he could hear the man buzzing—as if under his dark, unruly shock of hair, a swarm of bees were at work.

"And who might you be?" Longarm drawled.

"I am Charles Ogden Stewart. And just who are you? Visitors were not to be allowed in until further notice."

"I am Deputy U.S. Marshal Custis Long. And you'd be the fellow I've been sent over here to see, I reckon."

"Sent by whom, might I ask?"

"Marshal Billy Vail—and the U.S. State Department."

"The State Department? Why?"

"Heard tell you were about ready to start a war with the British."

"Speak sense, Deputy."

"Well, that's what Marshal Vail told me."

Stewart's eyes narrowed in sudden comprehension. "Ah!" he cried. "I see what you mean, Deputy. You are referring to Dorset and his gang, the British expedition that is about to plunder Dragon Bluff—to loot it of its precious lode of fossils and take them back to Britain. Those are American treasures, sir. And they belong to this country. Of course I will do all that I can to stop them!"

"Then you admit you are responsible for the attacks

238

on the British expedition that have already taken place?"

Stewart smiled. "I am afraid I cannot take the credit for that, Deputy."

"What do you mean by that, Stewart?"

"Yellow Horn and his Arapahos are in the vicinity of the dig, I believe. And also a truly belligerent Reverend Wilson. In addition, I have a most meddlesome scientific rival, Deputy. He is as anxious as Sir Thomas to spirit away those fossils that are rightfully mine. Another rival for those treasures would be a most unwelcome turn of events, as far as he is concerned. His name is William Edward Pope. He is of the Quaker persuasion, though of late one would hardly believe it."

"And you figure any of these parties might be causing the British expedition trouble. Is that it?"

"Yes."

"But not your expedition?"

"Why, sir, how would I know that for certain? They are zealous men, indefatigable diggers, and I pay them well. Already you see before you the fruits of their labor."

Longarm glanced back up at the towering skeleton, then back at Charles Ogden Stewart. That this little man and his assistants had hauled this pile of bones from a quarry north of Denver and then propped the whole damn thing up inside this exhibition hall filled the deputy with a sense of wonder—and also a sense of incredulity at the many foolish errands some men will expend their energies to complete.

Stewart frowned as he read correctly the skepticism in Longarm's eyes. "You wonder why I would go to such lengths to present this magnificent specimen to the city of Denver. Is that it, Deputy?"

"More than that, Stewart. Why not just leave the bones where you found them? Why dig up half the

West so you can prop this dragon up inside this drafty hall?"

"I would not expect you to understand. You are a simple lawman, after all. What do you know of science, or the scientist's imperative need to brush aside the darkness of this age and peer into the past?" Stewart chuckled. "But to answer the question you put to me— I am presenting this specimen to Denver in gratitude to the many public-spirited citizens in this great state who have aided me in my endeavors over the years." He smiled. "Of course, many of these bones, the majority in fact, are simply plaster copies of the originals. I have long since sent back to Brown University the original fossils. There is much work yet to be done with each, you see. Classification, photographic plates to be made, and so on."

"And so on. Well, maybe I don't know what makes you fellows tick, as you say. But you better do what you can to keep the members of your expedition off the backs of them British scientists, or I'll just see how many bones your men can dig up in a jail cell."

Stewart's face reddened with alarming speed. He was obviously not used to being addressed in this fashion. "Are you threatening me, Deputy?"

"You and your men, if need be."

"Sir! Do you realize who I am? I have over three hundred publications! At present I am the chief paleontologist for the Providence Naturalist Society. I number Charles Darwin and Thomas Huxley among my collaborators!"

Longarm smiled gently at the little man. "Now don't go get your bowels in an uproar, Stewart. I heard of some of those men, and your reputation is mighty impressive, I must admit. But out here, Marshal Billy Vail is the law, and I am his agent. I'll check out those other hombres you mentioned—them Indians, especially. But I want you to realize that I am going to

240

hold you responsible for the actions of your men. Is that clear, Stewart?"

The man was fuming. "Perfectly," he managed.

"Fine," Longarm said, and turned to go.

"Deputy!"

He turned back to face the paleontologist, who said, "Am I to understand that you will exact the same discipline from members of William Pope's expedition? That you will not countenance any misconduct on the part of any of his crew, either?"

"That's right."

Stewart drew himself up to his full five feet five. "Well, then, sir—you will have your hands full. And I expect you to live up to that promise."

"Stewart," Longarm said softly, "I may be just a simple lawman—but I don't need anyone like you to tell me my job. Is *that* clear?"

The man swallowed, seemed ready to explode, then gained the upper hand over his emotions and nodded stiffly.

"Bravo, Deputy!" cried a tall, rakishly attired individual who had just stepped out from behind the great skeleton's enormous thighbones. "That's the way to handle that pipsqueak!"

"And who the hell are you?"

"William Edward Pope, your servant, sir!" As the man advanced on Longarm, he held out his hand.

Longarm clasped it and the newcomer shook it warmly. Then he grinned at Stewart. "It's about time somebody cut you down to size, Charles. It was a pleasure to see this gentleman do it! You are a fraud and a liar! I propose to reveal that fact to the world!"

Unable to control his fury at this charge, the smaller scientist flung himself upon Pope with such force that the taller of the two was sent reeling back. They both thudded to the floor with a loud whack, and began pummeling each other like school kids, and with just about as much effectiveness. Longarm pulled the two

241

apart with some difficulty, then hauled Stewart to his feet. He had both men by the nape of the neck. Stewart dangled for a moment from Longarm's powerful grasp with both feet off the floor.

"Get out of here!" cried Stewart. "Both of you! Get out!"

"I guess," said Pope, picking up his wide-brimmed hat and brushing off his buckskin jacket, "that we are no longer welcome, Deputy. Join me in a cup of coffee?"

"I'd like something stronger," commented Longarm as he strode away from the fuming Stewart, Pope keeping pace.

"I am afraid that strong drink is forbidden to a man of my convictions, sir," replied Pope as he held the door open for Longarm.

"Coffee it is, then," said Longarm, following Pope out onto the sidewalk. "But I won't keep you long. I reckon I might have a train to catch."

"Of course," Pope said, as he fell in beside the tall lawman.

Longarm was somewhat over six feet tall, which made him at least half a head taller than his companion. They were a perfect contrast. Pope was dressed in a flashy, fringed buckskin outfit, a broad-brimmed sombrero, and finely tooled leather boots, into the tops of which he had tucked his trouser legs. He wore no sidearm. Now, as he walked beside Longarm, he took out a pipe. Longarm still had his cheroot in his mouth and was trailing a thick cloud of smoke as he strode along Colfax Avenue.

He was wearing a snuff-brown Stetson, tilted slightly forward, cavalry style; a brown tweed suit and vest; a string tie knotted at the neck of his light blue shirt. His cordovan leather boots were low-heeled army issue, and had none of the sheen of Pope's boots. While Pope's face was lean and clean-shaven, Longarm

242

sported a newly trimmed longhorn mustache, its tips flaring dramatically.

Pope's eyes were hazel and bright with excitement. He seemed eager to talk with the tall lawman, but was busy filling his pipe as he hurried along at Longarm's side. Longarm's face was, in contrast, brooding. Pope seemed to be at least ten years older than Longarm, but the scientist had a kind of eager bounce to his stride that belied his years. Longarm's gunmetal-blue eyes were smoldering some now, and he made no effort to break the silence between the two of them.

Nearing a restaurant familiar to Longarm, the lawman turned to his eager companion. "We can get coffee in here, Pope," he told the man. "Is that all right with you?"

"This place will do nicely," Pope responded.

They found a table in a corner. Longarm sat down with his back to the wall and watched as Pope carefully removed his hat and placed it down on the empty chair alongside him. Longarm studied the scientist carefully, not knowing what to think.

He knew he didn't like Charles Ogden Stewart, and this fellow Pope had not acted with any great self-control back there in the exhibition hall, but Longarm had long since learned to hold his judgment about any man. At least until after he had had a drink with him. He wondered if coffee counted.

The waitress took their orders and left them. William Pope smiled broadly at Longarm. "You have no idea," he said, "how pleased I was at the way you handled Stewart. He is a charlatan, a man who takes credit for the insights and hard work of others, who uses his wealth to prevent others from advancing their careers, even though they may be far more deserving."

"I reckon that means you."

"It could, and that's a fact. He has tried to keep me from Dragon Bluff."

"How do you feel about that British expedition, Pope?"

"They are welcome to whatever they can get." William Pope smiled then, and Longarm immediately caught his drift.

"I see," Longarm replied. "Like Stewart, you don't mean to go out of your way to help them."

"I will not."

Their coffee arrived. Pope insisted on paying.

"Did you hear what I told Stewart?" Longarm asked Pope.

"I overheard everything. But you see, Deputy, I have no doubt that my men will be able to get what I need from that bluff, despite Sir Thomas or that fraud, Stewart."

"Your crew is tougher, is that it?"

"Yes."

"Where did you find your men?"

Pope smiled. "That would be telling."

Longarm finished his coffee and leaned back in his chair to study the scientist. If Stewart was pompous and arrogant, this one was dangerously unaware of the forces he was setting in motion. From the way Pope dressed, he seemed to be playing a role he relished, but not one he really understood. These two dragon hunters might be brilliant enough, but in things that mattered, they both seemed woefully ignorant. It was a damn good thing, Longarm reflected, that they were chasing the *bones* of dragons and not the real thing.

Longarm got to his feet. Clapping his hat back on, he said, "Stay put, Pope. I've got business that won't wait. But I want you to know that if I have to tangle with either of you two again, it will be against my better judgment. And listen good now—I will not take sides in any of your damn fool arguments. Is that clear?"

Smiling up at Longarm, the man seemed unwilling to take offense. "Deputy, I understand your position perfectly. It is really quite clear. Of course I did not expect you to take my side against Stewart. After all, if you simply keep the man in his place, you will be doing me—and Sir Thomas—an inestimable service. You can count on my support in that endeavor, I assure you."

For a moment Longarm stood over the dragon hunter, studying him; then, with a shrug, he said goodbye and left.

As Longarm strode past the pale young clerk with the plastered-down, center-parted hair, the door to Marshal Vail's office was flung wide and Billy Vail stood in the doorway, an anxious frown on his red face.

"Get in here, Longarm. You got a train to catch tonight. Did you find those two scientists?"

Longarm swept past Billy Vail and slumped into the chief's red leather armchair. A glance at the banjo clock on the wall told Longarm it was close to four o'clock in the afternoon. The train Vail was talking about left at six that evening. But Longarm was hoping he could talk the chief into sending someone else to Dragon Bluff.

As the heavyset chief marshal closed the door and hustled around behind his desk, he glanced unhappily at Longarm. "I got another telegram from the State Department. *They* just got a telegram from the British government. Sir Thomas is having great difficulty, and the State Department wants to know what I'm doing about it."

"What's happened now?"

"Two wagonloads of fossil bones were lost. The telegram didn't say how, but it seems there is no doubt that those Americans at the site are behind it. Longarm, our government welcomed these British scientists, actually invited them to come. Hell, there's eight miles of ridges and bluffs filled with those damn fossil bones. There's enough for everybody."

Longarm shrugged. "Maybe, Billy. Say, how about you sending Wilson on this one? I just met Stewart and Pope. I suspicion this business is going to be a sweet mess. Send Wilson. He's a sight more diplomatic than I am."

"You met those two scientists, did you?"

"I met 'em."

"And what happened?"

"I tangled with Stewart. He's an arrogant son of a bitch. I also pulled him and that dandy, Pope, off each other. They were scrapping like schoolboys in the exhibition hall. They may be bright, Chief, but all they are going to cause anyone who's near them is trouble. I don't want any part of it."

"You are the man I am sending, Longarm. That's final."

There was an iron gleam in Marshal Vail's eyes as he peered out at his deputy from beneath his bushy black eyebrows. Longarm met the older lawman's relentless gaze for a moment or two, then shrugged and accepted the inevitable. "All right, then, Billy. But how about giving me something more to go on than I have now?"

"What do you want to know?"

"What's the law on this kind of operation? Does anyone *own* that bluff? And who owns all those bones they're hauling out? Also, Stewart said something about Chief Yellow Horn of the Arapaho. First I heard he was this far south."

"The chief is in the area, all right."

"How close to the diggings is he?"

Vail smiled thinly. "Dragon Bluff is on Indian land."

Longarm groaned.

"As for the law, the nearest I can figure," Vail went on, "is that the bones belong to whoever digs them up and ships them out of there."

"There's no such thing as claims or titles?"

"Not on this find," Vail said, polishing his bald head with a pink, pudgy hand.

"So it's every collector for himself."

"That's right."

"How many men have been killed so far?"

Vail frowned, pawed through the pile of documents on his desk, then pulled forth a large folder and flipped it open. He ran a finger down the first page, then looked with upraised eyebrows at Longarm.

"Three, so far. A driver of one of the wagons, a digger, and one of the British guards." He paused and glanced back at the folder. "And one more. A rattle-snake got him. He was shoving his nose along the ground with a whiskbroom in his hand when the rattler caught him. But of course there's nothing you can do about that sort of thing."

"I don't like this, Billy. I wish you'd send Wilson."

"Get on that train, Longarm. Keep those Britishers healthy, and get the State Department off my back."

Longarm stood up. "And if I can't?"

"Don't come back here," Vail growled.

As Longarm strode through the outer office, he reminded himself that Billy Vail had just been kidding.

Or had he?

The scream came from beyond the next ridge. Longarm spurred his buckskin hard and, leaning well over the horse's straining neck, topped the rise and saw the Arapahos—and the small wagon train they were plundering.

As he thundered down the slope, he snaked his Winchester out of its saddle boot and worked the lever. The Indians saw him coming. For an instant they paused in their plunder, then broke for their own mounts and weapons. As they did so, Longarm saw a clutch of Arapaho run from the white men—and the one white girl—who had been driving the bone-laden carts. It was the girl who had screamed.

Galloping closer, Longarm fired over the heads of the Indians, wanting at this point only to frighten them enough to send them on their way. There were at least a dozen braves, more than a match for a lone lawman. And then, as he rode still closer and loosed another round over their heads, he had an idea. Twisting in his saddle, he shouted back at the ridge and waved his arm. There were no other riders behind him, but he hoped the Indians wouldn't know that.

Whether they did or did not mattered little, as it turned out. An Indian bullet struck the tip of Longarm's rifle butt, tearing the weapon from his grasp and sending the butt swinging with numbing force into the back of his head. He was aware only of a punishing blow that sent him flying backward off his horse. The ridge he had been looking back at tipped crazily and changed places with the sky. Longarm slammed heavily into the ground and was flung in a rapid tumble down the slope. He crushed to a halt against the side of a boulder.

Hovering on the brink of consciousness, he shook his head and peered around him. The solidity of the rock grew, and he found that he was clutching it frantically. It seemed to anchor his swimming senses as the horizon spun sickeningly about him. At one moment the onrushing Indians were below him, riding with wild yelps up the slope—and the next moment they were behind him, charging crazily off in another direction. At last his head cleared enough to enable him to struggle to his feet. Dazed, his legs spread wide to balance him, he awaited the Indians' charge.

The Indian in the lead was heading directly for the upright Longarm, a series of high, keening barks coming from his savage throat. Longarm recognized his cry.

"A-he!" the brave cried, "A-he!" *I claim it!*

As he closed with Longarm, the brave brandished his beaded, brilliantly decorated coup stick. He had already counted Longarm out, and was now about to touch his enemy with his coup stick to prove his valor —and his right to a woman.

But Longarm had a surprise for him. The sight of the onrushing Indian helped marvelously to clear his head and concentrate his attention. At the last moment, as the Indian leaned over with his coup stick, Longarm snatched up at the stick and managed to grab its beaded end with both fists. Then he leaned back, planting his feet firmly in the rocky ground, and while the mounted Indian swept past, he yanked hard. The Indian was lifted from his horse's back and went sailing over Longarm's head.

Longarm released the coup stick and spun to face the Indian, who seemed to have landed crouching, ready to spring. Swiftly, Longarm clawed the .44 from his cross-draw rig and covered the brave. He straightened defiantly—and waited for Longarm to pull the trigger. By that time the rest of the war party had thundered down upon the two, and in an instant Longarm and the brave were being circled by the rest of the Indians.

Longarm smiled at the waiting brave and then calmly holstered his double-action .44-40 Colt. At once the Indian folded his arms across his dark chest and relaxed. About them both, clouds of white dust billowed as the Indians brought their horses to a halt. One Indian, older and apparently wiser and wearing a chief's bonnet, stepped down from his pony and strode imperiously toward Longarm.

"You have good sense for a white man," the chief informed Longarm coldly.

"Would you be Yellow Horn, chief of the Arapaho?" The chief nodded gravely.

"I am Deputy U.S. Marshal Custis Long. I crave no trouble with the Arapaho or their famous chief, Yellow Horn. When I rode upon your warriors, I fired over their heads to warn them. I had heard a white woman's scream."

The chief nodded gravely. "Yes. Foolish white girl. One of my braves took a close look to see how white she was. He would like to take her, but he knows now that she screams too loud for his ears." He smiled thinly then. "And for the ears of this chief."

Yellow Horn turned then to the brave whom Longarm had unhorsed, and waved him back onto his pony, which another brave had caught and brought back to him. The unhappy brave swept up his coup stick and flung himself onto his pony's back. Once astride the animal, he glared down at Longarm and said something to the chief.

The chief answered him with a sharp word or two, undoubtedly a rebuke, and the brave spun his horse about and broke through the ring of impassive Indians. Not one of them, Longarm noted, had yet lowered his rifle, and it looked as if almost every brave had one. The chief looked back at Longarm.

"Black Horse says next time he will shoot the lawman, and not bother with the coup stick. I think he talks foolish," Yellow Horn said, the shadow of a sigh in his speech, his eyes suddenly troubled. "He is a young brave and must show courage, must count coup —or no woman of our tribe will have him. But the Arapaho have no more enemies to fight. They are all in the government agency, sleeping under thin blankets and eating bad agency beef. Now the white man comes to the Valley Where the Giants are Buried. It is sacred Arapaho land. But the white man does not care. He comes to take our dead giants away. Tell me, lawman. Why does the white man always take what the Indian has? We do not take what you have! We do not *want* what you have."

"Reckon that's the reason," Longarm replied wearily. "The white man wants what the Indian has, so he

250

takes it. These bones the white man takes—do you know what he does with them?"

Yellow Horn shook his head.

"The white man puts them together, so the giants can stand once again. I will take you to see this wonder someday."

The chief's eyes gleamed. "Yellow Horn would like that. It would be good medicine!"

"Fine, Chief. It's a deal, then. Now, would you tell your braves to lower them guns and let me get on my way? I took quite a spill back there, and it feels like a few bolts are loose."

Yellow Horn nodded quickly. He turned to his braves and spoke sharply. The rifles were lowered at once. Then the chief mounted up. He looked down at Longarm. "You have made a promise to Yellow Horn. He will wait for you show him the Standing Giants. He will not wait long." He saluted Longarm with an upraised palm, pulled his pony around, and led his party away at a sudden gallop.

As Longarm squinted through the dust at the departing Indians, he wondered how much time he had before Yellow Horn and the rest of his feisty braves would call him on that promise. He had had no idea how taken with the prospect of seeing a rebuilt dinosaur skeleton the chief would be. Longarm just hadn't been thinking clearly. He was thinking clearly now, however. Of course the Arapaho chief would be anxious to see one of the Standing Giants. It would give him great prestige with his tribe, and an agency chief didn't really have all that many opportunities to gain prestige.

So that meant Yellow Horn would be waiting impatiently for Longarm to deliver. Longarm swore softly to himself and started back up the slope after his horse.